Trial by Fire

Also by Frances Fyfield

Trial by Fire

A Helen West Mystery

FRANCES FYFIELD

WITNESS
IMPULSE
An Imprint of HarperCollinsPublishers

This book was previously published in 2012 by Hachette Digital.

EPub Edition AUGUST 2014 ISBN: 9780062301147

Print Edition ISBN: 9780062301178

10 9 8 7 6 5 4 3 2 1

Chapter One

THERE WERE FOXES as wild and shy as wolves in northeast London, haunting the dead railway lines by night in search of sustenance, running into gardens when the need was great, abandoning the petticoats of the city to forage in bins. In the crowded outskirts where city clawed at country in a flurry of picnics between mismatched towns, the presence of summer and constant supply of discarded food lessened necessity and made it negligible. High summer for this fox, sufficiently fed on old hamburgers to cope with present hunger, but nothing in her stomach as compelling as this fruity stench, this rich smell of carrion. She quivered from the sharp, vicious snout of her to the down-pointed tail, eyes bright with curiosity, hair stiff with anticipation, a predator salivating in the darkness.

Fox scratched at the loose earth, dry and unresisting around the human hand. She examined and sniffed. A mottled set of fingers, earth-stained but still delicate white and shiny in the waning dark. Her firm teeth gripped the fingers, bit and gnawed the splintering bone within, then paused, shy and wary. In sudden urgency, she closed her jaws over the knuckles of the hand, dug paws into the ground for purchase, and pulled. Better a prize to carry home, not to eat but to bury, less greed in her now than pragmatism. The hand was weighted by a heavier body, resisted beyond the elbow as the earth resettled around the form with a sigh. Fox grasped the forearm, encountered larger bone, pulled again to the tune of a slight cracking sound. Growling softly, she persisted as the light grew, shaking her head from side to side, unable to shift the obstacle. Pausing in the struggle to survey the problem, she tested the air, heard in the distance a car on the road, the infinitesimal dawn sounds of human life gathering force far away, yet too close for comfort.

She turned her head from the carrion and spilt soil in sudden disinterest, scratched, twisted, and danced in the new warmth spotting her coat between the trees, a ritual dance in the rising light, graceful and carefree in celebration. Then she cleaned the earth from her jaws and slipped away into the undergrowth for home. Sunlight, warmth, freedom and safety were preferable even to food.

The grave she left untidy, as if a sleeper had turned the blanket in the middle of a dream. Beneath the surface, the larvae continued their slow and steady movement, out of sight, busy, busy, busy.

ONE HAND REMAINED visible above the ground, finger splintered and chewed, knuckle browner and stickier than before, softened by teeth and the abrasive tongue. It was the shroud of flies that indicated a presence, buzzing in a furious crowd and attracting the dog running through the woods when the sun retreated. The arm protruded crookedly, the wrist at right angles like a signpost. The owner of the dog, once a poacher, regarded the sight with laconic curiosity only slightly tinged with shock; he sat and debated with his slow soul what to do next, holding his animal firmly by the collar as it twisted to escape, enraged by the smell of fox, frightened by the presence of death. As the man rose and plodded towards a telephone, he was relieved he had not seen the remnants of a face, relieved the fox had not done worse. Such a pale, slender arm, the colour of a well-hung, badly plucked bird. Once a woman's.

AT EIGHT FORTY-FIVE in the evening the village of Branston was already somnolent. After seven-thirty, the trains from Liverpool Street via twenty-one stations east, a long and rattling ride in carriages with dirty windows, became less frequent, and even the alternative route, Central Line to Epping, equally elderly rolling stock and even noisier, had diminished its reluctant service. The commuters had faced their last hazard of the day: none remained in city wine bars on an evening like this. 'We live in the country,' they said. 'Wonderful, have to get home. Ever heard of Branston? No? You haven't lived. Marvellous spot, hasn't really hit the market yet, house prices not bad, why, we only paid ... You must be mad, living in Surrey. Go east, man, go east, the only place to be.' So they laboured uphill from the station carrying tributes to spouses and children, wine in carrier bags held by men, while the women carried decorative materials and ornaments in endless pursuit of style for the solid-built houses, some old, some hideously new, which formed the fabric of Branston. Flanked by woods on one side, flat fields on the other, approached by three roads hidden by hedges, Branston nestled quietly. There was a main street, comfortably ugly and mellow. The Coach and Groom, Bario's plush pink and grey restaurant – 'Terrific place, better than anything we've found in London, I mean, there's everything here' – and a few miles beyond all that, the wider consumer vistas of Chelmsford with Marks and Spencer, Habitat, and all the disguises the human soul could require, places where Branston refugees escaped on Saturdays to avoid contact with Mother Earth. Branston consisted of workers, a village of respectable and ambitious house-owning commuters, pushing themselves ahead by sheer effort, taking advantage of still old-fashioned schools for their new-fashioned kids, watched with amazement by the few High Street natives for their habit of leaving their homes empty for all of twelve hours a day.

Branston did not possess a history. It mirrored the taste of its current age and was resurrected from oblivion by the need for housing an Olympic stone's throw from London. Previously its three streets had almost died, deserted by young and old alike, the young from boredom and lack of opportunity, the old from pneumonia induced by dampness and the right time to go. Now the remnants found themselves revisited, adopted, and conquered by the descendants of their more ambitious children. In addition to those with no instinct to go south or west, there were those seeking the nearest patch of greenish field to the East End convenient for market trade, a touch of fraud, or a place to own a house acceptable to a mother still locked in the fumes of Bethnal Green with her pub and all the blacks. Branston had never been much of a community, simply a place. Now its inhabitants tried to make it into a village. The village format was slightly unconvincing, with the High Street boasting one confused supermarket, one small branch of Woolworth's, a shop selling kits for homemade wine and beer, and alongside the restaurant a kind of café called La Taverna, a pizzeria, and a burger bar, also selling kebabs for those who preferred foreign. The rest of the ten shops included one featuring swanky tracksuits for the unconverted East End wives, one more prosaic and expensive sportswear, an upmarket greengrocer, a jeweller, a delicatessen, and two newsagents, the only ones that were there in the first place, source of all gossip. Aside from these establishments, which maintained half-day closing and lunch hours, the rest strove to cater for the custom living in the newly developed housing estates. Parallel to the shops was a small green, usually hidden by buses panting at two stops before turning around to return to bigger things. People gathered on this green trying to make village gossip, hampered by their underlying London reluctance to know one another.

She could see the point. Occasionally she enjoyed the prettiness and the space, succumbing to the instinct to enjoy all aspects of life whenever possible. But much of the time Helen West, émigré from the dirtier streets of Islington and grimy offices of very central London, found herself hating Branston with a quiet passion that surprised her.

Not at every moment, and not during this one. Whistling, with her hands in the suds covering last night's washing-up and looking out through the diamond-shaped windows of the modern house in Invaders Court, Helen told herself she had no excuse for hating any place – places were not important enough for the expenditure of that kind of emotion. She slammed a dish on the draining board and did not stop it slithering back into the water. What the hell, better things to do, sun still shining. Bubbles of soap attached to the front of the loose jacket that swung from her slim figure with comfortable ease. Helen was at home in a suit, wore one like a glove, far better adjusted to the professional role it symptomized than she was to the kitchen sink, which she approached with all the caution of an enemy unwilling to do battle. She was small and dark, dressed in the black and white required for a courtroom, enlivened as always with one splash of colour, like a magpie with crimson in the tail. There was a dishwashing machine, which she dared not use in Bailey's absence, so terrifying were its instructions, and she missed his presence slightly the more for that. It was the slightest missing, a constant and distinct preference for the pleasure of his company, abnormal in her to resent time spent alone, and it stemmed from her impatience with the ever unfamiliar sharp edges of this streamlined house. Squinting through the window, she could see Isobel Eastwood toiling past the house on the way to her own, laden with carriers. Oh, goody, I wonder what she's bought today. Where on earth do they put everything she carries into that house? Ducking below the windowsill, Helen avoided the necessity of a wave, which was the closest she and Mrs Eastwood ever came to communication. Helen and Bailey had become gleeful gossips, discreet but avid in their curiosity about other people's lives. They were both unused to visible neighbours and found them the fascinating source for hours of comfortable speculation, their own amazement and observation never diminished. Now he had been called to a dead body, he had said on the phone, no self-importance in the announcement, just a statement of fact; he would be away until late, possibly all night, but at least they could spice the usual enjoyable daily accounts with something more substantial to discuss. In the knowledge of that, and the sudden lack of necessity to clear the kitchen now rather than later, Helen abandoned the attempt, gave herself a generous measure of gin, and purred with contentment in the first sip. Bet they're all pouring drinks, she thought, looking beyond the window at her vista of new brick.

It was an equally sound bet that none of them would invite her to share. The inhabitants of Invaders Court, Branston, were empire builders rather than sharers, and besides, their vague knowledge of the unmarried status and respective professions of Geoffrey Bailey and Helen West did not encourage them to warmth. 'What do you do, Mrs Bailey? I suppose we call you Mrs Bailey?'

'No,' Helen had said cheerfully, 'you call me Helen West. I live with Geoffrey, but we are not married. And I'm a solicitor. No, I don't do conveyancing; I'm a prosecutor. No, we don't have any children, and no, this is not our house, we've borrowed it.'

'Oh. And what does Mr Bailey do?' they persisted, beaming in benign, slightly wavering curiosity.

'He's a detective chief superintendent. In the police.' She could never keep a note of defensive pride out of her voice when describing Bailey, not for his rank, just because he was Bailey and she could never cease to honour him, in public at least, but she had watched the faces fall.

Mental head count of delinquent children, out-of-date road tax, and unpaid parking fines, end of conversation. 'Well, my husband works in the city.'

Helen's understanding of this reserve was complete. She knew it to be as natural as breathing, not indicative of malice or stupidity, simply a withdrawal capable of reversion if their other interests had been more communal. As the woman of the piece, like all the other women, it was her role to make the social effort, but chatter died on her like the end of sudden rain. She did not despise domestic bliss, but, having ploughed the furrow of thoroughly professional life for a dozen years, remained puzzled why anyone with choice settled to anything else. There was so little to discuss: she and Geoffrey had no children, no company car and, although the details of their identical houses would be enough to fill conversational hours, she did not, as they did, love or treasure her home. It was rented for twelve months, half of them gone. She would never have bought it in a million years and would never have filled it with these fat, hard, uncomfortable, but ludicrously expensive things chosen by her young and absent landlords who were pursuing the upward path of their success on foreign territory. Helen did not feel like a successful woman, didn't expect she ever would, wondered what it was like. Her own environment, lost for this experimental year, reflected only what she liked, rich colours, plentiful pictures, and an element of disorder. In Helen's mansion, it would take at least a year to mend a broken object; here, anything flawed would have hit the reject heap and been replaced within hours. The pale harmonies of the walls, grey carpets, cream sofa, jarred on her, also the lack of anything middle-aged, let alone old.

She sat on the offending sofa and thought that if it had been taken out of context, it would have been quite nice. The same sort of thin description would apply to Branston itself. A village that was not quite a village, one of a series of villages, this one in particular was caught in a time warp of house prices because of the triangle of motorways and trunk roads that had somehow isolated it with a few miles of protected woodland. But it was still not a real village, because the heart went out of it every day when three-quarters of its occupants remembered it was only an outpost and pushed themselves into taxis and trains. Well, thought Helen, cheerful at the alternative prospect, at least I don't do that. I get in my clapped-out car, drive it to the office as rarely as possible, then to magistrates' courts in Cheshunt and Epping where I prosecute the daily list of thieves, burglars, and even, occasionally, poachers, all at snail's speed to suit the magistrates, saying everything twice.

It was in that respect that the contrast was most marked – the pace of it, the deliberation behind decision, the endless repetition of facts. What would have been allowed half an hour in front of a tetchy stipendiary magistrate in Bow Street or Tower Bridge took half a day here, with somewhat dissimilar results. Here they were swifter in sending the offenders to prison, heavier on fines, and inclined to hang them for careless driving, but she had to confess that law and order prevailed after a fashion, not unjust, not innovative either. Less bark, slower bite, more civilized.

Nor did she mind the subtle demotion that her move from central London had involved. Helen was not designed to succeed on the crude hierarchical ladder of the Crown Prosecution Service, or in any branch of the uncivil service, had never progressed far in grade, owing to an embarrassing frankness in interviews and a deliberate ignorance of whom she should please and flatter. Securing further promotion was a Machiavellian exercise demanding paroxysms of sycophancy for which she had no stomach. Bailey's similar indifference had propelled him through the ranks of the police like a secret missile, but Helen's had kept her still and, in the old office, rewarded in a way she had preferred. She had skills beyond those of her superiors. They recognized and exploited her skills by a division of work that took advantage of them, leaving Helen with a host of difficult and dangerous cases. Here in the outback, her sheer competence, the experience of murder, mayhem, drugs, and fraud, unnerved her employers more than slightly and they tried to bar her from the mainstream as far as possible. It was Cheshunt, Epping, and the juvenile court for Miss West. Keep her out of the office; she knows too much. Helen smiled and defeated them further by genuinely not minding. There was a purpose to this beyond career, after all: she had only wanted to stay alive and to see if she and Geoffrey Bailey could make a success of living together. Nothing was more important, nothing more absorbing than that. If some of her remained unused material, it would have to wait.

'Oh, damn.' For the second time in an hour she had gone to the wrong cupboard. Freudian slip, the product of undiscussed home-sickness, making her behave as if she was in her own home. Which she wished she was, even with all the attendant arguments – your place or mine? – that had bedevilled the last year. What an unlikely pair of lovers they were, policeman and lawyer, too scared, the pair of them, too suspicious, and far too independent to begin to decide which house should be home, miserable apart, tricky together. She had thought of abandoning it, could not contemplate that; thought of marriage, could not contemplate that, either. A marriage of true minds, all right, but pulling in opposite directions. Then Bailey was moved to this parish; this very house fell vacant for rent. They would try it for a year, borrowed premises, borrowed time, no commitments. Helen as housewife, the idea made her choke, but there was a nice novelty to it. So far so good in this isolation, though it would have been better if he liked it less. Bailey, after all, hailed from the East End; he might have the same aspirations for a better life. Helen hailed from nowhere and believed in very little.

'WE MAY AS well go home,' said Superintendent Bailey. 'If we search in the dark we may ruin the chances. The doc will be here shortly after five a.m. So shall I.'

'I've left Smith and Peters here to peg out the area. All that.'

'And shoot foxes,' Bailey added, smiling.

'With what, sir? It's the ghosts worry them.' The inspector grinned, comfortable with Bailey as few were, grateful for the pragmatism that was going to allow some of them to sleep instead of messing around all night, talking about it until daylight revealed anything they would miss if they moved now.

'Seal off the footpath and the carpark, will you?'

'Will do, sir. Bowles will do that. Funny thing is, it was only opened again yesterday. Been resurfaced, out of action for weeks. They've all been taking their cars elsewhere.'

'Good. More chance we'll find traces of whoever put that body in there.'

'Poor cow.'

'Yes,' said Bailey, looking at the protruding hand sealed with polythene. 'I wonder who she is.'

The inspector grinned. 'Was, sir.'

Bailey sighed. 'Definitely past tense. Was. Come on, let's get some sleep before we have to look at the rest of her, presuming it is a woman. See you at five. Tell them to walk carefully. He may have left some souvenirs on the footpath.'

Eleven p.m. now and too many boots for comfort on that footpath already. Tell them not to deviate into the woods either, for God's sake, crashing about and standing on anything that might have been left by the performer of these rude and hurried burial rites. Looking at the shallow grave, flattened earth, and bent branches around it, Bailey supposed there would be traces. No careful undertaker this; no wonder the fox had found her. Tomorrow would be soon enough for discovery, when all the willing troops were deployed to their worst after brief sleep. All except Peters, Smith, and Bowles, who would not even have their turn to sleep in the morning. Bailey tried to forget them all on the way home, tried, on his way to Helen, to forget that offending, blotched stump of a hand pointing its accusation above earth.

IN THE CARPARK, half a mile from the grave, Police Constable Bowles tapped on the window of the single van parked beneath the trees, stood back politely. Inside, beyond the condensation on the glass, he could see movement, a breast rapidly covered, an arm in guilty movement, a face pressed to the rear window, eyes wide at the sight of the buttons on his uniform. More movement, until a youth scrabbled out of the front, buttoning his shirt, furious in the face of Bowles's half-smile.

'Wha's the matter, for fuck's sake? No law agin it, is there? First I knew.'

'Just hope she's sixteen, son. But you've got to move. Got to clear this carpark, see. Sorry about it.'

'Why? Why the fuck … why should I?' His fists were clenched, aggression on display like a fighting ram.

'Less of that. This your car, son? Or your dad's? Or your gaffer's? Been for a drink, have we?'

'All right, all right, all right.' Querulous fear rose in the voice. A girl's head, young but not childlike, appeared at the window. Bowles relented.

'Found a body in the woods, miss. Dead. Got to clear the area, seal it off. Hop it.'

The girl shrieked, short and shrill, an eerie little sound, then curled back in the passenger seat, pulling the boy in beside her. The engine spluttered, van spitting away full of the boy's fury, leaving profound silence. Extending the yellow tape across the entrance to the road, Bowles missed the company and wondered how they had failed to see the police car parked in the far corner. Shame on you, boy, you could have done better than that.

THE PURR OF Bailey's diesel engine at the door was a welcome sound. By the time he had collected his case, gazed at the sky,

gathered his wits, wondered if Helen was still awake, and opened
the door, she had padded into the kitchen, found the Scotch, run
the bath, and filled the kettle. This was not the first body he had
found in their six months' sojourn in this not so peaceful place,
nor was it the first late evening to give Helen the opportunity to
practise domestic solicitude, which Bailey neither demanded nor
expected, but which secretly delighted him to the marrow of his
strong and slender bones.

Bailey welcomed these attentions like a child. It felt like having
the wife he had seen described in fiction, a true comforter never
encountered in his life until now, and not even a wife in name.
Bailey regretted that, and respected it. It was Helen's decision,
not his. Sleep, even after thirteen hours of duty, was less important than news and the long embrace of dear familiarity. One day
they would discuss his reservations about the place, this frightful house she seemed to like, but not now. There is nothing, he
thought, more delightful than a woman who is happy to see you.

There is nothing, Helen thought, more becoming than the
wrinkles on Bailey's face.

'VERY MACABRE,' HE told her, sitting up in bed with Scotch and
coffee, Helen curled beside him, as welcoming as the night had
been chill, both of them indulging in a frequent if decadent night-
time ritual. 'Macabre with the usual comic overtones. It always
makes me laugh when the divisional surgeon turns out. You know,
he who precedes the pathologist and gives us licence to continue.'

Helen knew.

'Dr Flick, busy little man, looks at his hand, this suggestion
of body, far from fresh. "I think she's dead at the moment," he
says. "I'll do a certificate." Very pompous and Irish. I don't know
why we needed a doctor to tell us that. "I'll pronounce it lifeless,

I think," says Flick, just as he would if faced with a pile of bones. Pretty clever diagnosis, I thought. Has a swig of this out of his back pocket' – Bailey raised his own glass to illustrate – 'then scuttles away as fast as his legs will carry him.'

'Back to the living. Or the pub. Can't blame him.'

'No,' said Bailey, turning to her. 'I don't blame him. The living have more to say. I'd rather be with you than keeping vigil in a wood.'

She smiled at him, forgetting her preoccupations, seeing him anew as she did almost every day. 'Well, if that's the case, I'm glad you've no other choices.'

'Who said I haven't?'

'I did.'

LATER IN THE warmth, his arms surrounding her. Geoffrey murmured sleepily into Helen's ear, 'You didn't have to run a bath for me, you know. I don't have to touch the bodies. Not these days.'

She stirred. He could feel her frowning. 'But you do. They touch you, and you touch them. You always do.'

'Yes,' he said, remembering the spasm of anger as his own fingers had touched that pathetic and pleading mutilation of a hand, felt the ice-cold mottled forearm in the dark. He had wished her goodbye, disliking the prospect of tomorrow's disinterment, wishing they could simply leave her alone.

'You always do,' Helen repeated.

'You're right,' he sighed. 'I always do.'

Chapter Two

Detective Constable Amanda Scott arrived early by fifteen minutes, always in advance of the boss, careful in this and all things to preserve the good opinion she had tried so hard to deserve. She stepped out of her neat car, unaware of its highly polished gleam, but pleasantly conscious of the shine on her leather pumps and the curve of her waxed and tanned calves as she stood away from the door with her precise movements. She checked her hair in the side mirror, reproving herself for her own vanity while locking the car with automatic care. Miss Scott was dressed as she was always dressed in sensible but feminine clothes. White long-sleeved blouse with buttons, pleated cotton skirt in navy blue, matching the handbag and shoes, offset by tiny pearl earrings. Nothing flashy about Miss Scott – not a Mrs or a Ms – clad in good chain store clothes with an eye to economy and perfect presentation rather than the luxury of flair. She had liked the less nerve-racking days of uniform duty, still reflected in her conservative clothes, but she liked this better and knew herself to be modestly, only sometimes raucously, admired.

She sniffed the air. Woodland smells mingled with fresh Tar-macadam in the carpark, completed when? A day or so before, she would have guessed. No common access to the woods from here for over a fortnight. She gazed around her, saw the footpath into the trees, and mentally propelled herself above it all, forming in her mind a plan of the area. Maybe they would need an aerial pho-tograph, but with a facility all her own, she imagined she could see herself and the scene of this demise from the air. A triangle, body in the middle. I stand, she told herself as she would have told a class, one mile from Branston on the Epping road, on the edge of Bluebell Wood. Here is a carpark, a picnic spot provided by the council, and here is a footpath that leads into the woods but peters out after half a mile; only proper walkers go farther, to their own disappointment because there isn't that much of it, really. Only another half-mile, then a valley, uphill to a small field and a bit more woodland surrounding that awful hotel. You could walk straight across to the hotel if you could ever get through that jungle of a garden. About a mile from here to there, with woods extending a mile on either side of where I point, two more pic-nic spots on the other side. Not a particularly beautiful or pleas-ant place outside the footpath and even with the dearth of green trees on this border of London and country, strangely unpopular. Might have been less so if the establishment on the other side, which insisted on calling itself a hotel rather than the unfriendly pub it was, actually welcomed guests. Amanda's single visit had coincided with that of a cockroach. She had never returned and could not remember what they called the place now – the name changed with each renewal of the licence and the whim of the owners. The Crown, that was it, and no one, surely no one, would brave entry into the woods and fields through their garden. Compared to that wilderness, the woods were as easy as a street.

Detective Constable Scott paced three steps left and three right, small, clipped steps. Should she stay and greet the troops or walk down the path to the muslin-sheeted grave? She hated being still: she would walk; no, she would wait for the boss and walk behind him. Bailey would talk and think at the same time, dividing the wood into sections for searching, throwing ideas and instructions over his shoulder, and Amanda would remember them all, watch, and learn. She was only there to learn, would never miss a single scrap of knowledge or let past her sharp blue eyes the slightest opportunity for making a quiet contribution. She would be as she always was, his calm, efficient shadow, earning trust. It never occurred to her to wonder if she actually liked Bailey, or any of her colleagues. Amanda's concentration was streamlined. Her own feelings were irrelevant, suspended as Bailey arrived and greeted Dr Vanguard as an old friend. Both their cars were parked crooked, and she wondered why, on such respectable salaries, they drove such shabby vehicles.

The team assembled like the cast of a play, Bailey leading and Vanguard following, as daylight grew sharper, the signal for a hot day. More speed, said Vanguard. The sooner we get her out the better. Police Constables Bowles and Peters rose stiffly from camp chairs as the rest arrived in single file, not deviating from the footpath, as Bailey had told them. Photographers, exhibits officer next with bags, labels, gloves, tweezers, strolling behind the ambulancemen, who were the only ones talking.

'As I said, Fred, it ain't really my turn to do this shift.'

'Never mind,' said Fred. Ordinary grumbles in the mist.

The searchers, combers of undergrowth, pickers of detritus, carriers of bags, would follow, foot soldiers behind cavalry.

Vanguard never seemed to mind the dirt. He who had waded into stinking Thames mud to recover half-submerged limbs, who had pulled a leg away from a hip joint in a cesspit, found this dry earth relatively innocuous. He knelt by the grave and began uncovering the form beneath the soil with all the care of an archaeologist, sweeping away handfuls of leaves with systematic energy until the shape emerged. The photographer recorded each stage of the process. The others watched from either side as the figure came into focus, lying straight with legs uncrossed, face turned flat against the earth as if refusing to watch what was being done. She was recognizably female in limbs if not yet in detail, and as Vanguard's hand dusted the face, Amanda could not suppress the rising nausea, glanced at Bailey, and maintained calm against her shiver of disgust. The face was discoloured green and black, alive with bright white maggots twisting in the cavities of empty eye sockets, active in the distended nostrils, full of hideous and indignant movement in the eyes and lipless mouth where their destruction had exposed teeth bared in an obscene grin.

Bailey wondered why they had attacked the face first, what dreadful lack of mercy; render to earth what must be rendered, but first distort, make unrecognizable what was once so human, may have been beautiful. No greater damage than the face; apart from the half-chewed hand without fingertips, the limbs were intact, stained like green marble, but whole. No doubt the larvae would have found the other orifices, liquid, vulnerable private parts.

Amanda turned her head away as pathologist and assistants lifted the body on to the plastic sheet laid ready to receive it. She was ashamed for the woman's nakedness, knew disgust and contempt for one found in such condition, almost an acute dislike for the dead, resented her own squeamishness and the constant struggle to suppress it. Thank God Vanguard would not be taking his vaginal and anal swabs here: they would be spared that sight until the thing was finally devoid of all humanity on the postmortem table. In the haze of her own disgust, holding her breath to avoid the stench, feeling her skin itch as if the larvae had attached themselves, Amanda shook her senses, forced herself to look harder. She was not there to feel pain, noted the gash on the forehead, the gaping throat. Well. They would soon know better. The exhibits officer collected larvae from the face, put them in a bag without a word, treating them with gentleness. Amanda wondered what manner of man it was who analysed them.

'How long, Doc? Can you say?'

Vanguard was continuing a cursory inspection, calling up the ambulance boys for the tiresome walk back to transport, grumbling under his breath. 'How long? What, for a report? Oh, I see, how long dead? Difficult to say. At least a week, probably more. Depends if she was left uncovered first, speeds up the decomposition a bit. Do we know who she is?'

'No, not yet. No one local reported missing, except children.'

Vanguard grunted, scratched, and Amanda wondered how his wife ever let him inside the doors. 'Well, look for a woman, fortyish, dark-haired, bit big in the bum, but otherwise shapely, probably pretty.' He cackled, Bailey grimaced. He liked the man, had time for him, but occasionally the humour was hard to take. 'And a knife, I would think. Also something blunt. About three p.m. OK? Got another one first.'

Bailey felt the hangover of familiarity. Another session with formaldehyde smells and all the ceremony of an abattoir. His own aversion to the necessary witnessing of the pathologist's knife owed less to squeamishness than to a sense of indignity. Sad enough to be buried, slaughtered first before time, terminally abused, without being disinterred and cut apart, so distant from the dignity of laying out and decent burial that was the ordinary hope of ordinary men. No saving grace for the murder victim, none at all, no stateliness in death or anything that followed and from the disgrace of secret killing there would follow more. In Bailey's mind there grew the dull and familiar anger against the dealer of such treacherous cards, the perpetrator of such brutality, which carried this in its wake. Pitiful nakedness. Not a stitch on her or with her. Not even woman's comfort, the everpresent handbag.

He turned, issued his orders. Start here, fanning out in sections, eyes to the ground. Cigarette ends, notable footprints, broken branches suggesting haste; a week is long enough to hide half the traces if there are any traces, and what a scrubby, mean, depressed bit of woodland this is. Not real forest or real country, not the oil-drummed, rubbish-filled adventure playground bombsites of his youth, either. He felt dislike of Branston and all its environs rise like a tide, sink in the need for action. Two dozen men, more if needed, comb the ground for a square mile. Amanda, organize a press release, meet me at the hotel, no, I don't need a lift, I prefer to walk, and I wish you were not so obsequious, or that I liked anything about this place.

Bailey had walked every inch of this ground, alone sometimes or with Helen, pacing the territory of his new home like a cat, fully aware that without butter on his paws, he would have aimed for home. For the wider territory of his professional manor he had made it his business to drive every road and take into his brain each landmark, street, pub, station, and anything else immovable. He knew the bus routes and the trouble spots as well as the areas of innocence. The manor extended far beyond Branston, slipped into the sprawl of northeast London where he was stationed in a building of monumental ugliness. The three other bodies whose removal he had witnessed in the last two months had been found, respectively, in a flat, behind some dustbins, and in the front seat of a car. Minicab driver with smashed skull, urban waste, sticky with blood, but found before the predators and the flies got to him. Not like this. This was beyond town limits and the zone of improved chances. The same was not supposed to happen here. For Helen, himself, and all who dwelt here.

An afterthought, catching the man's eye. 'Stay on and help, Bowles, will you?'

'Sir.' The grin widened on Bowles's face. Overtime and, besides that, work he liked, reminiscent of weeding and pruning, pedantic garden chores, which he also liked. Bowles was fifty, with eyes like magnets attracting him to anything out of place. A man of infinite patience which his children did not understand, so that he was forced to pretend occasional irritation foreign to a cultivator of plants and detector of metal objects on Essex riverbanks. Bowles enjoyed sifting lawn seed and grains of sand, also searching ground with his mole of a nose and brown long-sighted eyes, squatting and picking, sorting and choosing. A cursory search behind the carpark area had revealed cartons and Coke tins, hamburger wrappers, plastic bags, and several used contraceptives. Bowles was always amazed by the human habit of congregation even to deposit rubbish. The flocking habit was foreign to him, although his mating instinct was sound enough to let him recognize anything that might have been thrown from a handbag.

Ignoring all distraction, Bowles would waste no time looking for the obvious – what had Vanguard said? Knife, blunt weapon. Dimmer eyes than his could find these if they were there to be found, which Bowles suspected they were not, while his own would look for nothing in particular. He hitched his trousers and straightened his jacket, impervious to growing heat. Ah, yes. A plodder himself, he would recognize signs of haste, for a start, even over a week old, and distinguish between adult spores and the symptoms of tag-playing children. He shivered, accustoming a cold, stiff body to thoughts of activity, thinking slowly, remembering the couple he had dismissed the night before. Picnic spot or no picnic spot, this was somehow not a wood for children.

Bowles and the more conscientious of his companions knew they were looking for whatever they could find. Not an empirical search, simply a collecting exercise. Later, when they found the culprit – Bowles always said 'when', not 'if' – some of their souvenirs might fill in a corner of the picture. 'You never know' was Bowles's most infamous and irritating cliché; the phrase alone had quite rightly blocked his promotion, indicative of his preference for any activity without apparent purpose. In the event, it was Bowles, of course, who found the cigarettes, the packet and the two stubs, one with lipstick and one without. He put the stubs in a matchbox, like a boy with pet spiders, and carried them safely home.

Unlike Amanda Scott, with her preference for the wine bar in Branston High Street, Bailey had no objection to visiting The Crown Hotel, did not confess to his assistant his liking for the place, even though he imagined her discretion hid nerves of steel. Bailey had found the hotel attracting him from the start, a view shared by Helen to the extent that they had visited the place more frequently than any other local hostelry for reasons neither of them could fathom.

'It isn't the food,' Helen had remarked, happily and thoroughly entertained by wrestling with the crust of a cheese roll, putting it down to search for the cheese, finding a huge but dried lump of it in the centre.

'It isn't the beer, either,' Bailey had added, nursing a murky pint with some suspicion.

'What is it, then?' said Helen.

'Unpredictability, unfashionability, and anonymity,' said Bailey promptly.

'Oh, my, long words for a Sunday. You've been reading the papers again. Do you mean you can hide here without knowing what will happen?' Teasing him, grinning in contentment, Sunday a holiday.

'No, I mean I like it because so few other people do.' He gestured towards the bar with more spaces than people. 'And because I never know from one visit to the next what it will be like or whether it will still be standing.'

'I quite like it,' Helen said, 'because it has all the sod-the-customer attitude of a London pub. You know, the what-do-you-want-a-drink-for-this-is-only-a-pub-for-God's-sake approach. Clean glass? Fussy, are we? What's wrong with a dirty one? You antisocial or something? I only work here. Why should I care? Et cetera.'

'But they do care,' said Bailey. 'They care desperately, which is why it's so odd.' He had paused and grinned. 'Admit it, Helen. You really like it for the arguments.'

'Oh, I do,' Helen sighed. 'You know I do. I can't resist listening to other people's arguments. Especially loud, public, silly, insulting marital arguments.'

'You're well placed here, then, darling,' said Bailey with his smile. 'Seventh heaven for a nose like yours.'

'Actually,' she had said, 'I'm happy most places with you.'

He remembered the conversation with amusement as he skirted the hotel gardens, finally crossing the field at one side and climbing a fence to reach the front of the building by way of the road in preference to ill-mannered intrusion via the back wilderness of garden. Bailey was always courteous. His politeness was the coldest and warmest feature of his public face, giving him entry to numerous social pockets where courtesy could not be defined, let alone expressed. 'Always polite, Mr Bailey,' one streetwalker informant had stated. 'Always knows when you're in the bath.' Knew also when to accept obvious lies without comment to save face or save pain, and when not to intrude even as a friend, although in their bizarre fashion, Mr and Mrs Featherstone, licensees of The Crown Hotel and owners of same, would have welcomed him as such. Our man of taste, Mr Bailey the copper. Anyone who arrived at their doors, withstood the insults and the rows, the dizzying décor, the recitation of plans for improvement and instant riches, as well as the experimental nourishment, became in their eyes a man of taste. Bailey was aware he had reached this class, equated their definition of his taste in this respect alongside stamina and helpless curiosity, carried as always his own immunities.

Regarding him as a friend, insofar as the Featherstone family had friends, was no guarantee of politeness. As Bailey approached the entrance to the bar, door unlocked as both a sign of proprietorial carelessness by the owners and indifference to local burglars, he sensed beyond the pane the sound of an argument. Ten a.m., the Featherstones fighting, all well with the world. Revised licensing hours' allowing longer opening hours made no difference to the trading manners of the establishment, but then the laws had made no difference before. If the bar had been open in the a.m.s and p.m.s of life, the local uniformed police had used their well-known discretion to ignore the fact, saving the same laws to restrain only those pubs that caused trouble. There were no drugs or underage drinkers in The Crown, while the only fighting on the premises was conducted between the licensees. Even the authorities had neglected the place.

In the huge, potentially elegant bar-room, Mrs Banks, cleaning lady, sat in a corner smoking a cigarette and drinking the half of Guinness she had poured for herself, weary from flicking her damp duster. She let herself in at eight, stopped her indifferent labours when the Featherstone family emerged from their pits. 'Can't stand the noise, dear,' she said to Bailey, shuffling into her coat, draining the glass, which she was not going to wash, pointing in the direction of the kitchen. 'They're in there,' as if any announcement were needed.

'Oh, shut up, Harold, for chrissake. Feed your big face and shut up. Let me get on with this cooking.'

'Cooking! You call that cooking? You couldn't get a job feeding pigs.'

'What about you, then? Call this filthy stuff coffee? I wouldn't give it to the bloody cat.' A crescendo, followed by Harold's voice.

'Fuck off back to the smoke, then, why don't you?' Not screamed, but loud enough, calm enough to penetrate the deafest ears, shortened by Bailey's presence. 'Oh, it's you, Mr Bailey. Didn't mean you. I meant her.'

'Shut up, Harold. Shut up.' Very loud, louder than Harold's casual, vicious invitation. Bernadette Featherstone, shriller in voice but quicker to recover, forced a smile so fleeting a blink would have missed its presence. 'Yes, it's Mr West,' she said. 'Superintendent Geoffrey. PC Plod to us. Fancy seeing you. You don't usually need sustenance so early. Mrs West chucked you out, has she?' Bernadette took a delight in referring to Bailey as West, her own way of striking a blow for female solidarity. 'Can't think why. What do you want? Tea, coffee, gin, whisky? Harold's had one of the latter already. Sweetens him up nicely, you can tell.' Her clipped tones, educated, only the slightest undertones of Irish, betrayed a defeat that was marshalling forces. She had decided to allow Harold the last word, a decision made before Bailey's entrance. The why-don't-you-bugger-off-if-you're-so-bloody-miserable routine usually ended round one and heralded the beginning of round two an hour or so later. She never had the answers to Harold's final questions. Looking at her plump frame, wearied face, scarred hands, uncontrolled once-blonde hair, Bailey could see why she had no answer. Here and now might have been terrible, but here was an addiction, and in any event there was nowhere else to go.

'Business I'm afraid, not pleasure,' said Bailey, and to forestall some howl of protest added quickly, 'we've found a body three-quarters of a mile from here. Bluebell Wood. You're nearest as the crow flies, hence the visit. Simply a chance you might have seen something or know who she is. Which is more than we do.'

'A body? Oh, my God,' said Bernadette, sinking her weight into a chair, suddenly breathless, patting hair and chest as if to see that she was still alive herself, shooting a venomous glance at Harold, accusing him of every foul deed, including this. 'Really dead?'

'Very dead. Since a few days. Beyond artificial respiration.'

Bernadette crossed herself rapidly, last remnant of expensive Catholic education long since forgotten in her language, remembered in her fear of hell. 'Poor soul,' she said. Bailey liked her for being shocked, and for expressing pity before irritation.

'But why,' asked Harold, always the calmer but sooner provoked to suspicion, 'why are you asking us? Why should we know anything about it?'

'I don't imagine you do,' Bailey replied with casual patience and the smile that creased his face from forehead to chin. 'But you're the nearest building, and I simply thought if I gave you a rough description it might trigger something. She might have been a customer here. You might have seen a couple in here having an argument, oh, a week or ten days ago. Woman of about forty, dark hair, good figure. I'm only boxing in the dark. Maybe someone depressed.'

'Oh,' said Bernadette, brightening, 'was it suicide, then?'

'No,' said Bailey, 'not unless she buried herself, too.'

There was a little silence, sun streaming through spectacularly dirty windows on to Harold's pale skin. An innocent silence, pregnant with the desire to help, or so Bailey sensed it, not the hesitation of guilty confusion, but not a productive interlude, either. Unless this victim had sprung into the communal mind immediately it would be useless to expect either party to this soured but engrossing union to remember what happened the day before, let alone the week. Unless blows had been struck or walls collapsed.

Harold giggled. 'Only dark-haired lady comes in here is your wife,' he said, adding out of malice, 'sometimes on her own, too.'

'Yes I know,' said Bailey, 'but she'd resent the description of fortyish, you know. She's got a few years to go before that. Almost as many as I have the other side.'

'Couples,' said Bernadette suddenly. 'Couples. We never have women on their own unless they sit quietly and read a paper like

Mrs West. Think of couples, Harold, you git. There's one or two of the definitely over-the-side kind, always looking at the door in case they're going to be spotted, sitting in a corner pawing each other. Disgusting – well, sweet, really, in a way. Chance would be a fine thing, wouldn't it, Harold darling? One respectable pair – I mean, not kids – used to come in here, woman about thirty-eight, but not for a while, or at least not regular. Maybe last week, maybe not, I don't know, why should I? Only remember her because I tried to chat once, asked her name, and she wouldn't say. "What's it to you?" she said. "Suit yourself," I said, but I like asking names. Maybe last week, maybe not.'

Bailey could imagine some clandestine mistress recoiling from the suggestion she supply her credentials, especially to a request barked like the cross-examination Bernadette used in lieu of small talk to customers, smiled at the thought. 'Anyone else?' he asked mildly. The Featherstones sat at their long kitchen table amid the crumbs of breakfast, their faces a study of concentration.

Across the wooden floor of the bar came footsteps and a calm but carrying voice. 'Is your mother in?' A muttered response, heavier footsteps thudding upstairs, Amanda Scott pushing open the door with a pleasant hello on her face, fading as she encountered the glower from Bernadette, all at odds with the leer from Harold. 'May I come in?' she said prettily. 'Your son said you were here.'

William, son and heir. Bailey had forgotten him; he had a sad naïveté about children. William, listening at the door, poor daft child, a lifetime of listening at doors. Bailey had a vision of the boy – Harold's pale skin on a vacant face, none of Harold's cunning or vapid good looks, clumsy and lonely. A door slammed in the distance; a thump upstairs as the boy threw himself on to his bed. Found out, careless, bored.

Bernadette spoke rapidly, words addressed to Bailey while keeping her eyes and savage expression fixed on the face of Amanda Scott as if she would like to throw a blanket over that immaculate presence. 'Don't speak to William, will you, Geoffrey? Not today if you don't bloody mind. He's in one of his moods.'

Bailey watched Amanda, sensed her waiting in vain for some sign of authoritative insistence from himself, replied calmly, 'No, of course not, if you would rather I didn't. May have to another time once we know more, perhaps not. When it suits him.'

Bernadette relaxed and recovered. 'Who the hell are you, then, Miss Squeaky-Clean?' she asked Amanda in a deliberate attempt to embarrass. 'His bit on the side?'

Even Bailey could not suppress a hidden grin at the brief spasm of furious indignation on that smooth face. He added quickly, 'Amanda is the privilege of another, Bernadette. Miss Scott is my detective constable. Arrives in time to stop me drinking.'

Amanda was mollified slightly, but, as Bernadette intended her to be, uncomfortable, anxious to get on and out, mystified by the aimless chat that followed, disgruntled by Bailey's lack of desire to allocate tasks. There's been a murder, for God's sake, she said to herself, and you stand chatting in dirty kitchens. Not even insisting on seeing that lunatic thug who was listening at the door. Suspect if ever was, known for inclination to violence. Come on, Superintendent, please, come on. I don't like it here, and they don't like me. There are days when I do not care for you or admire you as much as others do, however handsome you are. There is nothing here, there never is. Come away, please, before I doubt you. Stood silent and smiling instead. Bernadette disliked her quite intensely. The feeling was mutual. Bailey was sorry for the discomfiture of both.

UPSTAIRS, HALF ON, half off his unmade bed, William listened with his ear to the floor and his heels drumming quietly on the wallpaper, his head uncomfortably full of blood and little else. William had chosen this small and unpromising room five years ago on the eve of his twelfth birthday, stuck in it ever since although he had outgrown both bed and furniture, and in this Edwardian barn he had the choice of other rooms far more dignified. There was a theory that most of the seven bedrooms were reserved for guests, but few stayed, only the odd misguided travelling salesman who failed to return, or the even odder couple whose passion could not withstand the discomfort, the breakfast, the inquisition, or William listening at the door. William liked the intrusion of the kitchen smells, ignored the noisy accompaniments, or turned the noises into rhythms inside his head, anticipating the next change of pace or silence. He particularly liked the whirr of the washing machine, which made his room vibrate, and he liked the childish chest of drawers, diminutive wardrobe, all ordered for a boy who was now the size of a man – a man five feet ten inches tall, equipped with huge hands, swollen genitals, the mind of a ten-year-old child, and hearing as sharp as an owl's.

They had gone. William heaved himself back on the bed, all anxiety banished. They had been talking about nothing, and whatever they had said would keep the peace. He knew the words of the conversation, could not always establish the links. Grown-ups were always talking about nothing. What took them so long never to remember anything important he never knew. And he would not be lectured for listening at the door, not today at least. They never noticed, Mum and Dad, never noticed at all, all those people who came and went, fiddled about, drank, got drunk, laughed, shouted, all that stuff. He was dimly aware of the limitations of his mind, conscious of the superiority of his eyes and the refinement of his senses, which found all others foolish, his own absorbing.

Spreadeagled on the worn candlewick bedcover, his bare feet grubby from padding back across the garden at dawn, William regarded his domain, still listening to the polite departing voices. He was the only Featherstone who relished his own being.

The washing machine downstairs began to rumble.

William scratched his groin idly, unzipped his jeans slowly, and began a quicker massage, fingering the thing he had always called his stump, for the second time that morning. Donkey William, they had called him at school, an unkind if accurate reflection on the size of his penis as well as his brain power. Silly William, happy as a baby in a sand pile, eyes closed, hands busy, his face in a grimace of repose, shooting stars.

Chapter Three

'IT'S THE LAWNMOWERS that get me most,' said Helen to Christine Summerfield. 'Lawnmowers in summer. Trimmers, hedge cutters, tree clippers, anything electrical. In winter it's hammers and drills. Lawnmowers are worse.'

'Did you have a garden in London?' Faraway London, as if it were another planet. All of twelve miles away. A lifetime.

'Oh, yes. Had? Still have. And a lawn, even. Well, a sort of a lawn. I clipped it with shears after the push-and-shove mower gave up the ghost. Rusted beyond repair, seemed undignified to use it in old age. I hope they – the tenants, I mean – look after it. But I never had a high-pitched machine, not like these things sounding like a swarm of angry flies.'

Christine was immune. She had lived here longer, relished the sounds of rural suburbia. 'Won't take a minute,' she said cheerfully. 'Only a small patch of lawn. Anyway, sitting still is so much my favourite pastime I can stand any accompaniment.'

'This is the point,' said Helen. 'I should formally thank you for your company. You saved my sanity in the High Street.'

'Thank me? It's your house, your coffee, your Saturday morning. Such formality. Does that mean you want me to go?'

'Oh, please don't. Have some more coffee, piece of cake, gin and tonic. Stay and talk. Otherwise Geoffrey gets an earful when he gets home. No, I only mean I'm grateful for a kindred spirit, if that's the right phrase. Eat the cake, anything to keep you.'

'Eat the cake? Encouraging me, you thin hypocrite. You can afford to eat the cake. I can't, but I'll eat it all the same.'

'Inside me,' said Helen, 'is a fat person trying to get out. Six more months of domestic bliss in Branston and this damaged butterfly will have gone back to chrysalis. Fat chrysalis. I can't afford cake, either. Cake and country: why do they go together? Eat your calories, get lethargic, sit back and listen to the butterflies. OK, for once I admit the pleasure of it.'

The two women were a sharp contrast to each other. Christine Summerfield bore a seasonal name for a buttercup nature, resembled an attractive advertisement for dairy food – pleasantly plump and fair, heavy bosom, blue eyes, and expression of shrewd honesty. On first sight her role as professional caretaker of man or animal seemed obvious: she looked like what she was. Helen had guessed nurse first, then social worker. Right the second time. Christine resembled the kindly guardian she was, sympathy implicit in every line of her face, while Helen – so easily ridden with pity, guilt, confusion, and fury, so prone to every surreptitious kindness or mercy her job or her life afforded – did not carry her compassion like a flag in her eyes. She was small and dark, slender but muscular, occasionally fierce. She had a slightly lined face full of hidden humour, huge eyes, and a scar on her forehead. Christine considered her beautiful; Bailey did, too. Helen's previous Boss had called her a stubborn little brute. Vividly attractive on any estimate, but unlike Christine, not a thing to be embraced soon after shaking its hand. She was too quick in wit, too articulate to present as the immediate comforter, the bosom for all sorrows, as Christine patently was, and yet they found Helen, the lamed and the disgraced, the troubled and the children. Can we play in your garden, miss? Can we sit in your car? Of course you can. Tell your mother where you are, and if you eat the plants or puncture the wheels, I'll brain you, understand? Any use for these biscuits, have you? Thought you might. Staccato common sense, endless generosity almost gruff in the giving, parameters firmly set. Old men in pubs, young women in shops talking while she listened and understood, patient with fools. An instinctive grasp of what was important in any tale. Christine the caretaker knew herself drawn in the same way to that calm understanding which was quite devoid of criticism, was charmed and relieved when the confidences that had poured unbidden from her own mouth and into Helen's ears were rewarded by confidences in return. Incomplete confidences, but still something tantamount to shared secrets. 'Dear God,' she had said to Helen, 'social worker and prosecutor, I ask you. By tradition we sit on opposite fences, but we manage to talk for hours.'

'Opposite fences?' said Helen. 'Rubbish. We're all on the same side. Two professionals doing a job. Tradition has a lot to answer for.' They had gravitated beyond such considerations, still discussed them.

'I like it here,' said Christine. 'But I can see why you don't. You're playing second fiddle to Bailey – professionally, I mean.'

'I've always played second fiddle. That's what solicitors do, after all. We never make big shots, in public at least.'

'But you don't even deal with big shots, not here.'

'True,' Helen admitted. 'It's a bit lower-powered than I'm used to, but that isn't what I mind, most of the time. Some of the time, but not most of the time. It's a bit of relief, and if the truth were known, the small cases are often as complicated as the big ones. Shame they don't get the same attention.'

'What about your little-shot clients, if that's the right word for them? Do you ever have any doubts about their guilt?'

'I very rarely doubt their being guilty as charged, if that's what you mean, especially here, where truthful witnesses are less at a premium. But I still think them innocent in many respects. Fault and blame are so often irrelevant.'

They were content to sit in silence, Christine waiting, Helen finally restful.

'Damn that lawnmower. I never understand how an age that forces people to live in closer proximity than ever before should give them all the tools to make it impossible. Stereos, lawnmowers, food mixers, such a bloody racket. London was quiet compared to this. Speaking of proximity, how's Antony? Come on, tell me.'

Helen was well aware that her companion had been waiting to tell for the last hour, only needing a cue, ever since they had met in the High Street, grinning over the heads of the shoppers, she buying for Bailey, Christine for Antony, Helen making heavy weather of chores Christine took lightly. Oh, I can't make up my mind. What the hell shall I buy? There's so much of it. Decisions in shops were far harder than professional ones. Even their love affairs were different.

'Antony? He's at home making lunch.' Christine blushed slightly. 'He likes cooking, actually.'

'Now there's luck for you. Still love, I take it?'

'Yee … es. With open eyes. Early days yet, very early, but optimistic. I know what he is, you see, and I don't mind.' She curled up in the garden chair, which Helen found the only comfortable seat in the house, settled to the telling. 'I know he's a dreamer, been a bad lad in the past. Knee deep in poetry, bewailing his lot teaching Shakespeare to reluctant kids. Likes it, really. He has this peculiar ability to teach. I'd forgive him a lot for having that.'

'What's peculiar about it? Any special technique?'

'He makes children want to write,' said Christine. 'I don't know how. He says that's the essence of teaching English. Gets them to write down everything they think and put some form into it. They seem to love it, although the results are hilarious and sometimes disconcerting. Tell it like a story, he says to them, and they do. Then, lo and behold, the little blighters began to like reading, too. Much in demand, our Antony. All for his talent of getting them to record their lives on paper.'

'I like that,' said Helen. 'He goes romping up in my estimation. So that's one thing you love about him. You were just beginning on the reservations.'

'Well, he can't help looking like Byron. It's rather turned his mind, given him this fatal attraction for the opposite sex, which includes me, of course. Says he is redeemed by the love of a fair woman, and provided I can put up with that kind of nonsense as well as the naïveté that seems to have survived school, which I can, he's a lovely, generous, open-hearted man. He'll do nicely for a frustrated thirty-two-year-old social worker once he's over the complications. I only wish he was more truthful. The rest I'm happy to take.'

Helen, who knew these diffident descriptions hid a great yawning gulf of love in the only Branston inhabitant to whom she had drawn close, probed further in gentle cross-examination.

'What do you mean, more truthful? Does he fib?'

'Well, they all do a bit, don't they?' said Christine doubtfully. 'Men, I mean.'

No, they don't, Helen thought. Bailey doesn't. Lies choke him. Unfortunately he prefers silence.

'I only mean he doesn't tell the whole truth. This affair he had – you know, I told you, before me – God, has it only been three months? I can't believe it, seems like for ever. Anyway, this married woman whose daughter he was tutoring, extra English lessons … you know, he was giving the daughter this knack and habit of writing things down, although I gather she was pretty clever already. Quite rich, this family; he won't tell me who the woman was, but she was older than he. He had an affair with her, more off than on, for a year. All tailed out. She was keener than he, he says, pursued him like a tank across the desert. He insists it's all off; he's met me, the love of his life, et cetera. Swore he never touched her after me, and I believe him. But he met her last week because she cried on the phone at school, threatened to tell her husband, suicide, the lot. He was a bit distraught. They met at The Crown – I'd been forewarned – and finished it for ever, he says, and again I believe him. He may be a bit of a womanizer, but only one at a time. I just wonder, that's all. Didn't see him for two days, and when I did he looked as if he'd done two rounds with a tiger, still does. Says he fell over a bramble bush while trying to mend a fence in his garden. Antony does not mend fences, not that kind anyway. He may cook, but he doesn't mend fences.'

'I see. No word of how the meeting went with the lady?'

'That's just it. I don't know. He refuses to elaborate. That isn't typical Antony: He relates every wretched shameful thing he's ever done since childhood. His honesty's pathological, exhausting at times. He makes his pupils enjoy mild catharsis on paper, and he enjoys it in words. But not over this, and I don't know why.' She crumbled the last of the cake, dispirited.

'He probably behaved as badly as anyone would when there's no kind way to say the things he was having to say,' said Helen. 'Spoke all the wrong words in the wrong way. Maybe honesty was his downfall, he should have lied a lot, and instead they ended up screaming, he for his skin, she for her dignity. No one would notice in The Crown, after all.'

'I see all that. But scratches? Antony's quite capable of violence, you know. Only when cornered. I know that,' Christine added hastily, 'from the confessional of his early youth, not from anything he's ever done to me. He's wiry, with all the aggression of a bullied boy. That's what worries me. If this rejected matron scratched him, what did he do in return?'

'I hope he didn't scratch back.'

Christine shrugged. 'I hope so, too.'

Helen looked at her friend, alarmed by a sudden premonition, a hateful vision of that corpse in the wood, encounters at The Crown, the disjointed memories of the Featherstones, all recounted as amusingly as possible by Geoffrey the evening before, all merging into the landscape of tragedy. She stripped her face bare of thought, dismantled and dispelled the premonition as it rose like an ugly monument in her mind, smiled, and spoke firmly. 'Nothing you can do now, whatever he did then. Wait and see. But ten days? That's nothing. I tell you, in the realms of male silence, especially if they feel guilty, really nothing. He'll tell you when he's ready, surely.' Sophisticated platitudes for a mature companion, not doubting her tentative analysis of a nasty event, too honest for that, simply suggesting that all sounds of alarm could be postponed, perhaps for ever. Allowing time for a good lunch, a peaceful afternoon, and with luck a peaceful lifetime, but not entirely omitting the doubt. Ointment for a troublesome graze, not suggesting a cure. The balm discharged Christine from the house in a state bordering on optimism, leaving Helen pacing the pastel carpets, full of worry without name. Putting a lid on it was as futile as attempting to suppress a jack-in-the-box with a wicked spring and cruel face, unsuitable for children.

Of course she would tell her Geoffrey, her own Detective Chief Superintendent Bailey, of course she would. Or maybe not. She would tell, feeling foolish for once in the telling, no more than an aside: Darling, do you know what else has been going on in The Crown … ? Nothing at all to add to the scenario that gripped him in the current search to find a face for this body, a signature for this murderer, preferably appended to a confession. She would tell him, nevertheless, as she told him everything. Almost everything, she reminded herself; no one tells it all. She might have learned to speak truth automatically and had not yet discovered the day when there would be a serious conflict of loyalties, a question of betrayal. So far there had been no conflict, but without conscious thought of Christine Summerfield or of the Branston way of life, which he seemed to enjoy and she to suspect for its very tranquillity, she feared the imminence of decisions.

One thought led to another. No potato peeling today; Geoffrey out on inquiries, plenty of freedom for thinking. Silly disconnected thoughts involving plenty of nonsense, seen as such. Practical considerations above all, such as what to do with a restless afternoon. I could go to London and get crushed and dirty in Oxford Street. Lovely, if I had the energy. I could stay here and pick daisies, worry a bit, sit in the jungle at The Crown, and pray above all that I never have a lawnmowing husband and that Christine does. No, I shall not wash the car, since the children would like it less, or clean out the garage, because of the starlings' nest, nor shall I deadhead these tidy roses; let them rot. I'll go and have a meaningless conversation instead or paint a picture.

Helen could paint. Charming scenes that tended to become caricatures with captions as well as faces. When words failed, she would grab pen and paper in her urgency to explain. 'Listen, it's like this' – gesturing with one hand as diagram or illustration emerged from the pen in the other, on a napkin, a tablecloth, best linen not immune, on the back of a brief or an envelope. In a lecture hall as a student or waiting in court, she would create a litter of doodles, noses, eyes, hairlines, and winks, summoning up for Bailey a presence on paper. 'Listen, will you? He looked a bit like this, as I told you,' producing a likeness of sorts with all the salient and funny features first. 'He had a nose like this,' or an animal face, catlike, doglike, snakelike, or blank, or a face resembling a car, or three lines that caught some angle of the features.

'As for you,' she said, 'you look like this on first acquaintance; you really do,' she told him, drawing three straight lines in a notebook at the head of a blank page, the lowest of the lines leading into a vertical line for a definite nose, a wide, curling questioning line for a mouth, and a short vertical stab for a cleft in the chin, forming at last a downward-pointing T to incorporate a strong and stubborn jaw. It suggested everything. A face full of hairline traces like overcooked porcelain: an infinite capacity for change within definite limits.

He had fingered this face, found the grooves she had displayed with her eyes away from them, laughed in disbelief and a tiny tinge of embarrassment to see himself depicted with such careless accuracy. 'Better than Identikit,' he said.

'Oh, I hope so,' said Helen. 'I know you better than some witness who might have seen you robbing a bank.'

'And the other people you sketch?'

'Them too, I expect. Surely I have a better recollection than anyone who is not being horrified at the time.'

'And Edward Jaskowski, Stanislaus, your clients, your guilty ones, all those you have sent to some kind of prison – can you draw them?'

'No,' she said firmly, snapping closed her notebook, 'not unless I must. Which is never at all, I think, unless they come and ask me.' Then she would draw more; he would try to copy. They would end as usual, entwined and absorbed in easy laughter.

So far these pictorial observations with pen and ink had provided little apart from relief from the frustration of words, with which she was unduly skilled. The most constructive relief was found on a day like this in a spare room, attempting to construct something with a hope of beauty. Helen painted and sketched on a day like this to rid her mind of everything else. Frowning, she quickly sketched the face of Antony Sumner. Widely spaced eyes, a long, sad nose, high forehead, full mouth and a slightly receding chin. A soft face, miscast and starving Labrador retriever, made strong by affection, a touch of stubbornness around the eyes, a temper. The exercise of bringing into focus that scarcely familiar face encountered only once in the High Street reassured her. Petulant, argumentative, clumsy with emotion, capable of eruption but only suddenly. Quite incapable, she decided, of the sustained rage and stupidity that were prerequisites in a true man of violence. She threw down her pen in the top room of the house, drew instead in her mind's eye the garden of her basement in London, full of overblown flowers, cat in the long grass of the lawn, animals instead of city sounds, some child crouching there awaiting her return. Then she went out to watch life on the reconstructed village green, not even really wishing she belonged, not unhappy, not rude, but not trying, either.

THE VILLAGE GREEN had been the creation of the property developers, a cunning thought, to give the place a focus, John Blundell had said. At the other end of Branston, comfortably far from this village green, standing aloof from the edge of the community and half turned away, the Blundell household did not resemble the miniatures of itself that clustered in Invaders Court where Helen dwelt and which Mr Blundell had helped to build. John Blundell, estate agent and developer, had put Branston on the map, first by selling its reconditioned houses, then by adding to them. Sympathetic additions, he said. His motives had not been bad, since although he had lined his pocket, the zeal to do well for ever and to become an elder of the kirk, if there had been a kirk, was foremost in his mind. This ambition for parish pump prominence had at least ensured well-constructed buildings and a manner in Mr Blundell which could be called honest; but recognition for his crusade was not received at home or abroad, since nothing he had commandeered into bricks and mortar could ever make him significant. He remained small, but became rich, pale, cunning, unhealthy, desperate to be liked, if not loved, and quite unable, for all that, to suppress a streak of meanness. Even while knowing by instinct what people wanted in their houses, he could never fathom the slightest notion of what they thought.

His large house, last of the genuine and best in Branston as befitted its only estate agent, turned away from the road into its own garden at an angle of forty-five degrees, just as John Blundell turned his face, always looking into the middle distance in suspicion of being cheated, vengeful if he was, rarely catching an eye. At the moment he faced his daughter Evelyn, failing to see the contempt in her expression, trying to know better, conscious of profound failure. He was dimly aware that the wheel of his fractious family life, maybe his whole life, was about to come off, that notoriety in the form of pity, rather than the respect he craved, was about to become his lot. And even after turning his head aside from the stern gaze of his daughter, he felt the accusation in it.

'Father, you'll have to tell them. If you don't, I bloody well will.'

'Don't swear, Evelyn, sweetheart,' he said automatically. 'It's unbecoming in a child.'

She clenched her teeth, drew breath sharply, banged her small fist on the table. The voice that emerged from her angelic teenage face was strangely mature. 'You'll have to tell them,' she repeated.

'Them? Who's them?'

'Don't be silly, Father. The police. Them. Whoever you tell when your wife's gone missing.' Her eye fell on the short paragraph in the Saturday morning paper: 'The body of an unclothed female was found in woodland near Branston on Thursday night, identity unknown. Police inquiries are in hand.' She did not draw the item to his attention. 'Mother's been gone nearly a fortnight. You've done nothing about it, absolutely nothing. She could be dead by now.'

'Don't be silly,' he repeated her words. 'Of course she's not. Your mother was unhappy, going through a bad patch. She's gone off for a bit of a break somewhere. She told me she would.' The last lie was transparent.

'You don't care.' Evelyn's voice was suddenly a shrill and childish treble. 'You don't care and you keep on pretending. She didn't tell me, and she didn't leave any food.'

'Darling child, she left a freezer full of it,' he said mildly.

Evelyn was shouting, 'She just went out one evening, and you don't know where she's gone and you won't do anything about it.'

He turned wearily, watery gaze and automatic smile fixed on her for the first time. 'And where do you suggest I begin to look? She went out of this house, wearing a solid gold bracelet and necklace worth a small fortune, probably a bit of money in her handbag, too. She could be anywhere. She went of her own free will. What do you want me to do? Have her dragged back in chains?'

'Report her missing, that's all.'

'It's nobody else's business. I don't want anyone to know.'

'That's it, isn't it? Well, it'll soon be everyone's business. What if she's hurt or lost? What if she's this woman here?' Evelyn stabbed at the page of newsprint, pushing it towards him over the table where they sat. 'Then you'll look an even bigger bloody fool, won't you? They'll think you did it. What if she's fallen under a train? When they find her, they'll think you pushed her because you haven't said anything, like you were trying to hide. Please yourself. Make it worse.'

'You've always had a dramatic imagination, darling child,' he said, trying to grasp the hand that pushed the paper towards him. Evelyn snatched it back. She was not there to give comfort. He was weak, ineffectual, indecisive: she knew all these words because Antony Sumner, her very own teacher, had taught her what they meant. Her father had retreated into silence for over a week, leaving her alone as she had always been left alone when he was not gasping for affection like a dying fish. He did not deserve comfort.

The kitchen was spacious and beautiful, solid wooden units with a dull gleam in the afternoon sun, quarry-tiled floor, dried herbs in a copper bucket, a perfect facsimile of magazine country life, showing signs of neglect, a tribute to huge expense and, finally, desertion. Tears gathered in John Blundell's eyes, rolled down his pale cheeks, blurring his vision of one magnificent room and one strangely beautiful fourteen-year-old daughter. She leapt to her feet, disgusted by the tears, snatched the phone from the bracket on the wall behind him, slammed it down on the pine table in front of his twisting hands.

'Do it,' she said. 'Do something for once. Phone the police, and when they get here, I'll speak to them, too. Do it now. Or you'll wish you'd never been born when they all start asking. Think of the neighbours, Dad. Do it.'

ANTONY SUMNER WISHED he had never been born. No, lying in the generous arms of Christine Summerfield in Christine's pretty little house at nine o'clock on a Saturday evening, he could never wish any such thing. But he wished he could take back the last year, and especially the last fortnight, and give it to her instead. Wished he had never set eyes on Yvonne Blundell, who looked like a gypsy; wished he had never agreed to give English lessons in the evenings to that daughter Evelyn who was the last to need them. Another gypsy. He was flattered, he supposed, to be asked, liked money for old rope, liked being flirted with, same old weakness. Christine darling, please cure me. Release me from a frustrated housewife who reads poetry, aspires to culture in a desert.

People should not read poetry on top of a bad life. It's like mixing drinks or eating cheese before sleeping, very bad for the emotional digestion.

Antony Sumner turned and kissed Christine. She was fast asleep, blissful Saturday evening torpor, rubbish flickering on the television screen, bottle of wine and a good meal gone. Peaceful, free in conscience. Yvonne Blundell was not like you, his mind continued fondly. She was looking for an affair before she hit forty, that daughter looking for learning like someone starving looks for food, both of them with wonderful eyes, fit to tear him apart. But the girl could write. He wished he had never bedded Mrs Blundell. It was like curling up with an octopus, then having to detach her one tentacle at a time. Oh, why wasn't someone there to save him? Walking in the woods after meeting her in The Crown, taking the argument into the trees. She always knew the way through that garden.

Antony removed a hand from beneath Christine's shoulder, watched her stir. Oh, God, what have I done? Shouldn't have lost my cool, shouldn't have shown all that disgust when she took off her clothes. Darling, I was thinking of you; the contrast was too awful for words. Antony felt the marks on his face, almost gone but still noticeable, the stigma of shame. Christ, what a cat; more like a tiger, hurling herself at him, but all the same, he should never have struck back, never used conduct unbecoming to any kind of gentleman.

Christine readjusted her position, ascending slowly and reluctantly from sleep, muttered, and smiled at him, one eye open. 'Feel like an old lady,' she said. 'Tell me when it's tomorrow and hand me a stick to get upstairs. Can't manage on my own.' The eye closed; she dozed as he stroked her pale hair, movements involuntary to hide the sudden heaving of heart, which was deafening to his own ears. Stick, she had said. Hand me a stick. The word 'stick' beat against his skull like a gong. Walking stick, his own, an affectation since teenage years and his first reading of Wordsworth striding about the Lake District and Keats stirring autumn leaves. Milton leaning on one in his blindness. He had clasped his walking stick like a talisman through his student days of floppy bow ties, floppier hair, and caped coats; kept it now to accompany the heavy cords, designer hiking boots, and poisonous French cigarettes he carried to school. The stick was his adolescent symbol, the adult prop to individuality, and the staff room joke.

Stick. Walking stick. He looked around the room wildly. Where was it? Thrust into a corner here? In his own untidy house? In his car? Probably in his car. Surely in the back of his car where it lay whenever he forgot it, as he had forgotten it often since Christine, forgotten it entirely over the last twelve days. Antony had a vision of the stick, the carved wooden handle – an elephant's head, quite inappropriately – smooth on the top from years of use, with a rubber ferrule that had perished and needed replacement. Everything he had tried to blank from his mind rose like scum on a pond: he heard the swish of the stick as he walked through trees, remembered gripping it tighter as she had moved toward him, shut his eyes and attempted one more time to see it lying in the back of the Morris earlier that evening, failed. There was no denying the last place he had carried that stick, the last thing he had done with it.

TEN-THIRTY, DARK. HELEN bound the files together with white tape, each complete, annotated with notes, consigned to memory in preparation for Monday morning. No matter how much she did in her office, homework always remained for the peaceful hours when she could give scrupulous attention to detail. She never made a conscious demarcation zone between home and work. If you were a lawyer, you were one all the time: nothing stopped when you closed the office door. She looked at the room and the empty eye of the television, content with the evening's work, peaceful without Bailey. Well, my man, I haven't had a hard week, but I think for once I shan't wait up for you. Surely you're allowed home before midnight after last night and the night before? I understand completely: I'd be the same in your shoes, but it doesn't stop me missing you by this time of night.

'All depends,' Bailey had said, whether we get any leads on this thing or not. Might know who she is, or someone might tell us. She wasn't wearing so much as an earring. No fingerprints left, but there's always the teeth. See how we go.'

To be fair, he had telephoned once about seven o'clock. Someone, he said, had reported a missing wife, same age as this poor body in the mortuary. Nothing, really, only a disappearance coinciding with a death. Well, something perhaps. Oh, and a daughter, tugging his arm, saying Mr Bailey, let me tell you something: she was always going to those woods. With a man, she went with my teacher, Mr Bailey; I thought you ought to know. My father doesn't know, Mr Bailey. Please don't say I told you. Poor child. Bailey, coolest man in the world, was always a sucker for girl children, especially those the age his own might have been had she lived beyond three months. For these, he suspended judgement and never got it back. What man? I'll tell you that, too. I'm almost grown up, and I've been so worried. And Superintendent Bailey, knowing the full extent of Helen's Branston acquaintance, recognizing the name of Antony Sumner, had confined himself to telling Helen he was likely to be very late indeed. Don't stay awake for me, darling; we'll try to do something interesting tomorrow. Hearing a gurgle of suggestive laughter in her voice, keeping out of his own the yearning to be home.

Now, at midnight, Helen in bed, shocked by the mean impera-tive sound of the miniature phone by the side of it, wondering if the owners of this ghastly house used to phone their offices from it at dawn, thinking they probably did – then wide awake when she heard not Bailey's apologetic tones, but the shrill, hysterical voice of Christine Summerfield.

'Helen, you bitch, you knew, you must have known. Why did you let me think it would be all right? How could you let me go home? How could you say nothing? What a fool I feel, never mind the rest. Why did you do that?'

'Do what? Calm down, Chris. I haven't the faintest idea what you're talking about. Whatever's the matter? Chris, don't cry. What's the matter? Come on, pet, tell me. I'm in the dark. Please tell me. I honestly don't know.'

The sobbing on the other end of the line dropped an octave, subsided into furious gulps. Then Christine summoned up fury in words, stopped, started, ended in a voice of drab sadness. 'Oh, maybe you didn't. I don't know. I don't know anything. I don't know why the hell I'm talking to you at all. I only know that your bloody man, your bloody paramour of a bloody copper, your bloody bandit of a fascist pig, has just come here and very politely removed Antony to the comfort of Waltham Police Station for assistance with his inquiries into a murder. That woman Antony met. She's dead. The married mistress I told you about so trust-ingly because I was worried. The one who gave him the scratches. Now who the fuck told Bailey?'

'I don't know,' said Helen firmly, 'but it wasn't me. I might have told him if I'd had the chance, but I haven't seen him. Calm down.'

The sobbing subsided. 'Oh, God, Helen, you're the last person I should ask, but what should I do? What the fucking hell should I do?'

'Get him a lawyer,' said Helen, crisply. 'I'll give you the number of the only one I know who lives in Branston. He's as good as any. Call him and then go to the station, wait for him, and ask him to see Antony; take anything you think he might need. And just be there. Got that?'

'Yes,' said Christine, doubtful and weary. 'Give me the number.' Then, as an afterthought, product of emotion: 'I hate you both.'

Helen ground her teeth, resigned herself to a sleepless night. She had just catapulted one pompous and obstructive solicitor into the middle of Bailey's investigation, an act of dubious assistance to him, something that was bound to slow him down. She had instructed Christine how best to make a nuisance of herself because she believed that the legal rights of all people were sacrosanct, whatever they might have done. She had also acted in the interests of a friendship that had become precious to her and that had been mutilated, probably beyond repair, by this evening's work. Bailey would not have sprung Antony Sumner from the house of a lover in the middle of the evening had he not believed there was something important to ask him. Whatever the outcome of the interrogation, her acquaintance with Christine Summerfield was unlikely to recover. She would also have to see how far Bailey's tolerance in civil liberties extended when it was she who had prescribed them in the full knowledge that Sumner might be too shocked to find out for himself. 'Damn your eyes, Geoffrey Bailey. Damn your eyes. Poor Christine.' She was speaking to herself, surprised to find the anger. It had just begun to occur to her – foolish not to have seen it before – that she and Geoffrey might not always agree. She found the thought a strange and lonely spectre, found in herself the desire to push him away alongside the desire to embrace him. For once, she wasn't eager for him to come home.

Chapter Four

SUCH SPEED, SUCH graceless speed in the wake of a slow-discovered death. Facing Antony Sumner in the detention room of an ugly police station six miles from home, midnight, himself tired but composed while the man opposite was pregnant with information, twitching with nerves, and pasty grey with anxiety, Bailey knew the familiar sense of defeat that whirred behind his eyes whenever discovery was imminent and early. So there's the truth. How banal, how utterly expected, and how soon. One phone call began it: my wife has been missing since this date; she is dark, forty, not in the habit of straying from home, and has never before stayed away. Amanda Scott, quietly excited, had whispered this could be the one, not another potential victim in sight, all of the others missing either fourteen years old or eighty, always the extremes who run away from home. The postmortem notes sat in the folder on his desk, smelling of the postmortem room, reminding him for no reason at all of the mature but childish voice of that man's daughter, so calm beside Papa's distress, pulling a sleeve like a discreet tart on a corner, but, oh, so beautiful. Mr Bailey, sir – a hint of respect in the 'sir', responsive to the wide smile he always bestowed on girl children – about that body in Bluebell Wood: it won't be, couldn't be my mother, of course it couldn't, but she went there, you see; she was always going there. How did you know? An expressive shrug. Never mind how I know, I just know, OK? Mother had a boyfriend. It worried me. Don't tell my father, but she did. Antony Sumner, my teacher. They both went to Bluebell Wood. Well, they used to, anyway. I thought I would tell you.

Slender but convincing, this information, like the child herself. It was enough to provoke Bailey himself rather than a substitute to knock first at the door of Antony Sumner's house, then at the door of Christine Summerfield. He was apologetic but persistent. 'I'm so sorry for disturbing you.' Then, joking: 'You can sue the commissioner for my behaviour, but may I speak to Mr Sumner? He may, just may, be able to help us. So sorry to intrude on your Saturday evening,' Bailey was ready to back away after two or three questions, abandoning hope of that as soon as his purpose was diffidently explained. Not a murder inquiry at the moment, of course, simply a search for a missing woman, but the man's face was white, old scratch marks to forehead, cheeks lurid, and he was trembling, trying not to weep. It was uncomfortable the way such signs of guilt, accompanied by the look of horror on the face of the innocent friend, afflicted Bailey so, like a sudden flush of fever, making him wish he could have pressed Antony back into the arms of the woman who was, after all, Helen's friend, and told him it had all been a mistake. Instead, he invited him into a car. It's not an arrest, you understand, but will you accompany me? Antony nodding, stroking the woman's head, casting a backward look into that inviting room of hers while Bailey detected on him the incriminating, rancid smell of fear and knew that behind that distinctive scent there were words that would justify the fear.

Detention room, transit room, not quite the same as an interview room, but almost. A room where a witness was detained, usually pending removal to a cell but still with the illusion of liberty, exaggerated by Bailey's habit of leaving the door ajar. From the other end of the corridor he could hear the tidy sounds of Amanda Scott working at her ancient typewriter, tapping out on its reluctant keys a prepared statement for Mr Blundell: 'My wife's dental surgery is at 5, Cross Street, Waltham. I give authority for that surgery to produce to the police any records appertaining to my wife ...' Amanda would use words such as 'appertaining'; she tended to use the long where the short would do. Proud proof of literacy, Bailey thought with a touch of impatience, while this literary animal across the ugly desk from himself, less disciplined than she, but better acquainted with a dictionary, used short, sharp words and expressed himself with ease.

Antony was vainly attempting to regard his polite interrogator as an ape, could not reconcile this urbane manner with his own view on police brutality, had resigned himself to providing explanations. There was nothing else he could do, whatever the advice otherwise: he was desperate to explain and be, in part at least, forgiven.

Bailey struggled with dislike for Antony Sumner's handsome face, dislike mixed with pity for his misery, a dangerous and subversive combination.

Caution the man: advise him of his legal rights. Fetch Amanda to make notes, and start the tape. Let us continue after all these interruptions, please. We were doing so well before.

'MRS BLUNDELL? I knew her because her daughter had been at my school. She asked me to give extra English lessons to Evelyn with a view to taking exams early, some such thing. I was skint as usual, so I agreed. Went on for a year. I started having an affair with Mrs Blundell. Why? I don't know why: I was lonely and bored, she was nine years older; it was flattering at first, me with the rich capital-ist wifey. We went out for drinks last summer, lay on a blanket sometimes in Bluebell Wood, sometimes at my place. She liked my place, she said, shades of Bohemia. Liked poetry, mad about sex. Anyway, I had to cool it last spring. It was never that much fun, and then I met Christine, finished everything else. But it dragged on, you know, and she frightened me with all her intensity. Yes, we did meet at The Crown; her husband, you see, wouldn't be seen dead in there. Oh, God, what a thing to say, and yes, we were there the other night ...'

Then there was coughing and spluttering, pause for cigarette before continuing. Bailey noticed sadly the crushed packet of Gauloises taken from the top pocket damp with sweat, remem-bered Bowles's pathetic offering: two Gauloise stubs and a half-full packet apparently abandoned on one side of the clearing. He leaned across and lit the wavering end of a crooked cigarette for his prisoner, listened with his face straight inside the lines of his skin.

'We walked from The Crown over the field and into the far side of the wood – been that way before, very overgrown. A little clearing, don't quite know where. She was frantic, terrible. She loved me, she said; I was her life. She loved me more than any-one or anything. What about your husband, your daughter? I kept saying, but she only screamed. "There's no one else but you, no one; neither of them care for me." But they do, I kept saying, of course they do. She would tell her husband all about us, then tell Christine all I had never told Christine. She and I would run away. It was madness, all of it. She was full of ideas, places, prospects, showing me money in her handbag, escape routes, all realistic, convincing plans to Yvonne, who'd never had to earn a crust, but not to me. I didn't want to say, "Don't be so bloody stupid; nobody escapes that easy even if I loved you back, which I bloody well don't, never really have. Just a bit of fun that has got out of hand." I couldn't say, "I think you're a silly cow." I gave her a cigarette to calm her. She pulled on it twice, threw it away, didn't like them, really. Started all over again.

'I was sick, turned away a few steps, smoked my own. Christ, I thought, this is terrible, worse than I expected. I wanted to go home. Then she began to cry. I kept my back turned, hoping she'd stop, until I heard a series of movements, frantic movements. I couldn't believe it: she was tearing her clothes off. She always wore quality clothes – dull, smooth, expensive lines – and she was tearing them off as if they were poisonous, screaming between sobs. "You wanted me once; want me again. I'll show you how much you need me, more than that tart of yours." I dropped my cigarette, I remember, when she launched herself at me half naked, bare bosomed, skirt slipping down. She was trying to kiss me. I kept turning my face away, I don't know how many times, holding her off, disgusted. I felt I was fighting an amorous sow, and after a while she began to stop. She was quiet for a minute. Then she spat at me, as if she had suddenly understood. She let go of me, and I turned to face her. She was spitting fury, lashed out and raked her nails down my face, reaching for my eyes, taking me by surprise. It hurt like hell: I could feel blood on my face and I was very angry indeed. Can't quite remember what I did, but I know I hit her then, pulled back my arm, hit her with all my strength and sent her reeling to the ground, watched her lying there, weeping and moaning, exhausted by all that rage and hurt, while I kept feeling the blood on my face. Yes, I might have hit her with the stick; I can't remember. All right, then, with the stick, but only once.'

Antony raised his eyes to the ceiling as if looking for inspiration in the fluorescent light, clearly embarrassed, but determined not to weaken his flow by voicing the apologies in his mind. There are elements of the actor in you, Bailey considered. Even now you half enjoy the telling of the story, you who so enjoy making others record their thoughts, maybe you are only pausing for effect. I can see you wooing this poor matron with all the power of poetry, unable to face her passion when she responded. 'What happened next, Mr Sumner?' A soft reminder. Bailey believed they were either near the end of the story or closer than ever to falsehood.

'I just stood there. Then I knelt down beside her, patted her. I told her I was sorry, but she should have listened, should have listened before. We had never been real, she and I, and it had always had to end. Go home, I told her, go home now, but she simply stayed as she was, absolutely inert apart from the crying, determined to be helpless. I was confused, irritated, if you want the truth. I could have – No, no, I didn't mean that.'

'Could have killed her, were you going to say?' said Bailey mildly.

'No, no, I didn't mean that at all.' Antony was angry at so obvious a ploy, Bailey angrier for the interruption. He had known far longer than he could remember how empty a gesture of intent was the threat or even the desire to kill, how different from the doing, how frequently relieved in the mere screaming of it. He had shouted these threats himself as a child to his mother, and he remembered more clearly how, in the depths of love for his wife, he had wished her death years before. Then as now he had been incapable of causing it. He had never actually inflicted blows on any woman. Perhaps the intention was provoked into action by the first step towards it. 'Go on, Mr Sumner. I'm not trying to trap you. Go on.'

Antony lit another cigarette, hands unsteadier than before.

'I didn't know what to do. She was so bloody stupid, so helpless, making it worse for herself. She was often like that, like a spoiled child who would scream and scream until she was sick to make someone listen, then say, "Pick me up. I can't do it; you do it." So I just began to walk away, hesitating at first, looking back. I thought it would make her move but it didn't. I saw her from the footpath, huddled there half bloody naked, couldn't bear to see it, and started to run through the bushes, away from the footpath, then back until I came to the carpark on the far side. I walked all the way back round to The Crown, collected my car. Went home.'

'Leaving your walking stick, by any chance, Mr Sumner?'

He looked up in guilty surprise. 'Yes,' he replied, 'leaving my stick.'

Bailey gestured. Amanda Scott left the room, returned with the cane. 'This stick, Mr Sumner?' Instantly recognizable object even wrapped in polythene and decorated with a large label for passage to a dim laboratory with all other blood-marked objects.

'Yes,' he said slowly, regarding the stick as he would a friend who had been transformed into enemy.

'That's enough for now, I think,' said Bailey. Amanda Scott shuffled her sheets of paper in obvious disapproval.

'Try to sleep, Mr Sumner. I'm afraid you must stay here.' Despite the pleas of your indignant lawyer who has already postponed all this, shouted advice, which you chose to ignore, interrupted to the extent that I barred him. No doubt we shall hear more of that. Never mind. No doubt, either, that dear Amanda was pleased to tell me the lawyer was called by Miss Summerfield at the behest of Miss West, your er, wife, sir. Well, well, they are friends, after all, but surely Helen knows me well enough to understand that I know by heart all that the Police and Criminal Evidence Act requires of me, including the fact that a man must be offered a lawyer as soon as he's offered a caution, and of course I did it. He grinned ruefully. Helen would also know there are some invitations that he, as well as custody officers, tended to make less audibly to a helpful witness than to a defendant. The rules were more malleable for a witness. Yawning and stretching, Bailey realized he needed his bed. It was three a.m., and for once he knew that he and Helen would not talk either this morning or tomorrow: there would be no time once he had turned back here for ten o'clock. Tomorrow, if they had raised that dentist and put a name to the corpse, he would be going for Antony Sumner's jugular, lawyers or no lawyers. He would ask Sumner, however politely, about his knife. About his shoes and his silly walking stick with the elephant head festooned with human hair.

Somewhere in all of that, he and Helen would have to make time. Time was a thief in the night, one he knew well.

BY SUNDAY AFTERNOON, Christine Summerfield was only weeping from time to time, and had noticed through the disfiguring filter of tears how dirty were the windows in her house. She wondered if the panes of glass in Antony's cottage were as grubby as usual, no doubt hiding the large uniforms who were taking apart the contents, finding God knows what apart from her own underwear and several dirty dishes. He had preferred lately to stay under her roof, enjoying all the obvious home comforts he had never secured for himself.

Christine contemplated telephoning Helen West, felt in her bones a spurt of loathing, which she recognized as unfair to both occupants of that household, and did not phone. Instead, she cleaned her windows. When Helen phoned her, the response was predictably swift, not actually rude, but not polite, either.

HELEN WAITED FOR Bailey to wake, both of them reassured by early morning affection. 'Trust me, darling,' words accompanied by a swift hug before he took his long body out of bed.

'I do,' she had replied, smiling at him. 'I do, most of the time.'

THE SUN WAS shining. Bario's pink and grey restaurant disgorged the last of the lunchtime trade into shiny cars parked on the green where mothers talked over prams and fathers pretended to teach cricket to sons, while the less endowed waited in vain for buses. One mile away, the carpark to Bluebell Wood was still closed by a tape, the fragile officialdom of which defied destruction, with PC Bowles thrilling the questioners with a brief account of the reason why. The body in the wood was gossip but subdued gossip, slightly irrelevant to any of them yet. Mr Blundell had not volunteered to others what he had volunteered to the police, or the gossip would have been sharper. Bailey had ensured that this particular husband was not left unaccompanied while he waited to see if he was a widower: a large constable remained in the Blundell kitchen, bored with reading newspapers, while upstairs, drunk and tranquillized, Mr Blundell slept audibly. Bailey should have organized a woman for the child, who was also upstairs. Evelyn Blundell had kept to her bedroom, as far as the constable knew, or she had declared her intention to do so before climbing nimbly from the window on to the outhouse roof, down to the ground, and away through a series of gardens and roads to the jungled garden of The Crown. Evelyn knew this secret route from her own house so well she could have managed it in her Sunday best, but today she wore T-shirt and jeans and, oddly enough, with such casual teenage attire, a pair of very bright, sparkling paste earrings.

Even The Crown had attracted custom. Today's lunchtime fare had been vegetarian, Bernadette's new ploy to attract the discriminating Branston customer, Featherstones' best with an Irish flavour. The fact that most of the food remained uneaten in relation to the amount ordered only reflected the Featherstones' deafness to complaints. 'Aren't they all fools?' snorted Bernadette, dumping slabs of her grey bannock bread into a plastic sack. 'Don't know a good thing when they eat it.' For once, she and Harold were in accord, a temporary but regular Sunday afternoon peace, especially in summer, when Harold was mellowed by whisky and custom, content to sit in the kitchen discussing plans, believing in the success of their joint venture until his head began to throb and the worse temper resumed. Evening customers received short shrift in The Crown, but for now, all was sweetness and light.

'Aren't they all fools, then? You're right,' he was replying, pinching Bernadette's behind as she passed him, dropping litter on her way to the bin and ignoring it. 'But we'll show them, Bernie, won't we? I've another idea. Now we've got the place in shape, did you see all the people in here today? They're cottoning on at last. I'll set on the garden. Somewhere else for the buggers to go. Might even go back and do something about that garden bar. The summerhouse, I mean. Few enough places with this much ground around, you know.'

Bernadette nodded vigorously but silently, content to keep the peace. Silence was always preferable on the subject of the summerhouse. Like Harold, she was aware that the most recent revamping of The Crown's bar had eaten up another segment of the inheritance misguidedly left Harold by a doting father, the same inheritance depleted year by year since they acquired the premises with the first chunk of it, abandoning their London jobs in the process, because of William, because of wanting a better life, because of all sorts of things they could not discuss, even now. Again like Harold, she was unaware that the same new décor – floral walls, heavy unmatched chintz curtains, checkerboard carpet, red upholstered seats with varied cushions – was a savage onslaught on the eye, almost psychologically disturbing to anyone who sat in it long enough. Helen and Bailey had counted sixteen different patterns in that room and wondered, with enormous, frankly snobbish amusement, how much expense had gone into the creation of such ghastly disharmony. Along with Harold, Bernadette thought it was beautiful, enough of the gypsy in her to adore dizzying colour but when it came to Harold's other plans, she was less enthusiastic. There had been so many, after all. Upstairs there were two unfinished bedrooms, one half-done bathroom, the same state persisting for years while other projects began and ended and the paint peeled on the banisters. The garage next to the kitchen was full of junk that Harold collected from all over Essex: woodworking table of huge dimensions, rusty machinery, old telephone cable, three-legged chairs, bundle of mildewed towels, fire-damaged sheets, chipped crockery, a trough. Anything going free or almost free Harold, scavenger of the world, would have. It was a curious and useless economy in one so reckless with large sums and domestic provisions. These objects never surfaced again, once acquired and put away. If only he could bear to buy something new and use it. 'You're always wanting something for nothing,' Bernadette had yelled, rarely careful enough to avoid trampling on his dreams, but the mention of the summerhouse kept her quiet on a sunny afternoon that deserved a share of shortlived quietude.

Quite simply, he had gone demented over the summer-house plan; it was even worse than all Harold's other fancies. How long ago was it? Eight years since he had started digging like a child searching for Australia, convinced it was only six feet away. 'This is it, Bernadette. We'll double the trade by putting a bar in the garden. No one else has one of those,' and even then she could see it was cockeyed, the way his plans were in direct proportion to the enthusiasm with which he attacked them. Harold's plans were born drunk like the man himself: they had no place in a sober mind. The idea had been to buy a kind of prefabricated pavilion. 'Makes them think of cricket, don't you see? We'll have them playing bowls.' Even Bernadette could see the impossibility of playing bowls downhill. The pavilion was to be placed over a hole. 'We'll do this properly, Bernie darling: a bar has to have a cellar for the beer and the fine wines. The stuff the new rich in Branston and all over will be flocking for.' So, with a little help, Harold had dug the cellar, faced it in brick, then purchased from a brochure at enormous expense a funny-looking structure twenty feet long and ten feet wide to surround the aperture, and constructed inside it a kind of a bar. That was the trouble with Harold: he could do so much, was so clever with his hands and his brain, contemptuous of those with less, but he had a strange inability to complete any project, always discouraged by the failure of reality to correspond with the picture in his mind. There was the same trouble with the summerhouse bar: it had a squiffy character similar to that of Harold's mind, the mind of a man drinking out of a crooked brandy glass, wondering was it he or was it the glass who could not manage a straight line anywhere. The finished product had a cellar the size of a small room, far grander than the structure upstairs, which looked more like an old-fashioned bus shelter than the thing of elegance first intended. The whole beast was odd. 'Cheap' and 'nasty' were other words that came to mind, but 'odd' always came first.

Harold could not hide his disappointment, nor could the customers who were privy to its progress hide their derision. Bernadette would always remember that she had not concealed hers. The summerhouse was comic, a silly little structure of ugly wood looking like a pimple at the end of the half-acre of wild lawn, a sort of hut with windows listing slightly downhill. 'They'll think they've had a drink already as soon as they look at it,' Bernadette had yelled, and William, poor twelve-year-old William, who thought the summerhouse the nearest thing to paradise, had screamed and screamed in fury and rage. Harold, too, had translated the rage of frustration into action by dealing Bernadette a sharp backhander she had never forgotten, while William shrieked in the worst tantrum ever, kicked his mother, and began a course of conduct that became depressingly consistent and frightening. It was not the first of William's spectacular furies, only the most violent. After all of that, the summerhouse was scarcely mentioned, source of mutual shame and failure that it was. Bernadette hated it, never went near it; Harold, the same, reluctant to examine its obvious decay. He could not resist in the early days storing things there, the way he reacted to any available space in order to justify its existence. The bus shelter bar contained kerosene against power cuts – they had no heaters in which to utilize it, but the stuff had been cheap and Harold remembered rationing – a couple of old beds he could not bring himself to discard, and a broken chair or three, all rotting in there, like the fabric of the thing, sloping under the force of gravity, about to disappear in a cloud of guilt-less smoke. Harold had not looked at it for years; only the whisky ever brought it to mind, and even then he remembered William's reaction. Remembered, and then discarded the memory. Too close to home and all the familiar spectres of failure.

William was sitting in the corner of the kitchen hoping that the subject of the summerhouse would drop into silence, relieved and grateful when it did and other topics, brightly introduced by his mother, took the place of a dangerous pause. He had slowly learned the value of silence, knew he had them in thrall with the tantrums they dared not question. He had only to begin kicking his legs against the stool on which he sat with his usual dull but insistent rhythm to reduce them to either sullen fear or resent-ment; either worked as well, but on this occasion there was no need, and he was grateful. William's mental development remained at the age of that of a cunning ten-year-old, untapped by the local schools who had abandoned him one after the other or the child psychiatrist whom he had abandoned, while his manual dexter-ity and physical strength overreached his years. The combination was frightening. Bernadette treasured his rare smiles, treated him with distant loyalty and affection, while Harold patted his black head occasionally and otherwise ignored him. Bernadette knew that in William's life the summerhouse had more than the signifi-cance of memory, but did not know why. She guarded her wilful ignorance on his behalf, aware that the abandoned structure was a lair to him. She suspected Harold knew, but they did not discuss the subject.

'What will you do this afternoon?' She scolded with questions she knew he would not answer, gentle interrogatives. 'Get out, son. The weather's gorgeous; we'll not keep you.' He surprised her with half a grin, half a grunt, slid off his stool clumsily, made for the open kitchen door. Fine if he was ordered out. He would have preferred to sidle away unobserved, but either way he was gone with a blessing, and no one could call him back.

The garden into which he strolled had been planned with an informality quite unsuitable to such a large and impressive house. A cracked and weed-filled path of slippery stones led down the shady side of it flanked by shrubs for the whole length of the fifty yards that led to the summerhouse. A line of small trees marked the end of the garden, perhaps intended to be magnificent but now a scrubby demarcation zone surrounded by thicket. The lawn was punctuated with more overgrown shrubs in islands, designed to be discreet, but now well developed into quarrelling bushes of enormous size, roots obscured by long grass that would have done credit to a hayfield. Cornflowers and cockles from the last year's barley in the field beyond had seeded among the grass, and a dead tree lay rotting across the path. William clambered over it, too old now for the fascination with termites that had once kept him for hours, and quickened his step until he yanked open the summerhouse door.

Inside, the floor was swept, not recently or well, but swept. Most but not all of the jars of kerosene were covered with cobwebs, as were the windows where a fly buzzed insistently. William picked up one of the dusters from the floor and killed the fly instantly. The last broken pieces of chair were piled in one corner along with sacking and newspaper, and through the aperture behind the bar, a hole in the floor normally closed with half a door mounted on a clumsy hinge, he could see a light. Leading into the cavern below was a household stepladder, also broken but still usable. He began a short but dexterous descent of the ladder, which had only three intact steps.

'William? Is that you?'

'Course it's me. Who else would it be, silly?'

'Don't call me silly.'

He clambered down the steps, face wreathed in the smile the world so rarely saw, stood in the light of the butane lamp, and surveyed their domain. There were mattresses beneath a covering of blankets, a chair, boxes doubling for tables and containers, a locked cupboard, makeshift shelves from wood and bricks, a camping cooker that had been another of Harold's bargains, a blackened pan, and a few tins of food. The floor was covered with an old remnant of carpet, dirty but swept, and on the mattresses sat Evelyn Blundell, paste earrings sparkling in the light, wearing her jeans and nothing else, her white pubescent chest catching the glow of the lamp.

'You're late, William. I told you four o'clock. I've got to go soon. I thought ...' For once the confident voice faltered. 'I thought you'd gone and told them all.'

The edge of fear in her tone sharpened into reproof, a terrible threat implicit in it, and he hurried, tripping over his feet and his words to reassure her. 'Evie, Evie, I wouldn't do that. Couldn't do that, Evie, I promise, not ever.' The sharpness of her face had carried tears into his eyes. He knelt beside the mattress as she sat up, hair tumbling to her shoulders.

'Promise?' she asked, her voice as sharp as a blade.

'Course I promise.'

'It's our secret place. Hide everything when I've gone. Promise. Cross your heart and hope to die in boiling oil if you don't.'

'I promise.' He was looking at her, his eyes filled with rapture, suffused with complete adoration as he sat beside her, fingered the earrings, laughed in loud relief at the softening of her features. Evie could look so terrifying, especially in this light, her tiny figure as threatening as a whip, eyes blazing with scorn, reducing him to one of those crawling beetles they sometimes saw on the floor, blinkered things, looking desperately for light as William sought relief. Not today. Today he could tell she was relieved to see him, had made him a cup of weak sugary tea, which he loved, even without the milk he was supposed to have provided if the kitchen had not been so wary. 'Couldn't bring any,' he explained, gesturing to the cup she handed him, never taking his eyes off her face.

'S'all right,' she said, her favourite phrase. 'Doesn't matter.'

Silence fell. He drained the lukewarm tea in one gulp, set the mug on a box, shuffled closer to her, smiling his beatific, hopeful smile, tentatively reaching a hand toward her, questioning with his pale and vacant eyes.

'S'all right,' she repeated. 'You can. Only today, mind.'

Then she lay back on the mattress, small nipples pointing toward the dusty ceiling, her eyes closed. William lay beside her awkwardly, stroking her slender torso with one disproportionately large hand that could have spanned her waist. She was so small, so neat, her skin seemingly stretched over bone and the taut and miniature muscles that held the flesh to this graceful skeleton. He placed his mouth around one of the nipples and sucked like a child at breast.

'Ow. That hurts.' But William was panting by now, one hand below the waistband of her jeans, button undone as she had left it undone. She always hoped he might change his mind, but gradually learned that there was as much chance of that as of her baby nephew refusing a feed; she considered both pastimes – that witnessed, this undergone – equally inexplicable and unnecessary, but she was prepared for foolishness all the same. The zipper of her jeans fell away at his touch. He felt lucky today: he had been so good, so very good; he did not know precisely why she should be so pleased with him, but she was. 'Can I?' he whispered. 'Can I really, please?'

'Oh, all right,' she was murmuring, eyes still firmly shut, 'but only if you take it out, you know, before. Only if you take it out.' Then she sat up abruptly, pulled the jeans off her legs while he pulled down his loose canvas trousers. 'Oh, God,' she said in the tone of a bored sophisticate, looking at him with a distaste he did not recognize. 'Hurry up, will you, before it grows any more, but touch me, so it won't hurt.' He touched, a rough and peremptory stroking, with his breath arriving in clumsy gasps while she lay supine, legs splayed, faint traces of Vaseline on her inner thighs, her arms loose by her sides in an attitude of resigned waiting. 'A little bit more,' she commanded, and he obeyed in an agony of impatience, then stopped, rolled on top of her, and thrust himself inside, pumping against her unresisting thinness, remembering her order in his final abandon, whimpering as he released his sticky souvenirs on to her stomach and the blanket. Then he rolled to one side, clutching her hand, and was almost instantly asleep, the smile transfixed on his flushed face.

The butane lamp guttered. Evelyn sighed in the silence broken only by his breathing, drew her arm from beneath him, slid down the wall side of the bed. She picked up his T-shirt, scrubbed at her abdomen with something like a housewife's disgust, and then, as an afterthought, placed it over the small remnants on the blanket. After that, she rolled the unresisting form of William on to his chest. She put on her clothes and turned off the lamp, leaving him in the dim glow of daylight filtering through the cellar entrance, and made for the steps. He would waken in minutes; she was only just becoming familiar with the pattern after these occasions. It was time for her to leave, avoiding all the tiresome affection that followed. He might wake on his own and cry for her and that was all for the best, when she came to think of it; it might make him more grateful for these rare privileges, these conversationless and far from invariable Sunday treats that seemed to matter so much to him for reasons she could not really fathom, given the vague distaste they inspired in her. They had learned thus far together from the pile of pornographic magazines in the corner, from pictures that had frightened poor William to death, but they had not quelled her curiosity nor eased his desperate longing.

'S'all right,' she said to herself, as if reciting a litany while emerging into the blinding light outside the summerhouse.

'S'all right, really. Time to go home now.' She remembered the fat constable in the kitchen, the snores of her father, wondered if she might have cut too fine her own timetable, broke into a run. Looking back from halfway down the length of the field, she was almost sorry to have left him. Then she thought of the ridiculous pictures in those magazines, giggled, paused and stretched in the middle of the windswept barley-field, sprinted home.

Chapter Five

A PILE OF pornographic magazines and videos, bagged in black plastic, sat accusingly in the corner of the office Helen shared with two other solicitors whose desks were currently empty. The day before, with a speed and deftness that annoyed her senior colleagues, she had gone through the pornography, drafted summonses, requisitioned statements, and demanded the material that was missing – two hours' work to Helen, a full day to anyone else. Now she immersed herself in another exhibit list, professional antennae twitching, gripped by the emergence of the narrative of the Branston murder, working on three levels, absorbing the story, but still ticking off the irrelevancies, isolating hearsay, sorting the appropriate order of witnesses, giving the thing its courtroom shape, conscious all the time of a mistake. Even while she listed the further inquiries and inevitable missing links, she was remembering that Redwood, the branch crown prosecutor who ruled her life, had been out of the office the day before and that was the single reason why she had been allocated the case at all. Redwood's deputy had sent her the papers only because he was free of the insecurities and strange chauvinistic jealousies that afflicted his boss, and he wanted a competent hand at the tiller. Sooner or later Redwood would intervene; the speed of the intervention would only depend on how soon he could find an excuse. Helen was prepared for something of the kind, had schooled herself not to resent it, and was determined to do her professional best for the case before interruption. In the meantime, what she had read disturbed her.

The resolution of the case was so neat, so complete, so quick. A faultless report from Bailey, the contents of which he had refused to discuss with her at home, like a writer being secretive about a new opus. She could see why. Dismissing from her own mind any knowledge of the protagonists, she was dismayed by the comprehensive evidence, the tidy jigsaw puzzle of it, ready to be assembled in front of a jury with no missing pieces. It was hardly the mandate of a prosecutor to query such a satisfying picture. Not for the Crown to show that Sumner didn't kill the woman, only that he did. The defence must raise the doubt if doubt was to be raised, but in Helen's perfectionist mind, that was never enough when life imprisonment hung in the balance. She believed the Crown must show it has explored every avenue, drawn a blank at the feet of any other possible culprit, examined the motives of many, looked closely at husband, woman rival, even children. God forbid. Here the target had stepped into the net without a murmur and never a sideways glance from the investigators for anyone else. Helen's instinct told her to insist that the police begin all over again: 'Where would you have looked if you had not found him? Look there now. We cannot rely on the defence to do it for us. It is the Crown that must see justice done, facts fully explored. Go on; turn a few more stones.'

Fidget, light a cigarette, debate the next move. Phone Bailey in professional guise, lace the conference with a colleague to make sure it is fully impersonal, get on with it before Redwood uses his undoubted knowledge of the West-Bailey relationship to justify massive interference. Still inured with belief in justice and a passion for the truth, Helen wanted to ask questions. Phone Bailey. It was always a pleasure, that amiable conflict between two highly tuned minds meeting on a similar level of legal experience. She relished it.

As she dialled the number she could have dialled blindfolded, footsteps sounded on the worn carpet outside her door, the familiar, clipped steps of the branch crown prosecutor. Helen replaced the receiver quickly, hating conversations with Bailey to be overheard as much as her chief hated the idea of one of his independent prosecutors cohabiting with a senior police officer. Nor did she wish for Brian Redwood – with his penchant for performance indicators, budgets, time spent per case per day, and that integrity of his which only operated at the least imaginative level – to be party to any decision she might make at this stage. He had a love of rectitude and rules, a chronic dislike of all police officers under the rank of chief inspector, and a profound suspicion of Helen West. In addition to all his other neuroses, he believed that if he pushed and bullied his underlings, they would work harder, having failed to see that no lawyer chose this work who could not lead himself. 'Our Brian,' as he was known without affection, remained an interfering and harrying boss whose meddling was not matched by any semblance of support or guidance. He resented anyone who did not share his tunnel vision.

'Not in court, then?' he barked accusingly.

'As you see,' said Helen. 'Paperwork day.'

'Oh. Wanted to see you anyway. Getting on all right?'

'Fine, thank you.' Maybe he simply wanted to talk and she was the only one to hand on a very quiet Wednesday; she would do as well as any, better than most, but with a sinking heart, she doubted that was all.

'You got a file from your, er, boyfriend. Whatever.' Disapproval was implicit in his tone. 'You aren't the right grade to deal with murders, of course.' Helen forbore to mention that she had already prosecuted more murders under the auspices of previous offices than Brian Redwood had in a far gentler lifetime than her own. There was no point remarking on it. She was in the habit of keeping her head down with Mr Redwood, anything for a quiet life, but while putting her in place with this initial salvo, he was clearly in need of her opinion, however much he hated asking.

'This Branston murder … Mrs Blundell … Do you talk to your detective chief superintendent about it? Bailey, isn't it? Very good investigating officer.'

'No, we don't talk about it,' Helen lied with convincing sincerity, wishing it was not almost true. 'It's better we don't.'

'Quite right, quite right.' He nodded sagely, swallowing the unlikelihood without difficulty and adding inconsistently, 'But you do know the facts?'

'Roughly, yes.'

'The case is quite straightforward,' Redwood said. 'Open and shut. Fellow wants to end relationship with older married woman, loses his cool, hits her, and then stabs her in argument. Funny place to pick, though, Bluebell Wood. He buries her and goes home, leaving enough traces for an army: walking stick covered with blood and hair, hers, of course; heavy footprints all over the place, made by his very distinctive boots; cigarette ends in the clearing, his brand.'

'Have the police found her clothes, jewellery, handbag?' Helen asked, knowing full well they had.

'In the compost heap in his garden. l ask you, what a fool. The handbag and clothes, all neatly packaged. Jewellery and money from handbag, gone without trace, greedy bastard.'

Helen was silent, allowing the exclamatory flow to continue, wondering on the nature of our Brian's problem. Not the same as hers. He never suffered from second thoughts or surprise.

'No alibi, of course, though the girlfriend did try.'

She remembered. Poor Christine had attempted to say Antony had been at her house before midnight on the night of the murder, gave it up when Bailey gently pointed out to her that he already knew she had not seen Antony for two days after the woman's death, a knowledge he had only cleaned because Helen had told him. In view of the prisoner's limited admissions, such a pretence was no help in any event. Any chance of Helen resurrecting her friendship with Christine had died after that, but that was not within Redwood's knowledge, nor should it be.

'One problem, though,' Redwood ruminated. 'Man won't admit killing her.' His voice was hurt, as if Sumner's refusal to confess guilt was a personal insult. 'Intelligent chap, too. Can't understand it.'

Intelligence had very little to do with it, Helen thought, while trying not to smile. Nor was it incumbent on any defendant to admit guilt in the interest of expediency and saving public money, even if he was guiltier than sin. He had the right to protest his innocence all the way to the grave, causing storms of fury and irritation *en route* if it helped him at all. Man must fight like a cat for freedom, fight dirty if he must, lie if he must. That's what I would do, she thought: I'd make them prove every damn thing.

'How inconsiderate of him,' was what she said out loud, the irony of her words quite lost on her companion.

'Quite,' said Redwood eagerly, forgetting in the loneliness of the office that he was in the invidious position of debating with the member of staff he could least afford to admire. In the dim recesses of his mind he suppressed the uncomfortable knowledge that Helen West could run this office better than he could himself, was the natural deputy he never chose, preferring to keep her talents in obscurity. For today's purposes he also ignored the knowledge that the junior troops already flocked to her for any kind of advice from the state of their marriages to the state of the law, and they would continue to flock to her even if Helen did nothing to encourage them. She was popular for her wicked mimicry in an office full of cigarette smoke, bad language, and plenty of shouting under stress; she was authoritative without effort – all the things he longed to be and was not – while all he could hold against her was a less than immaculate conviction rate. Watching her dealing in court, he could find no fault in her except for her turn of speed and what he called promiscuous sympathy for both victims and defendants, but she was as hard as nails when necessary. Yes, take a plea here, she would say, a bindover here; no, absolutely no bail; honestly, don't be such a fool as to ask if he has nowhere to live; I'd help if I could, but I can't. What do you want, blood? The way she had of letting them go, the toothy schoolboy barristers of the opposition, the shifty defendants, and even the megalomaniacal court clerks, gods in their own arena, all placated and left with their dignity. I don't want to humiliate you, she might have said, but I will if I have to; don't push me to be fair, there's no bloody need. Other advocates faced with weary thieves might have thought from time to time, There but for the grace of

God go I; Helen West actually believed it. She moved in pity, only occasionally expressing anger over the sad exposure of charlatans, fools, and youth. Redwood's beliefs were not the same. He did not see himself as the same humanity, saw all of the defendants on the other side of the dock as a race apart.

'I wonder why,' he was musing out loud. 'Why, oh, why won't he admit the killing?'

'Well,' said Helen cautiously, venturing a further grim joke, 'he would radically increase his chances of a life sentence if he did. Or maybe he's telling all he knows and he didn't really kill her at all.'

'What?' He looked up, outraged, saw Helen's eyes fixed on her hands, and dismissed the last remark as one made simply for the sake of argument. 'Of course he killed her. He's charged with murder.' As if that was all it took. Helen struggled with the ridiculous corollary: if you want to kill someone, simply get yourself charged with that person's murder and regard the deed as done. Save yourself the trouble.

'Of course he killed her. Mud still on those boots he never wore afterwards, though he wore them every day before. Stick with silly handle thwacked across the brow, his stick, no one else's stick. A sweater full of brambles in his laundry box, and scratches on his face. And after a God Almighty row like that and her acting like a cat, he says he walked away and left her for someone else to kill? Come off it. Besides, who else had a motive? He, on the other hand, was frightened that Mrs B. would tell that girlfriend of his, whom I must say, he must have been fond of, enough anyway to be terrified of her finding out he'd been screwing the other one all the time.'

Helen could not stand it, loathed all this superior supposition, as well as hating that demeaning word, which Christine would hate equally. Screwing whom all the time? 'He wasn't,' she said swiftly before caution prevented the words, regretting them as she spoke them, unable to stop. 'At least Christine – "the girlfriend" to you, my friend to me – said he wasn't. He'd told her. She would have known. She told me.'

He looked shocked. Our Brian rose from the desk against which he had leaned, as relaxed as he ever would be in the presence of a subordinate.

'She what?'

'She told me,' Helen repeated, still disobeying the careful impulse and following the instinct to defend. 'She's a friend of mine.'

'You, Miss West,' he said majestically, with a pomposity she found indescribably silly, 'you, in cahoots with a defence witness?'

'No, not exactly. Not in cahoots. In conversation, perhaps. Unfortunately no longer, I'm sad to say. But listen to me, you ought to know: Christine Summerfield did know of Sumner's affair. She knew from the start of knowing him. She knew he was going to meet Mrs Blundell on the night he did, and I can and will give evidence of that knowledge if necessary.'

'Helen – Miss West, I mean …'

'Well, what do you mean?'

'You are being naïve,' our Brian said indulgently. 'That is what she told you, but perhaps she told in anticipation of exactly this situation.'

'Oh, yes,' said Helen, temper running like a car engine. 'She's a soothsayer as well as a social worker. Bit of double leprosy going on there, Mr Redwood, I mean Brian. And a jury would see it as rubbish coming from a mouth as disingenuous as hers. I'm sorry, I don't believe Antony Sumner killed Mrs Blundell to spare

Christine the knowledge of his affair. I just don't believe it. He may have killed her, but not for that reason.' All of this emerged far more sharply than intended in reaction to Redwood's underlying prejudices and also to the fact she had never, but never yet in three whole weeks, had the chance to argue the same toss with Bailey. Our Brian was here; he would have to do.

'Well.' He was standing now, looking down at her with his best supercilious regard. 'At least you concede the possibility of guilt. I was beginning to wonder. I imagine it's preferable I don't discuss the case with you, Miss West. And a very good idea if you don't discuss it with … with your friend the superintendent, either. In the meantime, if you would send your copy of the file back to me, I'll deal with this case myself.'

A few seconds of silence, her hand fluttering around the dismembered papers on the desk. She'd had long training in not reacting, had just betrayed it slightly, would not slip further from the self-discipline of calmer silence. He was ready for an unprofessional outburst, disappointed by the brisk, dismissive nod of her head.

'After all,' he added over his shoulder as a mild parting shot, 'you don't want anything to interfere with a conviction, do you?'

She watched his uncomfortable departure, recovering her smile, slamming down her pen as soon as the door closed, then taking it up again and sketching Redwood's face on the lined pad in front of her. A smooth face, pouched like a guinea pig's with firm round jowls and a precious little mouth. A high, unlined forehead with thin hair, slightly coiffed to one side over creased little eyes. Soon to have tunnel vision, she thought through gritted teeth. Nothing must ever interfere with convictions, his or the court's. Nothing. Not even the truth. At the back of his head she drew a curly tail.

Three whole long weeks since the dentist had confirmed that the radiograph of teeth taken from the Bluebell Wood body belonged to the late Mrs Blundell. Life in the Bailey-West household had resumed some semblance of normality. Geoffrey's office hours were as variable as Helen's and were rarely spent in an office. She liked the variety, enjoyed the peace of solitude as much as he, provided there was no tension between them to fill the solitary interludes with unanswered questions, nothing to disturb the trust. Which was not the present state. She had tried to tell herself not to express undue curiosity in his current investigation, even when Sumner was charged and Christine Summerfield had abruptly avoided her on a Saturday afternoon in Branston High Street. A tension in the Bailey-West household had arisen from a situation in which Helen could not support Geoffrey's opinion, and this tension was quite sufficient to persuade her not to phone him after all for advice on a multitude of cases and questions of police procedure, as she frequently did. Helen was finding difficult the return to greater self-reliance and the gradual denial of the constant turning to Bailey in any moral dilemma that featured one of his tribe. He had always done the same to her: What should I do, Helen? What do you think? The most precious of things shared was this impeccable trust in the judgement of the other, a complete respect neither held towards any other person. Helen mourned the passing of this mutuality, prayed to her own version of God that its absence was temporary. On the calm surface of their lives, there was no more than a breeze, but in the new atmosphere of secrecy engendered by the murder, she felt as if the fingers and toes of her existence were growing numb, losing sensitivity in an early frost.

Bailey, when she first encountered him, had been a silent man, bursting the banks of his own reserve so slowly at first that she had not realized how much he had been giving and at what cost. Bailey's heart had opened to enfold her own in a gentle embrace, always ready to release her should she ever protest or demand freedom. A childhood of genteel poverty, a policeman's life in various sewers the full details of which she learned piecemeal and never completely, things of which he was ashamed, fewer where he was proud, never a member of the club that would let him join, never wanting to be. A marriage long past to a woman gone mad, a woman he had treasured and who was still an unknown quantity in Helen's mind. No jealousy, simply ignorance. The trouble was, he still tried to protect his Helen from hurtful information the way he might have shielded that vulnerable spouse; he would always try to do so, and this case, which touched their personal lives so closely, forced a return in him to the old hesitation that had been his hallmark before love for Helen had overtaken him so completely. He had set himself against any kind of silence toward her, but could not persuade his mind to the same course if the truth might wound or even offend her. In his dealings with Sumner, he had acted with the efficiency of the professional: he had charged the man with murder and known that Helen could not approve, could never have done the same. The charge had been like painting by numbers on a picture that was clearly incomplete, since all such pictures were incomplete without fingerprints or signed confessions. The police had more than enough numbers; therefore there was a charge. Helen would have called this process an upside-down drawing, told him not to stop investigating. And so the body in the woods created not a rift but a hiatus, a time when they took stock of each other's reactions, withdrew to save admissions or accusations, felt more than a little lonely, Helen more than a little disappointed in him. No hostilities; each would have gone to the end of the world to avoid a row, but in the fruitful ease of normal communication there was a blockage, a reversion to the native state of two pathologically lonely and self-sufficient souls who had once found themselves so utterly relieved by the discovery of each other.

AT HOME, THAT home she could not think of as home, she sat and watched. How gently the police had treated Sumner she could only guess. Gentleness of every kind was inherent in Bailey, perceptible even in the lines of that hatched face of his, so severe in repose, so transformed by laughter. Even his harshest and most obstinate interrogations never carried the slightest implication of violence, but he often used the persuasive force of fear. She imagined him with his pale prisoner, well aware of how intimidating Bailey could be with a minimum of words and gestures. Strong medicine for Antony Sumner, prejudiced, illogical, spoiled, selfish teacher and lover, surely unable to withstand such provocative skills. Few others did, usually those cunning enough not to open their mouths at all in a way she would never have managed. But there it was: Antony had resisted, been charged, and her guinea pig-faced employer found the case straightforward despite gaps such as the absence of a murder weapon. Helen did not: she felt that the evidence was brutally incomplete, the conclusions drawn so far woefully inadequate; she was determined to watch and see if her judgement proved correct, but she was a kind of prisoner, unable to discuss the case either at home or at work, since after a few early forays, Bailey discouraged her interest and Redwood forbade it.

Looking at Geoffrey now as he sat in an armchair after supper, reading a book, the way he was most often seen at leisure, she saw the concentration in his eyes. Sitting upright, reading a novel in hardback, while she felt in her veins the old but still new tide of love for him, she decided to speak.

'Geoffrey Bailey, I know that's a book and therefore the most precious thing on earth, but can you put it down for a minute? Talk to me, you brute. This doesn't feel like a talking house at the moment. Let's go to The Crown.'

He smiled at her with the whole of his face as if he had been waiting for his cue, stood, kissed her lightly, made for the door before she had time to draw breath. 'Come on then, woman.'

Such impressive sacrifice, putting down a book, made her gallop out of doors after him into the evening, grabbing his hand as he swung away up the street. Tradition of a sort dictated they walk to The Crown, a habit winter would change but a pleasant mile for now. Bailey pressed her hand inside his own, put it in his pocket with the usual show of embarrassment as they walked up the road. He, who was slower to volunteer affection and all those signs of possession, responded and returned them with interest, conditioned for ever by a childhood and adult life in which they appeared to have been forbidden. Helen felt the warmth of him, and no, she would not mention Antony Sumner, not on the way. Let them simply walk in the sweet-smelling light while it lasted, along the road that had become deserted. Then sit in the motley company of the garish bar and listen to the Featherstones fighting, or something of the kind. Normality, please, something to remind her of the daily release his company provided in assuring her she was not mad after all. Maybe she would tell him about Redwood and the humiliation of being removed from the murder case. Maybe not. He would worry on her behalf, jealous of her professional pride. For the minute it did not matter. She was back in her native state and happy to be alive.

But it was Geoffrey himself, in some faint effort to clear the air, who shifted the conversation to forbidden ground. 'Saw your boss about our local murder,' he said once a bottle of wine was open before them. 'You know, the man without a profile, Red Squirrel.'

'Redwood,' she corrected, laughing and sensing his irritation with the man in question.

'He has his legal credentials framed on the wall in case we humble policemen should doubt them,' Bailey continued.

'Some people do doubt them,' said Helen, 'especially other lawyers. And whatever the diplomas, they don't include any in the art of conversation.'

'Or the appreciation of humour, I noticed,' Bailey added.

A pause for wine, a sigh of satisfaction, speech resumed more hurriedly. 'He told me he considered the investigation complete – a sort of well-done-chaps-but-leave-it-alone-now lecture. Considers it all wrapped up. Advance disclosure of written evidence will be presented tomorrow, only a few scientific statements outstanding. Leave it to us from now on. He's instructing Queen's Counsel and junior, of course, wouldn't condescend to tell us who, mandatory expense for murder, I suppose. Asked me if I thought Sumner would plead to manslaughter. Arrogant man, Redwood. Had you noticed that he looks like a guinea pig?'

'Yes,' said Helen, 'I had noticed.'

'Anyway,' Bailey went on, speeding over his subject as if to subdue it, 'I told him a plea for Sumner was as likely as a good English summer.' He paused and grinned. 'I saw Mr Guinea Pig as a good vegetable gardener; that seemed about the right level.'

'I'm hedging,' said Helen. 'I do want to talk about it and I don't, if you see what I mean. Do you think Sumner would plead guilty but provoked, or diminished responsibility, or whatever? No, I don't really mean that; you've answered me already. What I mean is, did he really do it?'

There was palpable hesitation, a long pipe-lighting and examination of wine label. 'The evidence appears to show that he did.' Carefully said.

'The evidence as far as you've told me?'

'The evidence, as far as it goes.'

'You don't believe it, Geoffrey, do you?' She subdued a rising note in her voice.

He sighed as if he'd been anticipating this conflict for the whole three weeks of its incubation. 'Yes, I do believe it. As far as I need. I believe in evidence. Nothing else works. Speculation, doubt based on loyalty, affection, or hunches, they don't have the same validity. Besides, it doesn't matter what I believe.'

'I've heard you say that before, and it's the only time I catch you lying.'

He turned his brown perplexed face to hers, determined against seriousness, happy to be sitting next to her and suddenly preferring to be talking about nothing.

'Of course it's true, Helen. I record, I investigate, I repeat in court what I have found. I'm not asked for my opinion. I'm a highly trained parrot – homing pigeon, more like, carrier of messages that amount to the nearest thing you ever get to truth – as far as Red Squirrel and the whole panoply of the judiciary are concerned.'

'All right, all right, point taken for the evasion it is. But what do you believe about Sumner? You must believe something. You, not the parrot.'

'I believe what I've seen. What the evidence indicates.'

'You'll drive me mad. What about Mrs Blundell, then? What was she like?'

'Hardly Sumner's type, I'd say. The only thing they had in common was a blood type.' He was attempting to end the conversation, and she was well aware he would succeed. He was becoming remarkably skilled in doing just that.

From behind the bar, the Featherstone insults rang out, transcending the desultory conversation of the customers whose own sentences became subdued out of both deference and curiosity. 'He said a pint, Harold, not a half, you git.'

'Shut up, Bernadette, shut up, put a sock in it, will you?' – all delivered in hisses the one to the other, louder than any stage whisper. Beer drinkers always confused Harold. His face was red, tension in the fist that slammed down the drink into relative silence, frightening the customer with a glare. In the kitchen, there was a sudden resounding crash.

William Featherstone appeared like a bolt from the blue from the kitchen door, ran across the dizzying carpet toward the stairs, darting glances to left and right as he went. Bernadette moved from the bar towards him. He shook his fist and she stepped back, pretending she had not noticed. William paused in mid-flight on sight of Geoffrey and Helen, pirouetted, granted these familiar customers the benefit of an inane grin, and disappeared up the steps three at a time. The noise of him was thunderous.

'Aggressive lad,' said Bailey.

'Poor boy,' said Helen.

Harold Featherstone shrugged comically: Bailey and Helen chuckled simultaneously at the oddity, the chuckle growing into hidden and uncontrollable giggles in the face of Bernadette's withering look. No reason for it to be so funny, but it was.

'That's why I like this place,' said Bailey, watching Harold beginning to dry a glass half full of whisky, Bernadette watching him aghast, preparing words. Helen, suddenly almost content, placed her hand on the back of Bailey's neck and laughed into his shoulder. The smell of Bailey laughing, the touch and taste of him, was like a patent faith restorer. Let them speculate about the Featherstones and the neighbours, then. Let him win for now; she would not disturb the peace with talk of Blundells and Sumners, murders and lawyers. Dangerous ground, a smooth-surfaced cesspit. Varnish it with laughter, while in her mind there grew a dull sense of compromise. It had been the love affair to end all others; it was beginning to slip, the way of all others.

IN THE POSH house, love was a much insulted thing. Blundell's dwelling was three-quarters of a mile from The Crown and owned by a modern man who did not think in yards but made measurements in metres for anything but grief and liquid. Liquid was brown and ordered in inches, with or without ice. John Blundell stood in a room as distant in spirit from The Crown as Mrs Blundell could have made it. She had been addicted to *Good Housekeeping* and *Vogue*, her house bearing souvenirs of the former as much as her clothes reflected the latter. The widower was in their bedroom, which was filled with the same ominous silence that suffused this house and filled it with accusations. His daughter was asleep, he supposed: she had retired to bed an hour since with the minimum of goodnights. The house had become speechless, his own breathing noisy. John had opened the wardrobe – fifteen metres of wardrobe – belonging to the late Mrs B. Inside there were yards of clothes whose existence she would have denied in pursuit of more; a small selection, she would have said. She had favoured camel, cream, and black ever since her figure had reverted to youthful proportions in the last eighteen months. Before that, and for the last ten years, she had taken size sixteen and favoured fluffy pinks and reds. Expensive reds, but shrouds nevertheless. The new image had been streamlined and the new face almost sweet company. Nevertheless he had preferred the old – less demanding, less expensive.

John Blundell moved from the wardrobe to the dressing table where jewellery spilled from a box, slightly dusty but otherwise tidy. The accompaniments reflected the clothes. Unburnished gold was typical, earrings that resembled brass globes, but cost infinitely more, belcher chains in large but elegantly dull links, nothing shiny, the most flamboyant thing of all a double row of old pearls with a gleam only slightly less subdued than the rest. Notable for their absence were the solid gold choker, bracelet, and gold hoops, all discreetly heavyweight and worn on the night she had left, the same plain jewellery he had described to the superintendent. Bailey, having acquired Helen's habits, had made the subject draw the objects in mind, fixing them in Blundell's eye for ever. Fixing, too, his fury at their cost. He had bought them to placate her.

She had donned the gear of more established riches, turned herself into an old-style lady of the manor, with none of the traditional parsimony. The habits of dress had not extended to fornication with the gardener, not as far as her spouse knew, in any event. She had found herself another touch of class instead, had she not? She wore her precious dull metals in rebellion against diamonds, tried to improve her mind, she said. And then taken up poetry in motion in the form of some bloody man who read it. And thought John had not noticed.

John Blundell moved back to the wardrobe. Looked at the line of neatly pressed clothes: lean linen for summer, cashmeres for cool evenings, nothing if not organized, colour against colour in fully ironed harmony, not like his own shirts, buggered by the cleaning lady. He took a dress from a hanger, removed the belt, looked at both, then inserted the spike of the belt at the neck of the dress and tore it from collar to hem. Rich cloth ripping made a satisfying sound. With slow deliberation he destroyed two silk blouses in the same fashion, hung everything back in the same wardrobe as neatly as before, along with the other clothes, some already torn, most not, and walked unsteadily to his side of the kingsize mattress. On the reproduction table stood the whisky decanter, which he grasped in one pudgy fist. Now that she was gone – dead, if not buried – at least he could drink in bed. He might as well have done so for the last four years. Sweet fuck all else going on, always moaning on about housekeeping while spending all this. He wept into the pillow: You could have had anything you wanted; I told you I didn't mind. You kept wanting me to talk to you all the time, and then you wouldn't talk at all. You deserved what you got.

Chapter Six

POST WAS SLOW. That was why it fell to Amanda Scott at the behest of Redwood, whom she would never have compared with a guinea pig, to deliver a copy of the evidence in the case of *R. v. Sumner* into the offices of Messrs Amor and Harmoner, Branston High Street.

The title of the firm suggested love to all men with harmony thrown in for free, but Mr Amor was dead and if his name had ever influenced the practice with sentiment it was not apparent now. Henry Harmoner was the mainstay, a deceptively slow-mannered man who was grateful to John Blundell for the swift turnover of houses in Branston and thereabouts, which had trebled his conveyancing practice and his clientele. He was not yet grateful for the legal aid clients who followed, leaving these to his brother George who, for reasons best known to himself, appeared to like that distasteful kind of thing. Henry had been less than delighted to discover that George was the inheritor of Antony Sumner, murderer of Mrs Blundell, whom Henry himself had always fancied, especially at size sixteen: fine figure of a woman before she went thin. Been to dinner in his house after all. Husband author of much good fortune while remaining a frightful little shit, mean as hell when standing a round, but not to be displeased. So Henry ranted briefly at George for accepting the client and hoped John Blundell would understand how business was business and all that, the way he usually did without great show of scruple and hopping from one leg to the other. Henry and George Harmoner quarrelling, even as briefly as they did, resembled two bulls locking horns and swaying around with a certain lack of conviction, for the sake of an audience, grunting every now and then. Both spoke in short sentences while beetling their very full eyebrows, the only characteristic of a family not renowned for anything else except a healthy pomposity. This characteristic was passed on to all clients as a kind of reassurance. George was the brighter of the two, which made him very bright indeed although less prosperous for his slightly younger thirty-three years, graced with middle-aged stockiness nevertheless. He resembled his brother in weight, short phrases, and a perfect if painless passion for the way he earned his daily bread and wine. 'Nothing like the law,' he enthused once. 'Nothing like it, Henry, nothing at all.'

'Oh, I don't know about that, George. Other things as good,' said Henry, patting his own rounded stomach. 'Not bad, though, George. Not bad at all. For a living.'

Even at this early hour, George's voice was raised. 'Don't be silly, Henry. Fellow's murdered someone. Got to be defended. Only legal aid, but never mind. Phoned up at midnight, this woman did, in tears. Nothing I could do but pitch up and be a nuisance. Which I was. Couldn't help him then: not allowed. But I've got him now. Stuck with him. Don't mind, really.'

'Bit much, George, bit much.'

'See what you mean, Henry, see what you mean. The victim was John Blundell's better half, and she was, wasn't she? Ha. John won't like it much if I get the fellow off? Well, sorry about that, Henry.'

'Bit much, George, really.'

'I know, Henry, I know. Nothing I can do, see what I mean.'

They yawed at each other in this fashion, feinting halfhearted verbal blows for a while longer, standing in the modern foyer while three junior solicitors slipped in behind and a receptionist with tinted hair blinked into her telephone. Honour was about to be satisfied when PC Amanda Scott stepped through the door carrying a large buff envelope marked 'On Her Majesty's Service' for the attention of G. Harmoner, Esq. Amanda was wearing blue tights with patterns in lace, a frequent sly adornment to an outfit otherwise perfectly plain, and Henry thought she looked jolly nice indeed. He also felt she had somehow lost his argument for him. George came to the same conclusion as his brother regarding her appearance, apart from considering that her legs in those things looked as if spiders were crawling down them, and he smirked, obviously. When Amanda identified him so easily out of the two, George smirked even wider. Personal delivery from personable young women was not frequent in conveyancing: teach Henry a thing or two. Amanda, after being thanked by name for her service, left as courteously as she had arrived.

Henry barked incredulously. 'That's a policewoman?'

'It is, Henry, it is. Lots of them like that now.'

'Good God,' said Henry. 'I give up. Get the bugger to plead, George. He hasn't a chance in hell. First Yvonne Blundell and then a woman like that: they've done for him.'

George knew the sad limitations of brother Henry's criminal wisdom, but after a cursory examination of a relatively small file of evidence, mostly scientific with Sumner's written confession to half the deed, George tended to agree with the verdict given from the depths of Henry's ignorance. Not much scope here for contesting the evidence at preliminary proceedings; at least a *prima facie* case had been proved. Shame. No fuss in front of the local magistrates. George liked fuss in front of the local magistrates and was very good at creating his only chance as a mere solicitor to harangue the witnesses before the whole thing passed into the hands of a barrister and he took the back seat apart from instructing like an ineffective puppeteer, hand-holding some Queen's Counsel who earned twice his own salary. But if this fellow, this poxy fellow of a bloody poetry teacher – his statement as well as his curriculum vitae made you sick – had a thought in his head about pleading guilty to anything, he had another think coming. Not at George Harmoner's hands would he plead to careless driving *en route* to the pub, never mind stabbing to death a wealthy woman afterwards. George sat back and thought, saving the full and sickening details of pathology for long after lunch. Good business, this, even if it was a pity about Mrs B., but she was still a case bound to attract plenty of publicity, her and her big house and all. 'See here, Henry, the property boom is slowing down in this neck of the woods. Made us rich but may not make us richer. It may be time to revise the direction of Amor and Harmoner. Keeping an eye on the ever-moving ball of lucrative but discreet East End crime, shoving a name in front of all those big, dishonest market traders. Only money, nothing nasty; might not be a bad idea.' Again he thought, Pity about Mrs B., but not a time to waste pity, was it? He'd save the kiss of life for the turd who'd killed her. Not bad, the law: not bad at all.

He hummed to himself, undeterred by the pile of files stacked on one side of his desk. Nothing to it, method was all he required and a sense of order, and with those two qualities, everything was curable.

Then, from the lines of a statement in quite another case featuring the theft of a set of carpentry tools including a paring knife, a thought struck George sideways from halfway down the page. Knife. Stab wounds. He dropped what he was reading, picked up Sumner's file, one line stored in his head from the first hurried look at the pathologist's report. What had he said? 'Wounds probably inflicted with single-edge weapon, a knife.' That was what he had read, the very words his photographic memory had transferred to Compartment A along with the contents of the printed exhibit list. Sumner denied either using or possessing the knife. So where was this single-edge knife, eh? Not on the bloody list. Scrabble around a bit, a good eye glossing pages with speed. No knife: not in Sumner's house, in the dustbins, or on the ground; not the sort of thing a poetic chap carried about, if you see what I mean, especially in Branston on the way out for a quiet drink at the pub. Not a bloke to fish, either, as George was; single-edge sharp knife handy there. Fishing line, that sort of thing; cuts it. Has to be very sharp. George was sharp, too.

He sat back and flexed his fingers. He could see the chance for a showy pretend contest in front of the magistrates after all, if only to find out about the knife. Good bloodthirsty stuff, even if unreported in the press; there'd be enough of an audience at the back of court. Make you gasp and stretch your eyes: wounds, causes of wounds, blade of knife, the very sound of it an incantation.

PASSING THE OFFICES of Amor and Harmoner, sitting on top of the bus, William Featherstone, otherwise in a placid state, ventured a glance at the law firm's windows, scowled, and turned back to face the road before him. While his parents were not aware of one George Harmoner, William was and knew him as more than one local notable who would not have graced their establishment for a funeral. William had met the man in circumstances unfavourable, a fact his mother would have to learn sooner or later, he supposed. George Harmoner had stood above him in the interview room of Chingford Police Station, called by the police as was perfectly proper in the case of a young shoplifter only just across the boundary of seventeen where the calling out of parents was mandatory. William's response to the question, 'Do you want a lawyer?' had been, 'Dunno.' Quickly appreciating his uncertain temper, the police had been careful to call a lawyer who was local to where the boy lived. He gave them the village, not the address. It was also known that Harmoner never refused a case, but on sight of the pale-eyed William plucking at the fraying crotch area of his grubby trousers and gazing out of the window with genuine vagueness, he wished he had. William did not like George, either. The man had shouted at him slowly as if he was deaf. 'Do you understand, William? They are not going to charge you. You told the lady here' – indicating a very young probationary woman police constable in the corner of the room – 'that you took those things.' William would have told the pretty probationer anything she wanted to know, and had. George continued. 'The big police officer' – here he gestured with his hands, making William imagine that the chief inspector he had seen once was shaped like a balloon – 'will give you what is called a caution.' Oh, he's a caution: William remembered his mother saying that and sniggered.

He had not absorbed what Harmoner was talking about, other than the strictures: yes, he would tell his parents, and no, he would not shoplift again. He told the balloon inspector he was sorry, because the inspector was a very big man indeed and that seemed a prudent thing to say. William was backward but, within his limitations, not stupid. He did not tell his mother: he expected he might be arrested again if this was the done thing, and he was not sorry at all.

'Come with me, Evie,' he had said earlier.

'No, don't be so bloody silly. Why would I want to do that? And besides, someone might see us. We'll go on the tube another day.'

Pity Evelyn did not care for riding the buses when she had nothing else to do. Coasting down country lanes, a mile or two of fields between mini conurbations, leaving Greater London behind and then joining it again, sitting above the driver and the throbbing engine, William was in seventh heaven. The No. 61 took him from Branston to Chigwell. From there the 134 – pay as you enter, nasty flapping doors that prevented jumping out between stops, another game denied – would take him to Epping via Loughton. Epping had a long High Street full of closed-in stores. He didn't much like that, either; he could not prowl in shops where they were always asking if they could help, the request made in expectation of denial, a mere shooing-away exercise, which he recognized. Worse than market stalls where he could not get a look in. The No. 206, green this time, a dull colour but a nice old bus with a bell, took him all the way to Stortford where there was a perfectly normal modern arcade, the sort he preferred. Shops were open at the front; he did not have to push open doors and announce his presence. Today was Waltham Cross, at the opposite end of the line from Stortford via the 65 from Theydon, but still as full of glittering things. The heavy hand had fallen on his shoulder in Stortford, so it seemed better to leave it alone for a while. All else failing, he could return to Branston High Street or nearby Woodford, which was probably his favourite. There were endless opportunities for changes of mind. He liked that, too.

William's purposes were confused when he approached the shops. Whether he approached from the front or the rear, he never knew quite what he was going to do next. Heart-beating, nail-biting suspense. His grin so wide that anyone catching sight of him wondered if he smiled in recognition of them, then turned away embarrassed, wondering who he was and should they say hello. Back entrances did not carry such traffic although he still smiled automatically. William had been a clumsy mimic as a child, never picking up more than half the idea, but he had mimicked and now mastered in different form his father's scavenging instinct. Bins filled with combustible paper, straw, and polystyrene foam, bits of wire and yards of tissue, and, oh, so often at the bottom of a box, something forgotten, lost in the packaging, or in another, something slightly damaged. At twelve years old, he had played for hours with discarded tapes, holding the endless ribbon of plastic to the light and winding it around his head. At fourteen, he had begun to carve shapes in packing foam, faces and robotlike hands with angular fingers, cut by a Stanley knife too blunt for any use but this. At seventeen he could spend secret hours in the manufacture of wonderful, if tiny, things made from wire and glass fragments, glittery items half resembling rings, bracelets of bottle fragments, but he was far more selective in what he acquired. Bringing home his own bulk along with more under the arm was too conspicuous these days, even for parents such as his own. He purchased or stole in miniature, all of it acquired with a purpose, and never once did he see it as theft, not even when he took an item from a shop counter. He only grabbed from the shop when it was clear to him that taking one item left a dozen of the same, and no one could possibly want so many, surely. Theft was when you took it straight out of someone else's pocket. He had seen that done once, and it had shocked him.

'How are you today?'

'Very well, thank you. How's your cold?' Showing a mouthful of teeth in a smile as wide as a bay, William was known on the buses as a harmless freak. The motion made him talkative: he would chat to bus conductors if they existed, fellow travellers, if not. Yes, yes, they would say, never quite allowing him to engage their attention unless they were over sixty-five. The subjects of William's conversations were food prices, learned from home; poor bus service and lying timetables, learned as he went along; the weather, which was a constant disruption to his soul; public transport; and aches and pains, which he understood. He debated all these topics intelligently with the pensioners travelling on cheap off-peak tickets. On the last subject, William was highly sympathetic, even offered advice. He liked the elderly and the very young. Those in the middle were a sinister blur.

Chingford. Should he alight here and find a quicker bus to base? No, he hated this bus shelter; wait a few more stops, then change; half an hour at least between buses, but a nicer shelter farther down the road on this drizzly, damp day. An old-fashioned shelter with yards of graffiti on the concrete walls, plenty to examine from proper wooden seats similarly decorated. Dear, dear – a phrase learned from the pensioners – Waltham would be crowded. School holidays, teenagers on the streets poking fun, boys moving in gangs, girls with thin legs, flouncy hair, fat lips. Little bottoms and tiny bosoms in all those funny clothes. Just like Evelyn, but nothing like Evelyn. Nothing, no one, no jewel or treasured thing in his whole wide world compared to Evelyn. He closed his eyes for a moment and missed the stop.

WILLIAM'S TREASURE AND father's darling child was trying to listen to her father, stuck in his stuffy office which did not compare with the posher front of the shop – the good plain carpet, carved desk and chairs, banks of plants in bamboo shelving, a mixture of traditional and the new, blueprint for Branston, et cetera. So John Blundell had instructed the eager designer, knocking her down to a cut price for the job, since she clearly hoped for, and he vaguely promised, other jobs to follow in his modest chain of offices and show houses. None did. Having cheated her slightly, Blundell was perfectly happy with the well-textured result. Since no one else but himself occupied the office behind his, it was not important enough for expenditure. A part of John Blundell was very parsimonious indeed. The most expensive for show, the cheapest for private consumption.

'Daddy, don't be so bloody irritating.'

'Don't swear, darling child, please.' Automatically said.

'Well, don't be so slow, then. I do have ears, you know.' She was astride a pile of house particulars perched on a chair on the side of the desk that was normally his. He, like a supplicant, was slightly lower on the stool facing her.

'Get on with it, please, Daddy. I'm not upset. You can see I'm not.' This in a wheedling tone, a placatory voice she had learned to use especially with the opposite sex of all ages, including teachers and relatives. A little-girl voice. He was always seduced by it; he cleared his throat.

'All right, all right, darling child, I was just trying to explain so that you won't be in the dark more than necessary. People will talk, you see; they always do. They'll tell you something I should tell you first.'

She knew that principle already, but found the opposite to be true. If she went into any Branston shop, which she did frequently in the vacuum of school holidays, silence fell. She was aware it could have been the silence of sympathy, a response to her pale face, but she seethed with hostility, wanting to scream, Shut up, shut up being quiet. Shut up knowing things and talking about us. Shut up being so bloody sorry. Just talk, you bloody twits; pretend to talk if you can't really talk. Stop it, stop it, stop it.

Her father saw the tension in her shoulders, paused.

'Go on, then,' she challenged, irritation subdued to the slightest of edges.

'OK, darling child. This is how it is.' He coughed, rendering his own face an unimpressive red to match the viscous red of his eyes. She looked on without sympathy, waiting.

'Your mother. The case about her murder. Henry Harmoner, our solicitor, has just phoned me to say what's going to happen. The bastard.' He muttered the last two words under his breath, remembering too late his strictures to the child about language. 'Anyway, he thinks – God, he thinks a lot, Henry – that the case will come up before the magistrates in Waltham in about two, three weeks, for a hearing of sorts.'

'That's quick. I thought these things took ages and ages.' He looked at her, perplexed. He'd had a dim idea of the same, not so explicit, and wondered as he often did how it was she knew so much. To him, the interval since his wife's murder seemed a lifetime, but he was able to recall that life moved slower for a child.

'Usually much slower than this, I gather. They must have speeded things up.' Perhaps there had been some deference to his feelings in this. He liked to think so, while knowing at the back of his mind it was scarcely likely. Victims of victims always come last, like the poor house-buyer at the end of some chain. That was how Henry explained it.

'What kind of hearing?'

'Don't really know, but not the real trial. A sort of trial before the trial. Won't be in the newspapers, but they mean to call some pathologist chap in to show how Mummy died or something. I'm afraid' – he swallowed, tears appearing at the rims of his eyes – 'she was stabbed before she was buried.' He looked at the pale and precocious face with its calm and disbelieving regard. 'I'm sorry, darling. It isn't very nice. That man, the one who did it' – he could not bring himself to say the name – 'says he didn't. Didn't have the right kind of knife or something silly. It won't be very nice,' he repeated finally.

'Is that man in prison?' she demanded with sudden venom.

'Yes.'

'Will he stay there?'

'Yes.'

She stood and walked around the office so that he would not see the look of grim satisfaction on her face, then went back to the chair, picking up papers and putting them down as she went. ''S'all right, Daddy. 'S'all right,' she muttered through perfect little teeth until she was back in the chair again looking like a miniature consultant. ''S'all right, Daddy, even if it does go in the papers. I'm going to be a doctor, after all.'

'Are you, darling?' First he knew. A moment's surprise distracted him.

'Yes, I am,' she said firmly. 'Also a writer. I have to know about these things so I won't be shocked, Daddy. 'S'all right.'

No, it wasn't all right. He was acutely uncomfortable with her calm authority and ghastly adult composure, felt the same frisson of dislike he had occasionally felt for her, oh, so dissimilar mother. Blundell was not a thoughtful man, merely cunning; he wondered for the first time what they had done, Yvonne and he, to create such a paragon. Should have been more children, he always said, there should have been more. 'Can I have a son, please?' But no, she hadn't liked the idea. Producing Evelyn had been traumatic; leaving the crowded East End in search of more money and clearer air for the child he had then adored had been more traumatic still. He wondered if the women in his life had been in competition and, if so, why? What was it all about with both of them, and were the survivors only pretending to grieve? Why had his darling daughter found her mother's death so easy to accept, mirroring his own lack of anguish? Tears of sheer frustration began to form again. He wanted a drink. His moist eyes slid to the cabinet in the corner, but he was interrupted by her words.

'Can I go, Dad? To this hearing, I mean?'

'To the what? The murder hearing?' His small mouth spluttered the words as his mind took in the meaning of her question. Surprise turned into outrage as his eyes slowly focused on her. 'The hearing?' he repeated, incredulity in each syllable. 'What? With all that—'

'I want to know what happened, and I'm going to write medical books, Daddy.'

'No,' he shouted. 'No you can't bloody go to any hearing, for Christ's sake. How could you – Stop being so bloody … so bloody grown up.'

'Don't swear, darling Daddy,' she replied lightly.

But he had burst into a kind of howl, sat on the stool like a lonely dunce, head in his arms, well beyond his own slight control, all of him heaving with anger and sorrow, fat with the desire to scream. Wearily she stepped out again from behind the desk to stand behind his bent back patting it like a fragile and unfamiliar thing, absent half-blows, half-strokes, as if trying to raise a cough. ''S'all right, Daddy, really. 'S'all right. Honest. Closing time now, Daddy. Go home to bed. Have a drink. It's good for you.'

EVELYN KNEW WHAT was good for Daddy. She could have chanted a list of what was good for Daddy, and did it to quell her own fury. William had guessed, as soon as they met at ten p.m., that Evelyn was very cross and very tired. He wondered if this not unfamiliar condition was one he could choose to ignore. 'Such a busy day,' she had said. 'Daddy's in bed now, goes to bed like a dog when it gets dark. What's the matter, William? 'S'all right, William, really it is. Stop opening your mouth.'

How could it have been a busy day if her daddy was in bed already by nine-thirty? William's father never seemed to go to bed sober, which was a nuisance, and he cried sometimes and drank a lot, like Evelyn's dad. Still, he couldn't see how her day could have been as action-packed as his own, the detailed recitation of which, including all the buses and every single one of the shops, had taken half an hour and clearly bored her. She was stiff with crossness and, for once, openly strained.

'Look,' he said placatingly, wheedling while postponing the other news, which he knew obscurely to be unpleasant, sensing without fully knowing why, that it would displease Evie more than most, dreading the disclosure. 'Look,' he said again, 'look what I've brought you.' Feeling in his pockets with stubby fingers, putting on the bed between them his small hoard of glittering things, trying to please desperately, giving it all away in one fell swoop. 'These were down my trousers,' he boasted. 'I stitched two pairs of trousers together, see? All these things were right at the bottom, by the hem. They didn't find these ...' He faltered on the last words, knowing he had blown it, told it all instead of waiting.

They were sitting in the summerhouse den, Evelyn cross-legged on the mattress, lit by the butane lamp, dark hair falling on her shoulders, ears sparkling like the objects on the bed, which she was sweeping to the floor in a luminous arc. One violent movement of her arm and the diamanté bits sprang into the air, hitting ceiling and wall, falling to the earthen floor in a series of uneven sounds. A gesture of contempt to his gesture of giving. Her face was the colour of day, two red spots and a tight slit of a mouth.

'Who's *they*, William? What do you mean, *they*? *They* what? They when? They where?'

He shifted away from her, cowering, starting to shake. 'They,' he said stupidly. 'Them, I mean.'

'Who's *them*?'

'Policemen them.'

'Oh, shit,' she hissed. 'You got arrested again, you disgusting little berk.'

'Please,' said William. 'Please, Evelyn, I didn't say anything. Just told them I'd found some things outside a shop. Griffith's shop in Woodford, you know, the one you like. A man stopped me, then a woman came, then—'

She leaned towards him and slapped his face very hard. The plain ring on her finger as well as the fingers themselves left an imprint on his face, stigma of a small remarkably strong hand. William shrieked briefly, a grunting little shriek of pain, louder than the sound of the falling objects, followed by a storm of sobbing. He crouched, knees to chin and head in knees, arms pulling self into self, hiding, hurting, and weeping, making his body as small as possible, shrinking away in despair with her strident voice in his ears penetrating his own enormous sobs.

'What did you say to them, William? What did you say?'

'Nothing, nothing, nothing. Only about the things I had and they found, nothing else. They didn't ask; I didn't chatter. Like you said. Like that big fat lawyer man said last time. If I said anything else, you said I wouldn't be able to see you, Evie, and I couldn't bear that. Didn't say nothing, nothing, nothing.'

The last was a rising wail. Evelyn began to recover. 'Promise?' she asked. 'Promise, promise, promise?' The din he made was terrific. They might have been heard for miles: they had tested the den for sound, found it safe, but there was still too much noise.

Her head ached. She began to pat his back, a circular motion with the palm of her striking hand but otherwise similar to the action she had used on her father only a few hours before. ''S'all right, William. 'S'all right, really,' repeated again and again in her best there-there voice, ''S'all right.' She was sick of saying it, speaking words like this and patting people, especially now with that monstrous fear stuck in her chest like an arrow bleeding into her lungs, making her gulp for air in the stuffy warmth of these dirty walls. All too much: she was not a grown-up after all.

She pulled his hands from his face, turned his head towards her own, stared at him intently. 'Promise, William?'

'Oh, Evie, I did promise before. Please believe me, please.' Broken words from a tear-stained, dirt-stained face.

She did believe. She had to believe, and in the reaction of relief that withdrew the arrow, she crouched behind him and hugged him fiercely, mind in an overdrive of impatience. Thinking how soon she could go home, plan, write her diary, sleep, maybe enjoy the luxury of crying herself, wondering if her bike, a possession quite secret from William, was still in the bushes where she had left it. "S'all right. Will, really. Honestly it is. Which shop was it, William? Tell me exactly which shop. It's important. Don't ask why, it just is. Sorry, sorry, sorry.' She repeated the word like a litany, until the crying stopped.

'I hate them all,' said William finally. 'Hate them, hate them, want to burn them down. I'll show them.'

'Nothing wrong in that,' said Evelyn. 'Tell me which shop.'

WIDE AWAKE AT three a.m., Helen wished that Branston were somewhere else, a foreign village, the kind she had visited and wanted to visit again, like a Spanish country village, where for all the silence and lack of light at this hour, the darkness seemed alive, a comfort rather than a dismissal. One long street where a dog would bark for a passerby, alerting the next dog in the next house, and the next, suspicious of movement, endlessly protective. Where sleep thus guarded was an end in itself, not a closing-down against the world as it was here, where all inhabitants were battened in hatches, pretending to sleep, their pets and children as silent as themselves behind double glazing, curtains drawn, blinds at full stretch. In contrast to the alien barking dogs and palpable breathing of real villages, Helen remembered next her own flat in Islington, a street where sleep was never universal. From her basement at any time of night she could hear traffic, distant trains, and from the other side of the house, footsteps on the pavement,

late revellers, early starters, walkers, joggers, products of the night
shift and city enterprises, living in a timeless zone. The bonus of
the metropolis: constant humanity barring the sensation of loneliness, while in Branston people closed doors on their separate
walls, switched a series of switches, and slept like battery hens.

Shuffling the pillow, putting one arm beneath it for comfort,
her body turned sideways, she pictured the rooms of her London
flat one by one. Did that ancient cooker still work? Would her
plants live? Would the tenants have taken down her pictures? Did
they tend the jungle of garden? Did children still climb over the
wall from the school beyond, a Montessori for vandals who were
too young yet to do harm. Her arm ached from lying across it, a
dull discomfort provoked further by sharp recall of one terrifying
night in her own home, remembering at the same time for how
long after that she had clutched Bailey in the twilight hours to
mitigate the nightmares, while now she merely clutched the pillow. The shock of her own withdrawal made her shut her eyes,
afraid to wake him.

'Helen?' His murmured and sleepy voice, a slight stirring from
him, suddenly intensified with the speaking of her name, himself
instinctively aware of her wakefulness, guarding her. 'Helen, love,
what is it? You're wide awake ... Come here, love.' Crossing what
had seemed a mile of bed, folding his long arms around her, turning her, pressing her against his prickly chest, kissing her forehead
and eyes. 'What is it, darling?' Saying to himself, If you will not
come to me, I am still here and I shall not let you go. 'What is it?'

She might have begun to tell him the half of it then in that
silent dawn, grateful for his knowledge of her need to be hugged,
for his constant reassurance, but as she snuggled into the embrace,
ready to speak secrets, he to listen, the phone shrilled. Bailey was

on call-out duty, worse than a doctor, a sound in the telephone buzz suggesting shattering relationships and bad news.

He kissed her once, disentangled himself gently, moved out of bed with the lithe speed that always distinguished his passage from sleep to action, answered with a few terse words, including a question: 'Can it wait?' A silence for the explanation. 'I see. It can't wait; fire still burning. I'll be there, fifteen minutes.'

Helen felt the rise of disappointment and loss as sharp as anger, but it was not anger, only sorrow for another opportunity missed, sad in a kind of inevitability. Back to bed with him, only for a second, only for a hug. 'What is it?' she asked in turn.

'I'm sorry, darling. One of those fires.'

'Which fires? Oh, I know, you told me. Backs of shops and bus shelters. That one? Why do you have to go?'

'Because I need to see one fresh. I asked Amanda to call if there was another. Will you be all right?'

'Course I'll be all right.' Automatic professional response of a woman who would have said she felt fine in the middle of an amputation. Smiling while her leg was cut off, everything perfectly OK, since that was what the onlooker wanted to hear. 'How many fires have there been?'

'This is the fifth.' Putting on his clothes with efficient ease, not like her, each morning a dozen indecisions.

'What time is it?' This wide awake, he was bound to know. Bailey was one of those who always knew the time.

'Four a.m. Go back to sleep, darling. See you for breakfast, I hope.'

She clung, arms around his neck, for a fierce moment, smiled to show she did not resent such departures. 'See you soon.'

Daylight was always too late.

Chapter Seven

MANOEUVRING HIS CAR out of its tidy space and down the hill into Branston High Street, Bailey regretted his own presence in it, regretted their sojourn in such a litter-free zone, and cursed the fire raiser who had caused him to leave his bed. Between a mishmash of thoughts that refused to assume any order of priority in his mind, he also considered dead Yvonne Blundell, Antony Sumner's committal proceedings, and Amanda Scott's efficiency. It was she, of course, who had telephoned, obeying instructions to the letter. Maybe Helen was jealous. He turned the wheel towards Woodford, smiled at the ridiculous notion of himself causing jealousy in the heart of anyone, wished it was so simple. The tension of his household was not related to anything so petty, more to professional disappointment. They were both trained to examine too much, and Helen West thought that he, Geoffrey Bailey, had passed the buck and was refusing to exercise either his mind or his energy to turn upside-down an unsatisfactory case, that he had concentrated on evidence rather than the more oblique prospect of truth. Ah, yes, he knew very well what she thought. That he was acting like a cipher in doing what he was told, trying to avoid those suicidal tendencies that emerged if he thought too much or became involved in other people's lives. Well, that was her theory, not one he had practised in this case or any other, and if she did not believe that, he was not going to tell her. She might know by now it was only his behaviour that was calm, while anything uncertain festered inside him like a wound. He had to confess an irritation with her for being as uncommunicative in her opinions as he was himself.

There was also this second nature of his, which held that an idea, once revealed, was spoiled, like an unexposed film shown the ruinous light of scrutiny. He could not tell her what he was doing with such badly focused images. The doubts and ideas that vexed him needed to develop in peace, immune from description and guarded like secrets. And if the telephone had not rung so imperatively fifteen minutes before, that is what he would have said twice as clumsily as he thought it now. I love you, my Helen, but I could never talk as well as you, and you cannot be party to everything I think without uprooting those thoughts. I know no other way; you must trust me. I could probably live without you if you did not, but the thought fills me with desolation and I cannot change my own slow machinery any more than you could limit your mercurial compassion, your constant vigilance, your strange fund of anger, and all the other things about you I happen to adore.

There they were as he turned down the service road, neat Amanda Scott in a summer jacket buttoned up against the chill of early dawn, standing with PC Bowles and two others, chatting in the cold, waiting. One badly parked car and a harassed key holder flapping his arms and looking upset, with Amanda placing a soothing hand on his sleeve to calm him, all caught in a stage set by the spotlights of the fire engine, which panted like a tired monster. As Bailey appeared, the tableau of faces broke, looked towards him expectantly. The five firemen began to retreat, ready to depart.

The fire had begun beneath a pile of boxes stacked against the wall for removal next day, all goods unloaded, nothing of value lost, sir, only rubbish burning other rubbish. The boxes had been lined up in rows against the brickwork of the yard, now scarred black by smoke, some of the tougher fabric smoking still, incompletely destroyed by the bright flame, which must have shot twenty feet into the air at least, such a lovely spectacle for the pyromaniac; it would have illuminated his watching face. Bailey did not doubt that the same first spectator was a mile away by now and still gloating. 'Anyone see anyone?'

'No.'

'Did you look?'

'Of course, sir; still looking.' Amanda Scott answered this time, but the fire must have been going ten minutes by the time the panda car spotted it, and the pyromaniac would have legged it long before then. Bailey felt weary and dispirited. They were looking to him for ideas and he had only one.

There was nothing unexpected here at all, simply another outbreak in a local epidemic. He asked questions, examined the obvious seat of the fire with the same sensation of dull familiarity. This was similar to the other four fires. Two were in bus shelters, which seemed extraordinary. Who could be angry with a bus shelter? The other three had been set at the back of shops rather like this. All five were clearly someone's idea of harmless fun – big high flames and no real loss, started with what resembled strips of cotton sheeting soaked in paraffin, judging from the overpowering smell. The same cheap washing liquid container used to transport the paraffin, then abandoned in the flames and half melted. For the moment, Bailey discounted the bus shelter fires, for which he could not guess a motive, turned to the key holder who was still flapping his hands, but looking less worried than mildly expectant. 'Sorry to keep you waiting, sir.' Always polite to a man worried about his stock, shot out of sleep without knowing if he faced carnage or a very small insurance claim, treat him gently. 'Could you tell me, were you working in the shop yesterday? ... Good. Was there any bother – you know the kind of thing: arguments with customers, anyone shoplifting, for instance? Common enough, isn't it? Yes, you might not be able to remember ...' And there, from the mouths of babes, sucklings, and shopkeepers, names tumbled. One William Featherstone, arrested here the afternoon before, same boy, same face cautioned for stealing a month before in another shop on the list, scene of the first fire. What was it Helen had called him, not watching him regarding the boy so closely? 'Poor boy,' she had said. That was the difference between them. Where she said 'Poor boy,' he saw a potential criminal. He was not without pity, but that was always his first observation nevertheless. Yet she, like him, should understand and know when to ration compassion. Can't be nice all the time, or even most of it.

As he kicked gingerly at one cardboard box, issued clipped instructions to send in another photographer later in the morning, he could see how clearly his next move could make life in Branston even less comfortable for Helen. He viewed himself as she might see him, the man who went around arresting the nearest and dearest of her tenuous Branston acquaintance. He wondered if she still slept while he raked the ashes of a silly little fire, wondering if two coincidences were sufficient to justify the pulling in of one William Featherstone. Amanda Scott was standing like Patience on a monument, waiting for a name and orders, which he did not pronounce. At least Helen never gave him this irritating and exaggerated respect. 'Think I'll go home,' said Bailey. 'Nothing for us to do.'

'William Featherstone?' queried Amanda, eyebrows an arc of surprise.

'No, not yet. Nothing yet.'

'I AM GETTING out of here,' Evelyn announced, 'as soon as I can.' It was the waning of the summer, visible in the days following William's arrest for shoplifting, and the first signs of dampness were apparent in the summerhouse den. William was shocked, watched while she continued. 'And if you're very good, you can come with me.' He brightened visibly. 'Only for a day, well, three-quarters of a day. We'll go on the tube, like I said. Not your silly old buses. We'll go to Oxford Circus on the tube.' He opened his mouth to protest, shut it again. He knew the tube, didn't like it. She knew how it frightened him, but with Evelyn with him it might be a different story. 'Only if you're good,' she added meaningfully. William sat closer, encouraged by the mood, put his arm around her shoulders. She did not resist. After all, it was Sunday afternoon, reserved for special Evelyn treats, with no one calling from the house. The news of his impending court appearance had alarmed his parents until Harold shrugged it away, but their vigilance had not increased in proportion to suspicion. William placed his hand on her left breast over the jumper; she let it remain. 'But you've got to be good,' she continued. 'You know, tomorrow at court. All these courts,' she added crossly. 'You tomorrow, me the next day.' He shot upright.

'What do you mean, you the next day?'

'You know, Mummy's case. No, don't talk about it.'

His eyes had widened in terror. 'Dead Mummy? Bad Mummy?'

'Yes, William, dead Mummy. Very bad Mummy. But after that – Thursday, I think – we're going out.'

His span of concentration, acute in some regards, was now as short as his memory, from which he plucked only what he wanted to retain, while his hands, arrested momentarily by the threat of bad news, continued.

Outside, the rain pattering on the wooden roof of the summerhouse was barely audible. Evelyn sighed softly, distancing her mind the way she normally did during Sunday afternoon treats, half her school days, and most dealings with Daddy. Daddy was not asleep and darling child was not doing homework. Daddy was being brave, sorting through all of Mummy's things, wanting no witnesses. She knew what Daddy would find in Mummy's desk: one hundred bills, all of them souvenirs of a bored life; thousands of photographs of Mummy when young, Mummy as teenage bride and infant wife, and among this detritus not a single photograph of darling child. If she had ever pointed a camera in Evelyn's direction, the results had never surfaced. Evelyn knew that with a spurt of rage: darling Mummy who had never loved her at all. Well, what was love anyway? Daddy's hugs, then William's more demanding hands, all to keep the bloody peace. Slowly she took off her jumper and closed her eyes. This was Sunday, after all. First church, now this. Life was full of chores.

FOR THIS SUMMER weekend, Helen and Bailey had fled to the sea, cruising the motorway into another county like children escaping the confines of work, armed with books, a picnic basket, shoes for walking, expecting rain and receiving sunshine like a blessing. They had called on friends, drunk a little too much, passed Saturday in a pub with Spartan appointments and splendid comfort, lost themselves in miles of pine-skirted beach. After two days of tranquil, sometimes uproarious contentment, Branston beckoned back a pair of lovers who had at least remembered who they were and why they were together. If there were subjects they failed to disinter from their own silences, it did not matter any more than shadows on the sun. Bailey had delighted in her and she in him. Helen went to work on Monday morning brown and refreshed, body tingling, mind alert. If there was something Machiavellian about her plan for the week, it had not yet begun to trouble her.

In such a mood, Waltham Court, scene of this week's endeavours, was the best choice. Although smarting a little from the actions of Redwood in making off with her murder case, Helen had refrained from either comment or complaint and simply concentrated more on the work that remained. Waltham's daily list offered a panoply of challenges, a picture of local life littered with dozens of decisions per morning, enough to tax the brain and leave it reeling. Waltham court was a favourite of hers. Approaching the façade of a building resembling a factory decorated with bird dung among stained concrete and flanked by vandalized trees, the local *palais de justice* did not look favoured. Inside, the worn floors were pitted with cigarette burns beneath No Smoking signs. The corridors were too narrow, the court rooms themselves airless and claustrophobic, the whole interior like a stained handkerchief left too long in a pocket, beyond redemption. But the atmosphere within it was full of jokes, the staff as cheerful as crickets, as if to forestall the building's determination to depress, the magistrates armed with a degree of realism, and the administration chaotically efficient. Despite a daily diet of misery and despite its carbuncular appearance, Waltham ticked with positive vibrations like a good hospital. The foyers buzzed; there was consideration for life, smiles among the anxieties. Even William Featherstone, sitting alone, had failed to lose his vacuous expression.

William was hers to prosecute this morning, product of the small world in which they lived, another unasked-for complication. She would have to confess her passing acquaintance to his solicitor. She hoped he would plead guilty, but she was recognizing a more than normal awakening of interest in his case as a teenage policeman, scarcely older than William himself, was showing her the exhibit bag, clear polythene, sealed once and for all with a label, containing William's choices from the worst of local shops.

'Can't open the bag before we go in court, miss,' the policeman said. 'Funny though, innit?'

'Yes,' Helen agreed thoughtfully. Very. Why on earth would William take these things? And later, at the very end of the session, with sulky, scratching, sadly unaccompanied William in the dock, unimpressed by the bulky presence of Harmoner, the worthy magistrates asked the same question.

The chairman of the bench, a local shopkeeper himself, had arranged the objects before him. 'I know he's pleaded guilty, but can your client tell us, Mr Harmony, why he took these, er, particular things?'

If he could, he wouldn't. William shrugged and, from the height of the dock, looked with regret at the display on the clerk's desk. There were four sets of earrings, mock diamond in green and white; three sets of very silvery bangles fit for a flamboyant slave girl; two sets of hair clips with silver and glittery buckles; two bright dip-on bows for shoes; and a necklace of shimmering paste. The collection sparkled in cheap harmony, reflecting the taste of someone addicted to *Dynasty* and young enough to mistake sparkle for sophistication. So: William Featherstone, a kind of human magpie drawn by anything brighter than his eyes, liked these pretty things.

'Got a girlfriend, have you?' barked the magistrate, profoundly suspicious of any other tendency this frivolous selection might imply. Helen looked at the pathetic collection with sadness, the sunshine of her weekend draining away. He had stolen the illicit fodder of dreams, poor child. Oh, yes, he could be cured by more pocket money or punishment or blows, like hell he could. Poor William. Stop dreaming, boy, it's illegal to dream with your hands. Goods and dreams, they have to be bought.

At the mention of the word 'girlfriend', William went into spasm, a stiffening of the body and such violent shaking of the head he looked about to lose it. He sat down – was pushed down, since he did not respond to orders – still indicating his negative while Harmoner preached mitigation.

Helen was relieved to see that William seemed preoccupied beyond listening, since like many of Harmoner's speeches on mitigation, this one sounded like a paean of insults: 'Poor child, not very bright, unfit for employment, unfit for anything. No parents here today, because he did not tell them the date, or if he did, they chose to forget. Lives in a dream world. Not much use to anyone, spends his days exploring on buses, he says. Should be given more pocket money, therefore less temptation to steal. Says he definitely won't do it again and is very sorry.'

More pocket money, simplistic solutions for incurable condi-. tions, a pat on the head for insurmountable problems accumulating over a small lifetime of not quite wilful neglect. Helen liked the eccentric Featherstones – she never criticized parental inadequacy, for lack of qualification – accepted the fact that William, like any thief, had to sit where he was, slumped as he was, beyond redemption by something as clumsy as the establishment, but for a moment she detested the ignorance that had put him there. William would have needed to be born beautiful to gain forgiveness at this point in his life, but his crumpled face was not beautiful. He was fined twenty pounds, repayable at two per week; handouts would certainly have to be increased. Law was law to be upheld; Helen believed in it, but in William's case, had the feeling it made no impact whatever. He was hereby made a thief before he knew what thieving really was.

Court emptied for lunch; William was gone in a flash. Yesterday in a relaxed moment of communication, Bailey had told her about the fires and William's possible involvement; she regretted the knowledge, hoped that questions on the subject could be postponed even while she watched Amanda Scott follow William from the room. She thought, What a close creature, Bailey, looking at everything. I'm sure that boy doesn't start fires; he hasn't the sense, and he has no resentment at all. Unless there's a connection between a liking for glitter and a penchant for flames. Why not? What's happened to you these days, my love? You're turning savage with suspicion, or maybe I never appreciated what it was like to live with a copper, especially a good copper like you. No good being resentful: you've a closer acquaintance with human folly than I. You're a graduate; I'm a student. She had thought it through a hundred times, not blaming Bailey, only the perceptions that made them different and him a stranger all over again.

'Ha! Miss West! Our delightful prosecutor for the day. Nice to see you. Nice of you to put your facts so fairly if I may say so. How you manage so many cases with such elegant economy ...'

Bit over the top, thought Helen. Harmoner, with his heavy bonhomie, chose this time to embrace her after eight months of rather more suspicious acquaintance. Woodford and Branston were almost country; they were certainly not town, where professional friendships developed perforce at greater speed, where trust or its opposite were bestowed in a glance, since you might never have seen that opponent before. She appreciated Harmoner's ponderous expertise and lack of dirty tricks, but could have postponed closer knowledge indefinitely. On the other hand, he appeared to have decided all of a sudden that she was good enough for membership of his club, which was not a club at all, simply the local fraternity of those thoroughly committed to their lifestyles.

'We're neighbours, I understand,' he continued with weighty familiarity, standing very close. 'My wife and I should see more of you. Marvellous place, Branston, don't you think? Do you ever have a drink at The Coach? You should come to the Rotary Club ... Sometimes a few of us get together; you know, good for business all round. Must get you involved more,' he boomed. 'Haven't made you feel at home, have we? Must do better. Jolly good. Lunch, eh?'

'Very kind,' said Helen, smiling convincingly. 'But I must go back to the office. You know how it is. But tell me' – seizing the opportunity suddenly with Redwood in mind – 'are you doing the Sumner committal here tomorrow or are you using counsel?'

'I'll do it myself. Why use a barrister?'

She replied diplomatically, 'Why indeed? You'll do far better. I'm not involved, of course, but you won't mind if I watch?' Best to secure some kind of permission, however worthless.

'My pleasure. Nice of you to ask.' He beamed, taking her inter-est in his case as a personal compliment. 'And after that, we'll arrange something for you and your husband in Branston.' He would know very well that Bailey was not her husband in the strict sense: Harmoner knew everything, and used the word as a token of forgiveness. 'Look forward to seeing you.'

Not if I see you first. Waving goodbye, watching him watch her make for the oldest car in the park. Nothing personal, dear Mr Harmoner, but the idea of involvement in Branston's social life makes me itch. Rural pursuits means clubs, committee meetings at the church, maybe. God forbid, wine and cheese parties, cof-fee mornings, and almost certainly dinner parties to show off the wonders of your house. Not likely. She had many acquaintances, few friends, but such as there were provoking passionate loyalty and the desire to entertain in the full knowledge of their toler-ance of burned food. The same was true of Bailey: they lacked the herd instinct. She swore to herself. Guilty side up today: first Wil-liam Featherstone, and then this wild resentment when some half-kindhearted soul tried to bully her into joining his club. Was she a self-protective freak or simply unclubbable, revelling in anonym-ity, missing her own city? Helen had a sudden and sharp yearning to escape, forgot the weekend's freedoms, wanted out and home to London, planned it quickly and furiously as she drove to the modern old-style house she could not call home. Later this week I'm off, not for good, mind, but off to the smoke for a day out. With or without you, Bailey, I'm going home. After I've had a look in court at the evidence you've gathered. Then I'll certainly need to escape for a bit.

She did not know why she wanted to watch the committal, but the desire to do so had been strong from the beginning, growing in proportion to Bailey's reticence on the whole subject of the murder and escalating sharply after she had seen the evidence. She could not remember when this current cycle of silence and countersilence had begun to feed her professional curiosity. Perhaps her own action in recommending a solicitor for Sumner had made Bailey distrust her, but she doubted it; he was far too fair for that. Somewhere along the line, his own doubt had touched him with obdurate reserve, had filled her with angry questions, and she was going to watch these preliminary proceedings to see the evidence in focus. Besides, she would one day return to the prosecution of murder and mayhem, and in case that day was far off, she was not going to lose her knowledge or any opportunity to test her judgement in the meantime.

She was better acquainted with the facts than other watchers at the back of another court in the same dreadful building, ghouls drawn by stories of blood, a local murder from a few miles down the road: would you believe we picnicked there once? Helen did not misunderstand the interest as she saw the ravens and the pressmen gather, felt it herself, this indignant, not always pleasant curiosity following violent death. Respectable blood, not a vendetta knife in the ribs or a drunken brawl resulting in death or domestic fury run riot with kitchen tools, all close enough to London to make them ten a penny. This was *crime passionnel*, illicit passion at that. That her own interest was less prurient did not stop Helen from feeling relieved by Bailey's absence from the court. She knew he was allowing Amanda Scott to assume the role of managing officer for the day, had come to consider he was bored with the whole thing and slightly ashamed of it. A purely academic worry was running riot on this score: she had seen before the catastrophic effect on a case of an officer who had simply lost interest.

Murder deserved better. Notebook in hand, making herself insignificant in the corner by the door in case Redwood should turn in his opening speech and include them all in his wide-angled view. She was not attempting to hide, but she felt like a trespasser and knew that was exactly how both he and Bailey might regard her presence. Spying on Bailey's handiwork, looking for some clue to his view of the world, seeking a perspective to show Sumner was innocent because she preferred to think that he was. They might have perceived it that way. Helen saw it as keeping her hand in.

Evidence recited out loud – marshalled into order, read like a story illustrated by faces and presented in court – was a different matter from evidence read in a book. To a casual reader it was not the same book; the overtones were familiar, but the style was different: level voices and the occasional inflection of emphasis or surprise, made as undramatic as possible – no emotion, gentlemen, please – by this quiet courtroom and these calm adversaries who brought it alive at the same time with their grave and silly gestures. My learned friend insists. I beg to differ. If my learned friend wishes, he may interrupt, but with all respect to my colleague for the defence, this is the way it is, brother. You might have the last speech, but I have the first. One defendant in dock, stripped of authority, almost of humanity, guarded on either side against escape. Poor frustrated Sumner. Bet he wished he never set eyes on womankind. Helen still could not see the murderer in him; could see no capacity for deadly violence in those thin shoulders even while she knew that that potential lurked in almost every soul alive. She watched Christine Summerfield sitting two rows ahead of her, wished she was close enough to touch, even offer the comfort she knew would be rejected. All the world's a stage and all the men and women merely players. Act One, curtain up, amateur thespians delivering expressionless lines, preliminary to final conclusion: sentence to death – sorry, life. Curtain down weeks or months hence. That was exactly what it looked like. Idly she drew her small pad towards her, pencilled a rough sketch of Harmoner and next to it, a cartoon of a guinea pig in a suit.

She knew by experience and instinct that the issues would be all about that knife. While she listened, she sketched, ever so economically, figures for the voices she heard. Come on, Dr Vanguard, I have had you described to me and we have met before. Do your stuff and tell us what you found. The doctor sounded shambly and tweedy with a compost-rich voice. Helen drew him as a gardener.

'The body was found in a small clearing among shrubs,' Vanguard said. 'There had been partial clearance of the soil before my arrival, revealing part of the head, shoulder, and right arm. The right hand had been eaten by predators and the head was infested with maggots, which appeared to be at the first stage, first instar. I proceeded to dig the body out of the ground, collecting soil samples in the process. My external examination revealed a well-nourished woman five feet four inches in height. The face was not identifiable because of decomposition. In the area of the neck there were two stab wounds on the left side. The top wound was one and a half inches, a lateral wound and the larger of the two, while the wound beneath was one inch, just above the thoracic inlet. On removal of the hair it was noted that there was discoloration beneath the front hairline with extensive bruising. There was also a laceration of the skin at the same point. There was similar impact bruising on the left shoulder ...'

And so on. Blows to head and shoulder with a blunt instrument, but the cause of death was the stab wounds to the neck.

So far so good: ponderous, mildly said, and dreadful. Then the questions.

Harmoner lumbered to his feet to cross-examine. 'You say, Dr Vanguard, that the stab wounds on the deceased were compatible with having been caused by a single-edge weapon, such as a knife? Indeed. Not the same weapon, if weapon it was, which inflicted the bruises and lacerations to the head?'

'I don't know. He could have used the knife handle as a club, I suppose, but the head injuries were blows, not cuts. There is a very obvious difference, you see.'

'I do see. Look at exhibit one. This walking stick. Could this have caused the bruising?'

'Certainly, yes, any stick, any blunt thing like this wielded with force.'

'Look at photo six.' Shuffling with usher and one glaring picture passed hands, described as showing two gaping wounds to a brown neck.

'How can you say these were done with a knife, specifically, a single-edged knife?' Harmoner asked.

'Ah. I conclude that from the wounds themselves. There is a single-pointed edge at one end of each wound. You can see it particularly clearly on the upper wound. In my experience the wounds have characteristics compatible with the knife used. The skin is lax, due to decomposition, giving them a gaping appearance, but it would have been a close incision, would have looked more like a slit ... No, I cannot possibly estimate the sharpness of the blade.'

'I am still confused, Dr Vanguard.'

'All right, I'll show you. See, the upper edges of the wound have some irregularities; the lower edges do not. The irregularities are similar. Thus a single-edge blade, not a stiletto, was used for both cuts. The sharp side causes a smooth line; the blunt side makes the other lip irregular, see?' Silence. 'A serviceable kind of knife. Single-edge knives are commonly used. You don't keep daggers, which would cut your fingers. A kitchen knife, if sharp enough, could have made these cuts. More likely a hunting knife, fishing knife, some such thing.' Silence again.

'My client does not have such a knife, Dr Vanguard. Never did.' A loud statement from Harmoner.

'I cannot comment on that,' said the doctor, clearly irritated by a question asked only for effect. 'You know I cannot comment. I did not know the man. I am only a witness to a body.'

Redwood protested about the futile and misleading question, his intervention also only a matter of form. Helen sighed. What a charade. If Antony Sumner's stick had inflicted the head abrasion, a fact that was already clearly established, then no one was going to believe he had stopped there. Even she found the rest of the story inevitable; so would the bench. The judge would commit him for trial and the jury would commit him to another prison. And then and then … She looked at her pad, found she had sketched the back of his shoulders, all she could see of him. She had caught in the lines the slump of a man quite defeated, beyond utterance of protest, rumpled despite the fine head of wavy hair. As she looked, she heard the sharp intake of breath from the seat to the left of her own, sensed eyes turned sharply away from her notebook.

She had been engrossed in the evidence, watching as she always did the style of its unfolding, admiring the dance involved. So absorbed she had failed to notice the small form that had curled itself neatly into the seat beside hers on the very edge of the public gallery, a latecomer, sitting still until the image on Helen's page had disturbed her composure. At the same time, Amanda Scott, turning in her seat to stretch her legs, took in the spectacle of the two of them at the back, visibly startled, making Helen prickle with guilty resentment until she realized that the surprise might not have been reserved for her. She turned and looked towards the creature crouched alongside her, conspicuous in her desire to appear otherwise, with her long dark hair curtaining her face, slouched forward, so obviously not raising her head. Visible beneath the hair was one bright earring, paste and mock marquisite, at odds with the clean jeans and dark sweater, worn like a good luck charm. Assisted by Amanda Scott's look of surprise and by her own memory of a face once pointed out to her, Helen recognized Evelyn Blundell.

There was palpable shock in the recognition, a tactile feeling of horror, no more or less than outrage at the thought of a teenager listening to grim particulars of fatal wounds to her mother's neck, glimpsing the colour of blood on the hideous photographs even from here. In one swift shaft of thought, Helen doubted if the deceased, let alone a single one of the living, would have approved. She was filled with a tidal wave of disgust. A child it was, a child, listening to this. She grabbed the girl's arm, leaned toward her, and whispered into the brightly decorated ear, injecting authority into a voice that might otherwise have shaken. 'Come on, sweetheart, out of here. We're off.'

'No.' A disembodied whisper, not revealing a mouth.

'Oh, yes,' said Helen, intensifying her grip on the arm, rising and pushing simultaneously. 'Move.' With Evelyn in mute protest, the two shuffled out through the door like a pair of conspirators. Amanda Scott had risen, sat down again.

'It is Evelyn, isn't it?' Outside, releasing the arm, Helen was confirming what she knew.

'What's it to you if I am? You've no bloody right … I'm going back in. I want to hear what he did. All of it, what he did.'

'I don't care what you want. You're staying outside.'

'No, I won't, I won't …' The intensity of their voices attracted attention even in a half-full vestibule well used to intense conversations.

'Look,' said Helen evenly, 'you may as well give in. You're staying outside that courtroom whether you like it or not and whether I've got the bloody right to move you or not. I bet your dad doesn't know you're here, does he?' A slow head shake, uncertain, the suggestion of a slight smile at Helen's use of the word 'bloody', a reversion of the face to a sulk. 'Oh, come on,' said Helen, 'I'll buy you coffee. A drink. Anything you want. How about Bario's in Branston? They serve coffee with too much cream and chocolate.' Instinct told her a bribe might work, especially if the bribe was a visit to a place from which teenagers were usually barred. Without waiting for a response, Helen touched the girl on the arm, waiting for her to follow. Evelyn shrugged and obeyed.

If the short drive was far from amiable, at least hostilities ceased. All Helen established was Evelyn's age, and the fact she was at school. She was grateful for the fact that Bario's, despite its recent attempts to augment luncheon trade by serving elegant coffee, was almost deserted at eleven-thirty, sensed that the girl was similarly relieved.

'My dad sometimes comes in here,' Evelyn muttered.

'Did you think you would get in and out of court this morning without him knowing?' Helen asked gently.

'Yes,' said Evelyn through gritted teeth. 'But now you'll tell him, I suppose. Whoever you are.'

'No, I won't, but someone will.'

'Who are you anyway?' The tone was more conversational. Helen looked at this old young face with its fine intelligence and steely eyes, decided against either secrecy or condescension. 'I'm a solicitor,' she replied carefully. 'I know you from living here with Superintendent Bailey. He's investigating your mother's death. You've met him, I think.'

A look of alarm crossed the smooth face and was dusted away with a flick of the head.

'But I don't have anything official to do with the case,' Helen added quickly. 'I just couldn't bear to have you sit and watch it. Here, drink your coffee.'

She was amused to watch how this self-possessed creature responded like a child when faced with a mountain of whipped cream sprinkled with chocolate, spooning it into her mouth with slow and concentrated enjoyment, delicately eking it out to the last, disappointed to find nothing but bitter liquid beneath it, not so sophisticated after all. The process took five almost comfortable minutes. 'You don't have to drink the coffee,' Helen reminded her quietly. 'The cream's the best bit. Want some more?'

'OK,' and the ice was broken.

Evelyn pushed her hair behind her ears, leaned her elbows on the tablecloth, looked at Helen squarely, and half smiled, not quite inviting questions, but at least resigned.

'Why did you want to listen?'

'I thought I ought to know. I don't think that was bad. Besides, my mother's dead. It can't make any difference to her what I know or don't, and I like forensic details. Pathology, anatomy, bones, all that stuff. I want to be a doctor. Or a writer, maybe. I've read about these things.'

'Do you read a lot?'

'Yes, of course. All the time. You have to if you want to learn things. Especially if you know more than your teachers.' Her expression added, You also have to reply to a lot of silly questions like these.

Helen was puzzled. Something was out of kilter, not merely the garish earrings, which struck an elusive chord of recognition in her mind. There was something else quite apart, a fact from her reading of the Sumner case, some part of his statement clearly recalled, which now seemed unlikely.

'I take it you're very good at school? I expect you are.'

'Yes, very good. They keep wanting me to stay down, but I'm far too clever. Teachers make me sick. My father should have paid for a better school. Better for science, I mean. He wouldn't, though. Mummy said it wasn't worth it. He probably couldn't afford it after all Mummy's clothes.' There was an overtone of profound if well-controlled resentment.

'And Mr Sumner? Why did he come and teach you out of school?'

The regard was suddenly very wary, then far too nonchalant. 'Oh, I asked if he could. My English isn't as good as the rest, you see, and I wanted to take the exam a year early, to get it out of the way.'

For a child so articulate, Helen found this unconvincing, but refrained from saying so. She was getting close to the limit of acceptable questions, but refused to resist the temptation to ask more. 'Did you like Mr Sumner?' she asked, but the child was uncomfortable.

'Like him?' she said loudly, voice full of infantile scorn. 'Like him? No, of course not. He's a teacher, isn't he?'

Evelyn bent her head to the cream of the second coffee, leaving Helen to wonder why a girl of fourteen, presumably with better things to do, should ask for extra tuition in a subject where she was highly unlikely to need it. She recalled in her own misspent teenage years avoiding official study like the plague, and remembered with sudden clarity her crush on a history master in the dim days of school. An hour alone with him would have been like an offer of paradise. Perhaps Evelyn had suffered the same, persuaded her parents into a course that offered contact with the beloved. An idle thought. She turned and looked out of the window. 'You can see the whole world pass by from here,' she remarked cheerfully, sensing she would receive precious little more response from the girl. 'Look at all these familiar faces.' Adding calmly, 'Your father is coming up the street, Evelyn. I should duck unless you want him to see you.'

The child leaned back, pulled Bario's pink curtain in front of her face, smiled at Helen in sudden appreciation. John Blundell passed into his office two doors down.

'All clear,' said Helen, and Evelyn released the curtain. One dislodged earring landed on the cloth. 'Yours,' Helen uttered as she proffered it back, turning again to face the view outside in order to hide the deliberately blank look on her face, forming one more question she knew would be the last. 'You do like jewellery, don't you?'

Evelyn was clipping the orb back on to her ear. 'Not this stuff, not really. I like the better stuff, but I have to wear this in case ... Well, never mind. I quite like it, really.' Fastening it back with fingers made clumsy by her distaste.

'Yes, I think I know what you mean,' Helen ventured. 'We sometimes have to wear things people give us. Just to please them.' In her mind's eye was the drawing of Mrs Blundell's missing jewellery, purloined from Evelyn's father, jewellery so different from Evelyn's own the pieces she had seen yesterday, glittering on the desk, exhibits in the short case against William Featherstone. Evelyn was regarding her with a look of fathomless suspicion. 'Oh, yes,' Helen continued artlessly, 'you can see the whole population from here.'

Evelyn accepted the distraction, looked outside. 'Nobody's got any time. They never stop painting their bloody houses, buying bigger cars, and having breakdowns. I hate it here,' she said suddenly and vehemently with a force recognizable as something more than childish pique.

'So do I,' said Helen.

There was a full minute's awkward pause.

Evelyn fidgeted, eager to move on. Home, then, to their no doubt empty houses.

Helen paid the bill. 'Where now?' she asked by way of farewell as they stepped into the street.

'Don't know. Lunch, I expect,' Evelyn replied, eyes fixed forward, secretive again, anxious to be gone.

'Not back on the bus to court?'

'No.' A brief smile, two retreating steps, a new anxiety as she turned on her heel and marched away. A definite, hurried walk, hands in hip pockets, lovely lithe figure that would have been the envy of a mature woman in its immature perfection, still childish nevertheless. On impulse, Helen stood in the next shop doorway, watching Evelyn's progress, partly to see if her anxiety would force her to break into a run, partly to make sure she did not board the

Waltham-bound bus, which had pulled into the stop a few yards beyond on the green. As Helen watched, William Featherstone jumped from the exit doors of the bus, bounding toward Evelyn, his face, even from Helen's distant view, alight with his best delirious smile, fading as the girl strode past him, a quick cut of her hand forbidding recognition, moving faster and out of sight. He started towards her, took two steps in her direction, pulled himself up short, and stopped with the guilty embarrassment of one who has remembered some broken code of manners, looking around to see if his infringement was noticed. Then he resumed his grin and crossed the road with studied carelessness, hands in pockets, copying the way Evelyn had walked but with none of her authority. Poacher's pockets, thought Helen: and you know that girl as well as she knows you. William Featherstone, what is your business with Evelyn Blundell and her earrings?

Then the next thought: tell Bailey. Back to the instinct to tell Bailey all the odd details of her day. If he would listen, that was. If he did not choose to listen these days to the neater and far more relevant conclusions of his pretty detective constable. If he didn't say, 'Helen, my dear, just because she has lost her mother does not mean I am entitled to cross-examine all members of the family about all the aspects of their lives.'

Helen went home, looking at her feet, faintly ashamed of spying. I must learn, she told herself, to trust nothing but evidence. Learn to do as Branston does: go home and shut the doors. Stop looking in people's windows. They do not like snooping. It is not the way of a community bent on privacy. This village togetherness hides a sad apartness. Go home, Helen West. Go home and close the door.

Chapter Eight

GOD, WHAT A poxy afternoon, Amanda silently complained, dreadful day from eight-thirty a.m. until now. What the hell had Bailey been doing all day, leaving her with all the legwork and, as it happened, a fair bit of humiliation thrown in? Perhaps he had calculated that last bit with the Featherstones. Amanda Scott pressed the horn on her car, tried to overtake a truck, realized her own dangerous speed, pulled back, and swore. She only swore in private, found it therapeutic but considered it disgraceful in public. The rage was dying, but she remained angry until she pulled into the forecourt of her block of flats in Woodford, where some sort of reconciliation with the world occurred as she parked the car. Come on, patting her hair in the mirror in an automatic gesture, it wasn't all bad: you might have found an opportunity today. But to be virtually chased out-of-doors by mad Harold Featherstone, behaving and appearing like a caveman, was humiliation indeed. On top of that last labour of the afternoon, she had found Bailey still absent from the office at five, unobtainable anywhere by phone for her to recount how comprehensively she had fulfilled orders and what a good girl she had been. Amanda needed support, needed him to listen to her achievements, and besides which knew very well that it was imperative for an officer as ambitious as she to have her efficiency on record. She would have to telephone him at home, and if she had earlier been of two minds about whether to tell the dear superintendent or nice Mr Redwood about Bailey's girlfriend bringing Evelyn Blundell into court, she certainly wasn't going to keep her mouth shut now.

Good: lipstick still intact. She smiled at herself in the gleaming window of her car as she locked the door, resigned now to her day's work and the prospect of an evening's wallpapering. Amanda spent half of her spare time in the beautification of her small maisonette. But maybe as a result of her afternoon, she might get lucky with a bigger, better flat. Or luckier still with a rich widower. She'd always known she was not designed for some fellow detective constable with a beer belly and long working hours. A lonely widower with a very large income would be good enough for starters. Chance would be a fine thing. The furore of the Featherstones passed from her mind. So did the fact that she had achieved none of her goals in either of the two households she had visited, omissions easily forgotten in the search for self-justification. Exhaustion, irritation, and conspicuous devotion to duty deserved their own reward.

No, it had not, after all, been such a bad day, Amanda reflected over the soapsuds of her three breakfast dishes – bowl for museli, cup and saucer for decaffeinated coffee – must look after the health. She had been the one in charge of the committal proceedings, subject of thanks from Harmoner, 'for favouring us with your presence, my dear.' Ya, ya, ya, nice to hear, but nothing he could say was going to enhance her promotion prospects. Better to impress Redwood, and even that was scarcely worthwhile. She did not consider it kind of Bailey to let her take the accolades for his immaculate preparation, suspected he had only done so to give himself a free morning after, and he had obviously taken the afternoon as well. Amanda had a suspicious mind. He was up to something. So what? The man wasn't married, after all. She wondered if his girlfriend knew. She had thought what a good-looking man Bailey was, had thought … Well never mind what she thought eight months ago. She closed the subject and put away her tea towel. She didn't think it now; ambition had moved on. So the committal was fine, no problem there. One murderer, fey-looking bastard *en route* to the crown court, quite handsome in a way, and everything hunky-dory, with the prosecution smelling of roses and the police, too, for wrapping it up so quickly. Then the rest of the day's impossible orders issued with a smile, while Bailey had the nerve to imagine that she did not realize he found her neither particularly likeable nor attractive. He was bound to prefer that little woman of his, 'a solicitor you might know'. Although Amanda did not regard police officers of any age as suitable for mating purposes – and Bailey was a bit old, let's face it – she was still mildly insulted by his preference for a bit of social status as well as the sort of casual elegance Helen West managed so easily and she herself could never achieve. You and I came from the same stable, Bailey boy. Stop pretending you didn't. She put the dishes back in the cupboard, looked at her neat kitchen with mixed satisfaction and discontent, admiring its shiny surfaces, stirred by the resentment when she thought of the splendour of J. Blundell's mansion. Come now, Amanda, you should be moving forward in life. You've come a long way in twenty-six years, but you should be further forward than this.

From Waltham Court, she had driven to Blundell's house. 'Call on the man,' Bailey had said, gauging to the minute how long the court proceedings would last. 'He goes home for lunch. Tell him what happened at court, be concerned. But most important of all, find some way to search the house. We've done it after a fashion, but not that thoroughly.'

'Couldn't PC Bowles do that?' she had asked, meaning quite plainly, I'm a detective, sir, not a trooper.

'Yes, he could. But Blundell understandably wouldn't like a few plods rummaging all over his house. He won't mind you. I want a thorough search for that jewellery. Explain to him the formality: tell him we have to eliminate the very remote possibility of her having hidden it in the house, dropped it, whatever, even if he did see her wearing it just before she went out.'

'Don't you believe him?'

'Yes, as far as he thinks he saw it.' Amanda felt a frisson of excitement. 'We don't know if she came back before meeting Sumner. Or whether Blundell was drunk or vague. But I want you to have a look in his room, and the daughter's. A good look in the daughter's. Doesn't matter why. It's important. Oh, and ask after the child. Find out what she does with herself. She's been given appointments with a kind of counsellor, but she never shows up. Don't tell him that, but try to find out why. Use your charm.'

Go and wow Mr John Blundell, in other words. Waste an hour of a sunny afternoon poking around his house looking for jewellery Sumner had clearly sold weeks since. Piss off. Then go and see the Featherstones – gently, mind – and ask them what their son does nights and days. What's that got to do with anything? Amanda asked silently. I'm on the murder squad, not the small-fire-and-two-bit-shoplifter squad. Leave those jobs to uniforms.

Not out loud, no point in complaining. Close as a clam, Mr Hand-some Bailey, good at delegating work, but not ideas. Dislike was becoming reciprocal. She only accepted the afternoon's dumb-fool assignments for the opportunity of a gander at Blundell's house. Dream house; she wanted it. Or if not that, something compa-rable. She deserved it.

Detective Scott had found the grieving widower in the kitchen at two o'clock eating a sandwich and drinking a beer, been greeted with enthusiasm, explained her mission prettily, and noticed that he looked a trifle lonely. Talking through the morning's progress, she managed to make Sumner's continued imprisonment sound like a triumph rather than the elaborate formality it had been.

'Good, good,' he said absently, 'I'm so pleased,' which seemed a mild response from the bereaved, but Amanda expected that was something to do with grief. She did not know much about grief, never having suffered such a thing in her life. He was certainly responsive enough to make a cup of coffee, offer a drink, which she refused. 'Quite right,' he said, and seemed suddenly disposed to please.

'How's your daughter?' Amanda asked.

'Oh … out, always out. She sees her friends, goes to her aunt, back about tea time. Then studies in the evening, darling child. Good girl, very good girl.'

That would do. Amanda was not particularly disposed to ask more about the daughter, felt capable of inventing details to fill in the gaps. Then she had complimented him on his kitchen, her wide smile and white teeth hiding the savage reflection on how her own abode had the same surface area in entirety, including her share of the garden. She put warmth into her remarks and felt him come alive.

'More coffee?'

'Oh, yes, please, if you're sure you can spare the time.' Charm him, Bailey had said. Looking at this kitchen, Amanda would have whored for him. He was smiling like an angel, quite bearable to look at, and patently well heeled.

'Where do you live, Miss Scott?'

'Oh, call me Amanda. I live in Woodford, actually.' Smoothing the skirt and patting the hair while his back was turned. 'Only a little flat,' belittling her pride and joy with a wave of the wrist. 'I bought it from you, as it happens. Your Woodford agency.'

'Really? What a coincidence. When was that?' Animated chat on what was sold when and where in their own six square miles, why it was sold and for how much. They were rolling on common ground. Both were fascinated by space and prices and value for money and floors and ceilings, he globally, she personally but with the same passion. They revelled in the respective merits of pitch or pine, sloped roofs or flat, whether the entrance was important. Enjoying herself hugely, she only just remembered to ease in the proposition about searching the house in which she was receiving such benign hospitality.

He moved the subject aside adroitly like a bill postponed to another day. 'Oh, no, not yet ... Must say, excellent commercial mind you have, Amanda. Ever thought of taking up estate agency? You'd be marvellous.'

'Do you think so? I've always been interested.' Flattered, she slid down the tangent, only resurrecting the searching-for-jewellery business ten minutes later.

'What for?' he asked, puzzled.

'For Mr Bailey.' She withdrew herself carefully from blame for the intrusion. 'He thinks we might have missed it somewhere.

Have to make absolutely sure it isn't here. You know, tucked in a drawer in your room, your daughter's room, one of the spare rooms. Or in a coat pocket or something. You know.'

He did know, turned away to refill the kettle and reach for a bottle of white wine from the fridge. She was bound to like white wine, not a whisky lady. Just a glass, come on, Amanda, won't do you any harm. What she would not like, nor would he, to ruin this budding relationship, was the sight of the bareness of his daughter's room. Pretty stingy furniture in there, disgraceful, really, when he came to think of it, rotten old desk, very small cupboard and child's bed. Yvonne had always said that was enough for her, and after a while Evie had stopped asking for anything else. It shamed him, the poverty of it. Much less would sweet Amanda like to see, or he to show her, the rows of clothes hidden by wardrobe doors in his own room. There were things he might have liked to do with Miss Scott in that room, but they did not include a search of coat pockets. There was not a single item of the dear deceased's clothing that was not torn to shreds. He was beginning to wonder how he was going to get the garments out of the house.

'Now listen, Amanda.' Placing a hand on hers, noting the lack of resistance. 'Why don't you tell Mr Bailey you've been through the place with a fine-tooth comb? Because I have, I can assure you, and you'd never find anything I'd missed. Turned over everything, I did. But fussy, your boss, is he?' She nodded vigorously, tut-tutting at his criticism, but smiling compliance.

'That's OK, then. What I was wondering … well, never mind. Presumptuous of me … I shouldn't.'

'Go on,' said Amanda.

'Well, I was wondering … It's nothing, really, but I do like to help. I'm sure we could find you a better flat than you have, you know, a good little bargain. In Branston, maybe. I always hear about them, always know when to pick 'em up, if you see what I mean. Interested? Nice girl like you, kind to an old man. Girl like you deserves to get on.'

Amanda's thoughts exactly. The rout of her distraction was complete and she beamed goodwill.

'Not at all, my dear, and do call me John. It's a pleasure to help someone I like, not all these toffee-nosed solicitors, city people, think they're the bee's knees.' A quick stroke of brilliance, stroking the chip on Amanda's shoulder. 'Tell you what. Perhaps when I've marshalled a few ideas we could have dinner and chat about it when you're not on duty. Ever tried Bario's?'

O brave new world: she had never been to Bario's, had dreamed of living among the select trees of Branston instead of in the service area of Woodford.

'I know a chap who does a wonderful line in discount furniture, too,' John continued, and they were off again, all thoughts of searching the house shoved downwind of his after-shave, her perfume, and the riveting discussion of bargains.

Amanda Scott left the Blundell house well pleased, sober on one glass of wine and three coffees, high as a kite otherwise, a tentative date with a rich widower and a plausible account for Bailey bubbling in the back of her mind.

J. Blundell made for the whisky and forgot his office once he closed the door on her, equally pleased.

Then Amanda made for The Crown and a rapid descent to earth.

'Yes? What the hell do you want? Oh, I know you. Old Mr Bailey's sweetheart, isn't it? The unofficial one. Dear God, have you only got one suit?' Bernadette Featherstone smirked in satisfaction, quick eyes recognizing the same navy blue suit at the kitchen door she had seen weeks since, and only briefly then.

'Hello, Mrs Featherstone, sorry to trouble you.' The pleasantry was like an armour. 'Superintendent Bailey asked me to call and ask you—'

'Don't hello me. There's no bloody need. And I'm busy.'

What a contrast of kitchens. Bernadette's kitchen was invisible to the downcast clients clinging to the bar outside and waiting for evening company, abused by Harold or ignored. It was as large as the Blundells', but twice as antiquated, extremely dirty, and currently full of the smell of baking bread and washing. Amanda, who had an eye for domestic detail, wondered how Bernadette could take such obvious trouble to make her sheets that dusty grey. She also wondered if the smell of the bread was going to be the only enticing quality about it. The washing machine in the corner was churning suspicious suds. Both of them were shouting above the noise; Bernadette was used to shouting, but it was awkward for Amanda.

'Oh, for God's sake, sit down. Stop gawking like a tourist at a monument. What do you want, and where's your bloody leader? Lets you out on your own, does he? In my opinion, policemen should be blokes.' Bernadette cackled. Flattery was obviously not today's menu. 'Have you come about William?'

'Well, yes, in a way.'

'What do you mean, "in a way"? Harold!' she yelled to no response. Bernadette picked up a cloth, dried dishes quickly and absently. 'Get on with it, then.'

'Well, Mrs Featherstone—'

'You're a bit worried about William, I expect,' Bernadette interrupted. 'Nicking from shops, little sod. Don't know why he did it.

But you needn't worry. Harold's going to give him seven pounds a week, and we'll be keeping him busy. We've solved the problem.'

'It wasn't so much the stealing, Mrs Featherstone.'

'Well, what then, woman? You suspect him of rape or something?' Another snort of laughter while Bernadette lit a cigarette, her instinct well informed enough to realize how much it would irritate while at the same time hiding her own jangled nerves behind the smoke. She had censured William as gently as she knew. He had erupted; she had withdrawn. He was beyond her control, but it was their battle, their very own, not for anyone else. She might have trusted Bailey with the worry of it, but not this peaches-and-cream piece of neatness who could go and boil her head for all Bernadette cared.

Amanda Scott could sense she was being intrusive. Even she could sense Bernadette's controlled rage, and she wondered if the reputed fits of William Featherstone were really an inherited mental deformity from a mother whose secret pastime was foaming at the mouth.

Bernadette was smoking at the mouth, deliberately exhaling a ragged cloud in Amanda's direction. Amanda opted for the businesslike approach. Keep this as short as possible.

'What does William do with his time, Mrs Featherstone?' The snappiness of her tone brought silence, followed by reluctant cooperation.

'Do with his time? I don't know. He's a grown man now. Everyone knows what he does with his time. I told Mr Bailey ages ago. He loves the buses. He goes shopping. London sometimes, Epping, Stratford, Waltham … well, you know about Waltham. That's where you booked him. And …' She scratched her head and thought. 'Oh, and he sits in his room thinking about things. And

I don't know what else. Apart from making things. Jewellery, as it happens.' Nothing else to be proud about.

She pulled open the drawer in the scrubbed kitchen table, a drawer full of assorted rubbish: tap washers, screwdrivers, receipts, fuse wire, wadded-up paper and half-finished candy packets. The kind of drawer Amanda Scott itched to clear.

'Here,' Bernadette said triumphantly. 'See what I mean?' There was a rough bracelet in her hand, upheld for examination with something like pride. 'Fuse wire and glass, baked in the oven,' she said fondly. 'Don't know how he thinks of it, really I don't.'

Neither did Amanda. There was a kind of primitivism in William's artistic efforts. Silver wire or fuse wire twisted, with small pieces of glass embedded in the twists, all melted to an uneven, unusual shine of colours, like crude enamel, the wire imperfectly smoothed by insufficient heat, the glass still uneven although no longer sharp. Rather uncomfortable Amanda thought. It might look strangely at home in some trendy fashion shop for punks where it could double up as an offensive weapon, but not on her own wrist or that of anyone she knew.

'He didn't like this one,' Bernadette remarked. 'Said it was dull. I don't think so.'

To Amanda the thing was distastefully bright; she did not like handling it, took it politely, put it down on the table with obvious distaste. 'What else does he do?'

'What else should he do? This stuff takes him hours.'

'Does he play any sport?'

'No.'

'Any other hobbies?'

'No.'

'Girlfriend?'

A very brief hesitation while Bernadette bent to scratch her foot. 'No.'

'Any friends?'

'No.'

'Does he work at all?'

'Not officially, no.' It was like a litany of negatives from which William emerged as blank as sky. The telling of it filled Bernadette with guilt.

'Well, what does he do in the evenings?' Amanda asked.

Mrs Featherstone rose in fury. 'Sits in the kitchen, sits in the garden, hangs around. Even talks sometimes. Helps me. Sits in his room and wanks, probably. Maybe he dreams of you, Miss fucking Scott. Harold!' she bawled again in the direction of the bar. 'Come here.'

There was a moment's silence, a heavy footfall, and Amanda felt the first trace of alarm. She was not proofed for insult from shabby, crabby Bernadette. She rose to her feet tight-lipped, Bailey's words in her ears: 'Always give up an interview if it seems entirely counterproductive. If they won't tell you, they won't. Wait for another time.' Amanda was content to wait for ever and to get out while the going was merely bad, preferably before the footfalls reached her vulnerable back. She moved, too late and too awkwardly.

'Ah,' said Harold behind her neck. 'It's Mr Bailey's moll. The pretty policeman. How are you, Moll?' And before she could turn, he wrapped his large, thick arms around her waist, wrists locked in embrace, his mouth in her ear. 'How are you, Moll?' he repeated softly, dangerously, but laughing, his breath whisky-laden, his skin damp and stale. 'Leave off our boy, Moll. Or we'll set him on you.'

She pulled at the wrists in sickening panic, tearing them apart, grabbed her bag, crashed against the table *en route* to the open back door. William's jewellery fell to the floor; she heard it clatter on the broken quarry tiles, and for a reason she did not fathom she bent and recovered the bracelet, slipped it into her bag as she ran for the daylight, slowed herself to a galloping walk, remembering dignity too late. Soon enough to turn and smile back sweetly, more for her own sake than theirs. 'You've been very helpful. Thank you.' Sarcasm in each syllable, hating the last glimpse of two laughing faces. Rubbing her neck where Harold had touched her, feeling diseased. Uncharacteristically close to tears, pushing through bushes, she walked downhill on a slippery path, spitting into the shrubs at the side like an angry cat. Then stood still, momentarily lost in the garden.

The straightest route to the car was the way she had come, through the kitchen, the bar, and the front door, but she could no more re-enter that furnace than she could fly over the moon. She paused, looking and listening. No choices as she drew breath and calmed herself. Walk to the bottom of this dark, disgusting garden, get through to the field somehow, walk back up the side of it to the road and the front of the pub. In common with most of her fellow émigrés to these country zones, Amanda believed in sanitized country life, disliked muddy shoes, brambles, and the slime of ill-controlled nature. The shrubs visible at the end of the path over a fallen tree held little appeal for exploration, but torn tights and a pulled skirt were infinitely preferable to the alternatives. Swearing silently, she persisted down the path, branches spitefully teasing her face, and came on the summerhouse by surprise, and stopped.

Christ. The shed was as mad as the couple in the hotel. No doubt a Featherstone project, with that drunken look, half done and then abandoned, like the kitchen. She was not interested or even disposed to look – the whole family could roast in hell, the sooner the better – but in passing silently she peeped into one of the windows, frightened but drawn. Through the damp grime on the glass, she could see a dim light, hear sounds of hammering subdued by earth as if coming from a great distance. From a hole in the floor, momentarily blocking the light, a head and bare shoulders, pale in the glow, rose away from her. Perhaps a Featherstone, perhaps an intruder, perhaps big William tunnelling out of the ground like a giant slug. Amanda could imagine white-skinned William, vacuous image of his father, an undressed grinning version of the lout she had met in court, but naked and rampant, lumbering towards her, a vision that was entirely in her mind, since only his back was visible; while she watched he remained terrifyingly still. She ran from the window, pushed through the shrubs, climbed a fence into the barleyfield, and thrashed her way uphill to the safety of her car. She drove well beyond view of The Crown before stopping, dusting down her muddy skirt, cleaning her shoes with tissue and grass, no longer trembling, feeling utterly foolish and simply angry.

Remembering now, looking at the mud on her skirt, Amanda decided on a weak gin and tonic, normally reserved for guests, to make it look as if she tried. The problem with the mortgage race was that it left over so little money for self-indulgence of this or any kind. She drank in tiny sips with relish, forgetting the humiliation as she crunched the ice. She had to get on, whatever it cost, and never mind the drawbacks. A job was a job and this was a good job, a passport. Featherstones or not. She had come a long way from the back streets of North London, and she was not going back. And as for her visit to The Crown, she would tell Bailey all she had learned about William, but not quite how the learning had happened.

'You DID WELL, girl. Really you did. Saw her off nicely. I was listening at you, you know, before I added my three penn'orth.'

Bernadette was lighting the fortieth cigarette of the day. 'Thought you might be,' she said. 'Harold, what are we going to do?'

She put her head in her arms briefly. He moved to her side of the kitchen table, hugged her quickly. Harold was sober and trade was dead at ten o'clock. Amanda Scott's afternoon visit had raised a brief laugh, but dispelled the taste for whisky.

'What are we going to do, Harold?' she repeated.

He slumped into the chair beside her, hating emotional scenes of the noncombative kind as much as he hated responsibility, suspecting most of the fighting was the result of his evasion of his duty.

'Do about what? The pub?'

'Oh, Harold, face up for once. Never mind the bloody pub. I mean William. Our son, William. I don't even know where he is.' She had a fair idea he might have been somewhere at the other end of the garden, and she was relying on the end of summer to bring him back, but even in this extremity she was not going to say. She knew Harold's limitations as well as his temper, felt she had betrayed William enough already for one day – she had even lost the bracelet she treasured, given her as reject gift from the pile of his creations, but still a gift.

'Well, what *can* we do?' asked Harold, mildly belligerent. 'Why should we anyway? All right, he pinched some trinkets. I've paid the fine, given him more pocket money, and that's that. He's not done anything serious.'

'Hasn't he?' asked Bernadette. 'Hasn't he, now? I wonder.'

'Like what do you wonder?' Irritation, a self-defensive and guilty anger, as well as a plea for forgiveness rose in his throat.

'Oh, I don't know, Harold. He's so empty. I keep thinking of that body in the woods, that's what I keep thinking. I don't like it, Harold. Don't know what to do.'

'There's a man in prison for the body in the woods,' Harold almost shouted. 'Stop thinking, Bernie. You're not good at it, honest you're not. And what the hell can we do anyway? If you stroke him he bites. If you pat him he scratches. Interfere now and we'll only provoke him. He's fine, Bernie, just fine. Look at him, always smiling.'

She was too tired for conflict. It was the story of her life, this incessant fatigue kept at bay by quarrelling. Better do as Harold did, simply avoid it and hope for the best.

'If he gets worse, pet, we'll take him away.'

She turned to him with mild and hopeful enquiry. 'Where, Harold? Back to London where no one would know us? Suit me fine. I'm sick of it here. It's like living with a whole load of cuckoos feathering their nest. Just like we do. If we hadn't worked so hard, and I might add for so little, we might have had a better son.'

He sighed dramatically. 'We'd be lost in London, Bernie. Wouldn't own a thing.'

'That's exactly why I'd like it, Harold. So would William.'

Harold hesitated, hating both the forward and backward trends of the conversation. 'You don't really think he's done anything more than thieving, do you, Bernie?'

'I don't know,' she said. 'I just don't know.'

BETTER NOT TO know, John Blundell had decided. If he did not look in her room, which was always carefully locked – 'I must have my privacy, Daddy' – he would not know if she was there or not, could kid himself she was, hunched over some encyclopaedia or whatever it was she did. Last time he had peeked in there, when Evelyn had permitted access to the cleaning lady, he'd seen a plastic skeleton, the only adornment visible in that Spartan room, before she'd caught him looking and frozen him off with her stare. She even supervised the cleaning. He had never really wanted to know anything intimate about her, and her eccentricities made more sense in the light of her recently confessed ambitions for a medical career. Thank God Amanda Scott had been fobbed off from searching. The sight of a small plastic skeleton in the room of a female teenager struck Blundell as a worse obscenity than a naked man. As for what was in the drawers of her locked plywood desk, he had a shrewd suspicion. There was something else of value as well as a lot of paper. She loved jewellery, and he had noticed how she hid the things she loved. Up here, she was forever writing and hiding. One day he would improve on his glimpses. Not now, later.

But he cared if someone else knew. If darling child wanted to be secretive about her own bits of rubbish, and if he wanted to tear up his wife's clothes, they would do so. Family was family. They had come here to preserve family, whatever kind of shambles this one had been for years. With the careful calculation of two whiskies down, he waited until ten o'clock, dialled the number left by Amanda Scott. He knew enough about the inside of people's houses to hazard a guess at her life-style, saw her with cold cream, cocoa, and nightie, rather liked the thought. Two birds to be shot with a single stone: avoid prying eyes on the one hand and cast a lure for a new woman on the other. Not a bad prospect, Amanda. Might at least know the value of money and be grateful. Yvonne, the bitch, only liked the best.

IN THE BAILEY-WEST household, peace of a kind reigned. A single phone call from Amanda Scott, bursting with the desire to report something or other, but guarded and satisfied when Bailey had said he would hear it in full tomorrow. No information given or received.

One of their neighbours was sitting on the sofa, complaining to Helen about her children. He was amazed at the picture they made, these two disparate women, even more amused when he contrasted Helen's obdurate unclubbishness with her complete inability to close the door on a visitor. No, she would not attend a meeting, be seen dead on a committee, sign a petition, but she would listen, pour a drink, and extend a welcome, unable to resist. At home in far-off London, her phone had never stopped ringing. Bailey had been irritated by it then, but found he missed it here. Listening to the neighbour, the well-meaning but harassed mother of two, despairing over the decisions made by local school authorities, he wondered at the implications of these empire-building residents of Branston, questioned whether fresh air and keeping up with the Joneses was really an improvement over life in London.

'He does so much worse than anyone else in his class,' the neighbour was saying. She was not tearful yet, simply indignant.

Stop pushing him, then, Bailey added silently to the conversation, wishing she would go. The boy is healthy. No one else is sick. What's the problem? Push, push, push, an endless spiral of improvement. Better houses, better cars and schools, all lined with the same amount of discontent. People nagging away: it's so good now; it can't possibly be good enough. We've come quite a long way, Helen; it might be time to turn back.

Bailey regarded the visiting woman with mild eyes she found slightly unnerving. He reflected that this brave-new-worlder was trapped economically in marriage, like a state-aided couple in a slum, neither with another place to go and no money to split up. The only difference was that one couple was more affluent and lived in a different cage where the padding didn't really help. There were plenty of murders in these situations, plenty of scope for them in cosy Branston. The upwardly mobile, striving for heaven, by some accident curtailing their choices rather than expanding them, leaving themselves no time to think. No time to see how the children thought, either. Would they prefer the posh schools or the concrete playground? Electronic toys or cardboard boxes? He didn't know. There was no time to judge your partner. Maybe Helen had time: she did not need him in the same way he needed her.

Since his contribution to this living-room chat was not required beyond an occasional murmur, Bailey was free to think of his own day. It had been pleasant in its way, a release from supervision, reports, delegation, and listening. Superintendent Bailey trying his hand at being junior detective and legworker – that took him back a year or ten. Getting on and off buses, amazed at how arbitrary they were, how patient their passengers all around the parish, buses that stopped at two burned-out shelters and took him to Waltham and Woodford armed with a copy of William Featherstone's photo, taken on his second arrest. 'Seen this boy, have you?' he had asked, showing the unflattering image in black and white. Odd how these new Polaroids were no improvement on the old in giving every subject the appearance of a villain. 'Yes, I seen him, guv. Often, as it happens, but he usually smiles, poor kid. Been seeing him for years, but he's grown a bit.'

Bailey had been surprised to find in William's travelling acquaintances something approaching genuine affection, at worst a mild tolerance. Perhaps in calling him 'poor boy' Helen had seen something he had missed.

He turned in response to a nudge from her. 'Pardon?'

'Mrs Levinson was asking if we like it here,' said Helen.

'Oh, we like it fine,' said Bailey. 'Lovely place.' Noting with surprise how Helen had passed that awkward question to him. Perhaps the space was not so important to her after all. He noted that, recorded it with amusement and something like hope. Perhaps – an impossible thought in the face of the evidence – she loathed the place as much as he did. And akin to this, a sadder conclusion: yet another day had gone by without real conversation; the weekends of life were lost so entirely by midweek.

Helen thought, I should tell him about the committal proceedings. Then she listened to his polite praise of Branston and held her tongue.

Chapter Nine

Shops. Oxford Street filth drifting on pavements that needed rain. Judging from the sky, they were shortly to be blessed with it. Of course, no one went to Oxford Street to look at the sky. All of them looked ahead or sideways, never upward, occasionally down to see what was entangling their feet, keeping handbag in front and pockets clear. Helen was streetwise, used to standing for hours in Marlborough or Bow Street court prosecuting queues of pick-pockets, dippers in every colour with quicker fingers than Fagin's children, smiling benignly as they passed on the escalator with a wallet already gone to the one behind, netting thousands a day. She was careful in the shops, too, once versed in the Can-I-help-you? conman: urbane and immaculate on the floor of a department store otherwise devoid of helpers, assiduous in assisting with choice of scarf, jacket, tie, before offering to take those traveller's cheques, dollars, yen, Visa card, whatever you were needing change of. Take a seat, ma'am, I'll be back shortly, and you will sit here for ever if you're waiting for me. Famous characters when not in prison. Policemen patrolling this fairground of shops for the parvenues of the cheap to the merely priceless called it simply 'the Street'. The Street was dirty, shabby, crowded, and jostling, downmarket, upmarket, middle market. No one spoke English or walked in a straight line. Rudeness was customary. Pretend stolen goods as well as real were sold on pavements along with tacky souvenirs, overpriced fruit and dangerous toys. Shop assistants either crowded around customers like flies or studiously ignored them. Litter bins overflowed, and the three underground stations were frankly sinister. Bargains and impolite robbery were equally available. There was nothing essential to life or decent to eat within a mile, and there were bomb scares.

Helen loved it.

Nothing better for a shopping addict. She loved shops, full stop. Here her essentially serious nature took off into harmony with the frivolous world. Helen could not shop with any precision, a facet of her that irritated Bailey to the extent he could never accompany her on any expedition unless she set out to buy one item in an emporium that sold nothing else – paint in a paint shop, for instance, nails in a shop that sold only nails. This suited Helen, who preferred to shop alone or accompanied by another female of kindred spirit who understood that when shopping you looked at everything: duvets and food in Marks and Spencer even when you went there to buy a skirt; washing machines, carpets and coats in John Lewis, even if you had gone for a plug. And if you had embarked on a vague search for clothes, there would never be an end to it, not even a beginning.

Bailey could not understand how she could return from such a foray armed with nothing but exhilaration, replete with things seen, people met, and everything else, but without a parcel in sight – although that was rare. Something always got hold of the purse, but it mattered not if the product of four hours' wandering was no more than two pairs of tights and a pineapple, one lipstick and a newfangled potato peeler, two light bulbs and a free sample of perfume. Today she intended to do better: this was a prearranged frolic with itching credit card. Helen was looking for the boost of a new autumn coat, replacements for down-at-heel shoes, and a new pair of trousers to make her look at home in ultracasual Branston. Having decided on that, she would not be disappointed to return with a tube of toothpaste. The looking was the thing: that was the way it was with shopping, the way she liked it.

Helen sat on the train, thought of the day ahead, armed with the inevitable book, forgetting to read in an almost empty carriage, so empty she felt the sense of secret holiday. Really, she and Bailey were equally bad. What harm would there have been in mentioning that she had seen part of his case and had met Evelyn Blundell in the process? But she had said nothing, and had allowed last evening's garrulous neighbour to exhaust them. They had gone to bed when she left, Bailey for an early start, she for a piece of truancy like this. What the hell. She was dreaming, gazing out of the window into a lowering sky, nothing ahead but dirty London and crowded shops. She wriggled a little with the sheer pleasure of it, ate an apple for late breakfast, watched the world. Thirty-five minutes by train on a good day from Branston into Oxford Circus, more usually exceeding an hour: never travel without a book for distraction or enough thoughts to fill the time. The Central Line rolling stock, running on Central Line rails, operated as a bone-shaker fit to disgrace any subcontinent, requiring restraints between stations, gathering speed with a threat to throw any unbraced passenger from her seat into the arms of the one opposite. Rush hours with strap hangers lurching around like drunkards only became more comfortable when passengers were packed like sardines, each avoiding the eye of the other as they stood in intimate stability, swaying in unison within the purgatory of the train, bottoms and stomachs joined like serried Siamese twins. Emptier carriages made others unwary: neglected parcels on a dozy afternoon would leap from their bonds between Debden and Theydon as the tube rattled and shook with the effort of speed, braked in fury for a deserted stop. Out of office hours the train was depopulated by the further reaches of outer London, as if places like Branston had ceased to exist. Once people moved away as far as this, unless commuting with the herd, they were supposed to remain where they lived. Otherwise, the floor-shaking, arm-bracing Central Line, as stable and sweet as a wagon train, became their punishment.

But in those languid hours, there was the mixture of views that drew Helen into the vortex of beloved London every time she caught the surroundings blurred by the consistently dirty windows of the carriage. Surprising fields around Branston, signs of harvest; then, seen near the rails, looking like an outpost, prefabricated 1950s buildings resembling Nissen huts, postwar construction still standing in lurid pastel colours. Debden melting into the background. Theydon Bois next, known locally as Theydon Boys, somewhat more settled than Debden, but scarcely visible. A tunnel of green approaching Snaresbrook, the presence of trees a sign of prosperity, homes with lawns, mock Tudor, mock Spanish, and older Edwardian houses with outbuilt conservatories, hidden to all but Central Line passengers. She had once sat in a train stopped by signal failure between stations, a frequent hazard of the Central Line, at this very spot, and watched mesmerized as a naked man washed while singing in front of a window, reaching to a shelf out of sight in all his glory, unconscious of the silent audience. Helen had nudged the woman next to her in case she missed it. 'Look at that,' she'd said, unable to resist sharing it, both of them sniggering like children. She thought of it every time she passed the place.

Greater prosperity still as the train chuffed away from Snaresbrook, downhill from the territory of lesser showbiz, and East End crooks seeking new life in security-alarmed houses, into the duller safety of South Woodford's narrower avenues. Earnest small blocks of flats to augment neat tree-lined streets, the territory of hopeful artisans, bank clerks, teachers, and the more modestly prosperous of the age. A tasteless place, safe and dull but green enough to pass. Then a quicker descent to reality: street after street of stocky row houses coming into Leyton, mean back yards bearing signs of loving devotion, covered in washing, a place of crowded roads. On the right, a vast graveyard that looked as if it might have held every corpse found in London over a hundred years. Plunging away from Leyton, another graveyard, this one for cars, bodies of metal in clumps piled up like weeds, rusty and shiny lorries, mangled cars, shells awaiting redemption, looking jaunty perched one on top of the other, cheerful scrap heap, metal stripped of all the aspirations and images once invested in the living machine. Mine belongs here, thought Helen; I might like it better without wheels.

Then Stratford and a quickening of heart among even meaner houses, the train plunging underground as the city began. The rest of the journey a crowded blur, onset of the true metropolis, train rattling slower, stopping to open its doors for engorging crowds at Mile End, taking in the city-bound people laden with bags and haversacks, holdalls and cases, bound on business, for shops, trains, aeroplanes. Liverpool Street, a pause for breath with more of the same in skin of every perspiring colour. Tick, tick, tick, doors closing, opening again as if indecisive, ever unwilling to take travellers from the east, unwilling to go on, sighing and moving with a jolt. Crashing into the gloom of St Paul's to collect a gaggle of brochured tourists speaking in tongues, panting into Holborn via Chancery Lane for lawyers' clerks, Tottenham Court Road for all the world plus wife, and then Oxford Circus, ever late for waiting crowds with shopping bags, four deep on the platform, doubting the train would ever arrive. The uninitiated pushed in and out, forever terrified of being carried on or left behind with doors closing on the skulls of half their families: 'Come on, Jack, we'll miss it. You'll be lost for ever. Get on, get on, quickly, quickly.' Helen stirred with the languor of a native, ambled off the train as the others boarded, unhurried, unfazed by multitudes, refreshed with the blessed familiarity, the sheer anonymity of it all. From the heaving mass of foreign confusion in the foyer, circulating in search of the right exit, she stepped leisurely into the roar of the circus and thus began the business of the day.

There was, of course, no method at all to the business of Helen's shopping; it did not matter how or where she started, stopped, or progressed. The nearest likely shop was the beginning, the last one the end. In the course of a very slow perambulation around dozens of departments she would stop for coffee in three or four different back streets, cappuccino or black as the mood dictated, teeth-defying bread or stale pastry for energy, cigarette for sheer joy, and back into the fray. Food was irrelevant but part of the haphazard pleasure. Over a space of hours she would try on an assortment of garments, most of them unsuitable; would be happily tired of taking off clothes and putting them on, wishing she had worn something better suited to the purpose like a track suit without buttons and more comfortable shoes; would look at herself in mirrors and detest what she saw, the existing skirt, even the clean underwear beneath it, dead and grey against the backdrop of all the newness. She would shake with suppressed laughter in communal changing rooms at the vision of herself looking like a dartboard in a dress of vivid yellow check; would give and receive opinions, joke, help to fasten hooks and eyes. She would rehang neatly on hangers everything she had taken off because she knew what it was like to be a shop assistant and she would try to be pleasant, however rude or pushy they were, making them laugh in the process. She would pull a dozen faces; considered herself obscenely fat on the beam, too muscular in the arms, too skinny in the shank; be hideously depressed by her own silhouette, obscurely and maliciously cheered by the vision of another infinitely worse, if she could find one. She would be shocked at the prices, discuss them with others in whispered tones, swear at buttons, zips, and the endless obscurity of the ladies' loo that seemed necessary at any given time; would drink her coffee like an addict while recognizing on her wrists the perfume sampled at counters under eagle eyes, by now a cacophony of scents. I smell like a tart's parlour, she told herself finally, while all original ideas of what she had wanted to buy drifted by the board. An excellent afternoon.

She had spent one thousand pounds in her mind and acquired no more than a bar of soap, admired fabric for curtains she would never buy, sat on a three-piece suite she could not own, wondered how the world could be as rich as it seemed and who bought these things, and debated the purchase of a microwave. She dreamed of eating a baked potato and promised herself chocolate on the way home. Not now, later. Stuck in the bowels of Selfridges, looking

There then followed a procedure as mandatory as it was point-
less, quite inevitable all the same. It involved Helen progressing
through the racks of coats in the hope of finding similar inspiration
in a cheaper equivalent, furiously calculating as she shrugged them
off on the hows and whys of affording the first, rounding up three
alternatives like sheep in a pen, and looking at them all.

'The first,' said the assistant.

'But the price,' wailed Helen.

'It's the best,' said the assistant. 'I wouldn't lie to you, madam,
honest I wouldn't. It does things for you, madam, And we close in
five minutes, madam. Nearly seven o'clock, it is. Long day.'

'Oh, Christ,' said Helen, 'late night shopping. I'm two hours
behind.'

'And the coat, madam?' She grinned conspiratorially.

'Yes, the coat, I'll have it. I have to have it, you knew all the time
I would.'

Taking home the jewel-coloured coat, skipping into Bond
Street station, she felt guiltily reborn, and bugger the bills. Bailey
would like it, Bailey never resented extravagance; always mean
with himself, he positively encouraged her to spend lavishly and
besides had a rare masculine eye for style. What else was there
to tell him that was fit for the retelling? The desire to relate her
adventures to Bailey was stronger than ever, which was saying a
lot. He enjoyed shopping as long as the experience was second-
hand. Ah, yes, she would describe the woman asking the seller to
wrap her silk shirt as small as possible so she could get it into the
house without her husband noticing. Assistant nodding without
blinking, understanding perfectly, a common request, folding the
silk into a myriad creases and the size of an envelope. At least
Helen did not have a spouse like that, and such reflections, plus

the comforting bulk of the coat, were enough to arm her for the rigours of the Central Line.

This red line out of London was ever erratic, as if sulking from time to time. Nothing unusual to find the thing promising to go to Branston, but fussing to a halt at Mile End and refusing to go farther: This is your Central Line information service. All change, please. This train terminates here. The few passengers were resigned. Seven-twenty in the evening, downtown London suffering a lull while the population arrived home from work, not ready yet to re-embark disguised in different attitudes, towards the night's entertainments. The platform at Mile End was a secretive, vulnerable place, double-edged, unguarded underground pavement for two sets of trains travelling east as well as west, a long and gloomy island punctuated by large flat pillars and copious freestanding signs giving directions. People leaned on the signs or lurked behind them seeking anonymity, making the station appear empty as Helen walked from one end to the other in search of a seat and the same anonymity. She sat down on a bench hidden by a pillar, clutching the coat bag and the overstuffed handbag, from which she extracted the book, reconciled to the world because of the coat, ready to endure the next forty minutes with the help of the printed page, when she heard whispering as diffuse as underwater humming.

'Oh, I'll be late, I'll be so late. They'll be cross. I told you I didn't like the tube: it never works.'

'Oh, shut up, William, shut up. I'll be late, too. It doesn't matter. Nobody's going to hit us, are they? Be sensible, will you? No one will know if we're late. We're often late. You watch out for the train, will you? You might make it come faster.'

Helen slid to the edge of her seat, craned her neck so as to look behind the pillar, caught a glimpse of William Featherstone at the extreme edge of the platform and only a few feet away, standing with hands in pockets, gazing down the tunnel as if willing a train to emerge. He was completely absorbed, tense with anxiety, looking first at the tunnel, then at the tracks.

'Oh, look, Evie, look: mice, real mice.' A whisper of excitement.

From behind the wall, where Evelyn squatted against the support, Helen heard a muttered expression of boredom. Her first response was amusement: two children at play, well, well, well. So they *had* known one another with the familiarity she had imagined; how coincidental to confirm their secret so far from home. The next reflection contained the thought that theirs was private mischief in which she should not intrude. The tube was as good a place for hiding as any; let them be. Helen might have moved away if their next moves had been as innocuous.

William knelt at the extreme edge of the platform, riveted by the mice who lived below the rails: a phenomenon that had often riveted her own eyes. While he watched, making odd little cooing noises to the mice, his voice echoing slightly in the tunnel entrance, Evelyn stood upright on her plimsolled feet, ran towards him, stopped short of him, turned and paced back to her spot. She did this twice, as if counting the yards between them, the second time retreating farther so that her distance from him was slightly greater. Then ran a third time, as silent and light as a bird, the extra yard allowing extra speed, retreated again, as if satisfied.

William was quite oblivious, still whispering to the mice. 'Come here, fella. It's not nice down there. I'll take you home. What happens when a train comes? Please climb up here, please.'

Evelyn was coiled like a spring in a sort of squatting race start, equally unaware of observation; both were utterly concentrated.

Helen watched, mesmerized, felt on her face the slight breeze that heralded the approach of an engine yet unseen and heard, knew it to be ominous, tightened her grip on her package, watched. She is going to push him; that is what she is going to do, push him over the edge just before the train bursts out of the tunnel. I know that is exactly what she is intending to do. She chose this deserted end of the platform, this distant platform, measured the distance. She planned it all. I know.

From the tunnel came the rumble of movement, the distant shriek and hiss of brakes, then growing sound. A slight vibration pushed the air forward, blowing strongly in Helen's face as she rose. William heard it, began to stand upright; Evelyn caught his intention in a glance, and was ready to run. Helen ran too, behind William, blocking the path between them, braced herself for the impact, felt Evelyn's tough little body slam into her from behind. She stumbled against William as the train crashed into the light, dropped the coat bag. The coat half spilled in a flash of blue. William shouted in anger. In an action quite as automatic as her running forward, Helen bent to stuff the coat back into the bag as the train strained to a halt, seeing at the same time from the corner of her eye one pair of jean-clad ankles hurrying away beyond the pillar. She rose, as the carriage doors slid open, to face the puzzled regard of the boy.

'What you doing? What you think you doing?' Furious, confused, looking around in sudden panic. 'And where's ... where's ... ?' The train tick-ticking, breathing impatience. People appeared from nowhere, stepping aboard, others, fewer, alighting. 'Where's ... Where's ... ?'

'She's gone, William. Get on the train, quickly. You're late.' Her voice emerged with brisk authority.

William's look of animal confusion vanished, replaced by a vacant gaze, the clearing features of a boy who has remembered well-rehearsed lines after a moment of panic. 'Who's gone?' he said loudly, jumping on to the train with unnecessary energy. 'Who do you mean? Must be mad …'

But as Helen followed, sat next to him, she watched him stretch and peer through the closing doors, scanning the platform as the train moved past, desperately seeking clues, a sight, a glimmer of the paste earrings or the plimsolled feet. Helen's limbs were trembling; so, she noticed, were his. They sat in silence, drowned by the noise of the train until it thundered through the tunnel into empty, floodlit Stratford. Outside Stratford, alongside the grave-yard for cars, motion ceased entirely. The lights in the carriage flickered.

September summer: humid, storm-filled, feeling like winter darkness, an inky daylight black, scarcely relieved in the heavy-breathing train. Even less light in this last of all compartments and no people, either; William and Helen sitting as silent com-panions, frozen with unease.

He turned and looked at her with cunning curiosity. 'No one's gone,' he said with conviction. And then, 'I know you. You come in the bar. I know you. And you talk in court. You're one of them.' He nodded vigorously; she nodded in turn. Sitting on a train, the two of them, lately prosecutor and defendant. Helen was glad that the resentment of the defendant was less often directed at the prosecutor than towards the policeman who felt the collar, and William was clearly feeling no resentment at all. Feeling nothing, apparently, apart from anxiousness to convince her in words of one syllable that he had been accompanied by no one. No one had gone: he had asked his questions of air.

'There are mice on the tracks, did you know?' he asked, beaming goodwill.

'Yes, there are,' said Helen. 'William, how long have you known Evelyn? I know her, too.'

'Evelyn? Evie … Don't know Evelyn. What you mean? No one's gone.'

'Evie, Evelyn. Evelyn Blundell, the girl with the earrings. Your friend.'

'My friend … Yes, my friend. No, she isn't. Which Evie? Don't know her at all. Stop it, that's silly. Stop it.' He muttered in agitation, squirmed, and looked towards the door for escape. The train was obdurately still, locked in a semi-silent signal-failure zone between one civilization and the next, a kind of no-man's-land, while someone was probably calling someone else out of a pub. She patted William's arm to soothe the quivering; she was not a parent after all, not here to cross-examine. To her surprise, he seized her hand, held it, examined it. 'Nice,' he said, 'very nice.' She felt the first queasy tremor of fear as he parted her fingers and scrutinized them, then saw he confined his attention to a sapphire ring, Helen's only piece of sparkle, Bailey's only gesture of ownership. 'Nice,' said William, twisting to look at her with the familiar vacuous grin, still holding the hand, stroking it now, sighing slightly. She smiled back; that action of face seemed prudent while she wished the train would move, which it did, slowly, clack, clack, a peaceful crawl, resigned to reluctant effort. William swayed with the carriage, abandoning himself to movement, suddenly relaxed by the motion, reminded of the buses and the soothing sound of his mother's washing machine humming beneath his room. The train exhaled and stopped.

'I like girls,' he said, apropos of nothing, and placed a hand on her thigh, hot through her skirt. Helen withdrew slightly, rummaged in her bag, discovered chocolate, and offered him some. 'Oh, goody,' he said. At least he was capable of distraction – not completely. William was feeling affectionate, inquisitive with it. He pressed his shoulder against hers, warm through her blouse, hotter to touch than his somewhat grimy hands. He had removed himself from Evie and everything else, attached himself to present company. He liked her.

'Do people ...' he asked, face contorted with the intellectual effort of formulating a question. 'Do all people ... people as old as you still do it?'

'Do what, William?' She was slightly fazed by the question, parrying for time without doubting the meaning of his enquiry.

'Do sex, I mean. I know some people older than you do it. I thought they got tired of it. They don't ever have pictures of them doing it. It must be horrible when you're so old.'

'Some people,' Helen replied drily, amused by the question despite herself and despite the hot hand on her thigh, which she gently removed, 'even older than me do it all the time. But only if they want to. Which means it can't be horrible or they wouldn't do it, would they?' The train, having started, slowed again. She felt an overpowering sense of the ridiculous.

'Even when they're more than forty?'

Which is, after all, very old indeed, Helen reflected with even more amusement. I'll soon be over the hill if forty's the limit. And Bailey's already only a few years on the other side. Bailey would enjoy this conversation, seems to enjoy that which William is discussing, come to that. Hope he doesn't think it's horrible. Shows no sign of it, or waning powers either. Must tell him this boy would imagine he is simply doing his duty.

'Oh, yes, even when they're over forty. Or fifty or sixty.'

'Ugh,' said William.

'Why do you ask?' she enquired in calm conversational tones, offering more chocolate.

'To see if I'm right.'

'About what?'

'Oh, everything.' He waved a limp hand, fell into silence. Perhaps they could talk about something different, but William's mind, master of the non sequitur, remained on its own peculiar tangent.

'Mrs Blundell liked it,' he remarked, picking up Helen's even tone. 'She liked it a lot, but we thought she was silly.'

Helen's reactions were suddenly sharper, her body stiller, her voice on the same even keel. 'Oh, did she now? Well, I told you, a lot of people do like it. I suppose you saw Mrs Blundell in the woods?' A good enough guess, judging from the nodding.

William was forgetting his lines. 'Yes. Both of us saw her. With Evie's teacher on a rug he brought. Very, very silly.' He giggled. 'She looked horrible. All bare. Evie was very cross. I told her my mummy would never do that, never.' She was silent, waiting for him to continue.

'I 'spect Evie was cross because they were our woods,' he added. 'She said if her mummy and that teacher went to the woods, they might come up and find the summer-house. Sometimes they passed it. I watched them. They were all silly, like people get after drinking in our place. They came through our garden and out over the field. Evie was furious. "What's she coming here for?" she said. "If she finds us, she'll kill us. You first, me after. No, Dad'll kill me, slowly." Never seen her as cross as that, but she does get very cross. Sometimes. "She'll kill us," she said …' There his voice faltered in a dim realization of too much spoken.

'Well,' said Helen, keeping her own voice as untroubled as her throat allowed, 'she didn't find you, so that's all right, isn't it?'

'Yes. I suppose so,' said William slightly mollified, still driven to speak. 'But we found her, though.'

'You? When?' Too late to prevent the give-away sharpness of tone. 'When was that, William?' But he was retreating fast, shrinking, remembering stricture and warnings, horrified by his forgetfulness of learned-by-heart promises.

'On the ground. You know, dead. Evie fetched me. No, she didn't; I was there. I'm not supposed to say that. Oh, stop it, stop it, stop it.'

He was squirming in agony, his movements accelerating with the sudden speed of the train, possessed by a pain beyond enduring, electrocuted by the gravity of his own words. Then he turned on her in a fury, punched her shoulder with clumsy violence. Placed both heavy paws on her breasts, pressing and kneading with a force that made her wince in pain. Paralysed by some dim memory of physical attack she suppressed the desire to scream and struggle, forced herself into an unnatural stillness. Even when he changed his tactics and grabbed both her arms, making odd, biting motions in the direction of her throat, his fingers clawing into her flesh, bruising delicate flesh with savage strength. A fan-tail of raw prints rose under her skin, and she felt a lacerating pain.

'It's all right, William. Calm down, now. It's all right, don't worry. It doesn't matter what you've said. I wasn't listening at all. It's all right.'

The words worked like a slow but magic formula as the train drew into Debden. He withdrew his hands; she resisted the almost overpowering temptation to rub where he had touched. William looked at the sliding doors opening to the dark world outside as if contemplating flight, then decided against it. She contemplated it, too, felt his hand stray to her arm, stayed as she was.

'Hold my hand, William. It's all right.'

'OK, then.'

They pulled away towards Theydon, the prospect of home becoming reality, swaying together in the new enthusiasm of the machinery, pitched and tossed and lurched into the next station. She was beginning to see what the motion did for him, felt faint and sore with the effort of keeping still, decided recklessly to risk one more question.

'Where's the summerhouse den, William?'

He gazed at her blankly. 'In the summerhouse, of course. Daddy was going to make it into a bar. Only the summerhouse,' he repeated, as if it was obvious. The noise of engine and track was a duet of such force that they had to raise their voices. He looked at her with sly affection, pushing his face towards her. 'You're nice,' he said. 'Nicer than Evelyn's mum.' The same hand had moved back to her thigh, squeezing above the knee, fingers spreading in exploration. She removed it again. Ten minutes at most before Branston: she wanted to make him forget all he had said as well as the movement of the train, cast about her thoughts in desperate search for words. Finally, out of the blue, a question emerged.

'What did you buy today, William?'

He sat upright. 'Nothing, I didn't buy anything for me. Not allowed today. You did, though,' he added, pointing at the fallen-to-floor coat bag.

'Yes, I did. I bought a coat.'

'Oh, I love shops, I really do. Will you show me? Please?'

In the bucking carriage, he released her and she released the coat from tissue paper, showed it to an admiring audience of one. William stroked the cloth, grinned at it, tickled the collar like a cat's ears, murmured compliments while she gabbled a little description, words only words, of how she had come to buy it. He folded the coat back into the bag, insisting, 'No, this way: you're doing it wrong. Got to be careful, see? Nice thing, very nice.' Just in time for the single light of Branston and a mutual falling off the train, he carrying the coat, which he immediately handed back, albeit with reluctance. Beyond the unmanned station, William examined his unused ticket, puzzled. Life on the buses was different. 'Here,' he said, 'you can have this,' proffering it to her – his version, she understood, of a gift.

'Why thank you, William. See you soon.' Then in a rush of sudden pity for his look of misery, as well as a desire to walk home unaccompanied, she added, 'You can tell them you came back with me, if you like. Say I asked you, if they go on about your being late.'

William's straight face widened into the vacant grin; they smiled in conspiracy. 'Goody,' he said, smiling and waving, embarrassed at parting. 'Bye, then.'

'Bye.'

She staggered uphill with deliberation. Her thigh tingled from his touch; on her upper arms the purple marks were forming that would show tomorrow over the bones of another possible statistic. 'Woman raped and attacked between Debden and Theydon.' The stuff of the local paper, the thought of it inducing a mild and comic hysteria. Not a woman with a coat, though. Ridiculous thinking: coats were meant to lend warmth, not protection; perhaps the mere existence of this one had lent her confidence. She was surprised to find herself giggling. One way to downplay this whole episode to Bailey: Darling, I bought this very expensive coat and avoided being attacked on the train because I didn't want to damage it. Or, having this new, very expensive coat enabled me to cope. Take your choice. Or, darling, I want to talk to you about William Featherstone and someone who seemed for a moment to want to kill him. He and Evelyn Blundell – they're conspirators. They found her mother, and William is violent enough to have killed her. He's been schooled into silence, but he's like a dummy without a ventriloquist until the action slips. What are you going to do about it? And while we're at it, what are you going to do about us, Bailey, you rat? Can we leave this improving place, please, where people do these things to their children? I'm sorry to disappoint you, but my spiritual home is Oxford Street and North London with all the Cypriots, and drunken Irish, the blaggers and the dirt. I'm frightened here as I never was there, more frightened now than I was on the train, which is extremely frightened, as it happens. I'm also ashamed. I have fingerprints all over me; please let me in. Her own fingers had lost their sixth sense for finding the keys. To avoid William, she had walked from the station, forgetting the simple fact of her car in the carpark. She was cold, it was dark, she was wet from the drizzle she had failed to notice on the train, and she was still preparing a smile. She dared not look at the time, expected it was well after nine. Dear God, the civility of London was a long way off. Life here was far too complicated.

Bailey wrenched open the door of 15 Invaders Court, feeling and looking savage, his face blank with fury. The smile fell:

Bailey's rage, whatever the degree or cause of that rare anger, was difficult to handle.

'Hello,' she said stupidly, and pushed damp hair out of one eye. He saw the scar on her forehead, implicit with dreadful memory. She remembered, quite irrelevantly, that the coat on her arm might be soaked.

'For Christ's sake, Helen,' he shouted, dragging her in through the door, 'I could shake you ... Where have you been?' And he was shaking her, gripping both arms in his own strong hands, as strong as William's, fingers extended in a grasp more exasperated than affectionate. He was angry and anxious and distant: she was in disgrace. Perhaps his concern for her was uppermost in his mind, but it made no difference on the sensitive spots. She hated him for this exhibition; it simply hurt, body and soul, it hurt. Helen yelped briefly in her own anger and profound disappointment, and in the flurry of the pain she shook her arms free. And briefly, sharply, and painlessly drew back one hand and slapped him.

Chapter Ten

THE DAY OF Helen's ordeal had begun well for her but not for Bailey.

'Get you, Amanda Scott! Who's the new lover boy, then? Look at that, flowers all over. Champagne next, is it? Boss gave them to you, did he?'

'Leave it out, Jack,' said with ostensible boredom and secret pleasure. 'Can you see Bailey giving anyone flowers?'

Police Constable Bowles paused to consider. Difficult, that, hanging on the door of the detectives' room, empty save for her. PC Bowles was one of Amanda's fans; most occupants of the room were not, preferring to work elsewhere when she was in. Prissy, clever, tidy little bitch. Iron knockers.

'Superintendent Bailey giving flowers? Yes, I can see him doing that, as a matter of fact. But not those flowers and not to you.'

'Push off, Jack. I'm busy.'

He blew a daring kiss in the air, ambled down the corridor whistling, leaving Amanda in contemplation of the bouquet, which he had delivered from the front desk, telling everyone its destination *en route*. Which was nice, to put it on record; so nice she was not about to diminish the pleasure by taking off the polythene and allowing anyone to imagine she had bought the flowers herself. Keep this up, J. Blundell, and we'll get along fine, really we shall. You're doing very well, what with phone call yesterday to celebrate the colour of my eyes and dinner tomorrow night. Don't know if I should. Bailey won't like it, but he'll have to lump it. If he knows, that is, which he won't if I don't tell him. Never mind, never mind, I know how to fix him.

Grabbing handbag, smoothing hair, making for his office with verbal report of yesterday's sojourns with Featherstones et al. already tidy in her mind. Not entirely fictionalized, simply glossed by judicious omission. She always presented the best profile to her information.

Good morning, sir; good morning, Amanda, how did you get on? Could ask the same thing, sir, but I don't, of course, even leaving aside the rude connotations of the phrase. Your days can be secret, mine bloody aren't. Instead of saying that, offering a rueful smile.

'Not much success, sir, in any direction. Apart from the committal, of course; you know about that. But I found out a bit on William Featherstone, our arsonist, sir.'

So did I, Bailey thought. Rather too much, really; can't afford to feel for a fire raiser. I know all about where he goes and what he chooses to buy and steal. He watched with surprise as Amanda produced a clumsy bracelet from a tidy handbag.

'In his spare time he hides in a shed in the garden, and he makes these things in the kitchen,' she said gravely, as if revealing the crown jewels.

The bracelet lay on his desk like a gaudy and lumpish pebble: Bailey wanted to laugh. 'Do they know you have this?' he asked quietly.

She flushed, furious to be caught at a disadvantage so soon. She should have begun at the beginning and gone on to the end of her afternoon, giving her report the authority of chronology. 'Well, no they don't. I sort of picked it up.'

'I think I'll return it at some stage,' said Bailey evenly. 'Someone's treasure, isn't it? Well, well, clever William,' putting the thing in his pocket, continuing. 'No jewellery in the Blundell house, by any chance? Was he helpful?'

'Yes,' she replied with sincerity this time, 'yes, he was. Very. We went through the place with a fine-tooth comb,' repeated like a parrot and, to forestall any further questions on that line, entered a rider that did not follow the question at all. 'Sir, there's something I must tell you.'

'Sit down, Amanda, please.'

So she told him with relish, keeping the spite out of her voice and her whole stance as she had learned to do as a child, wrapping it into a parcel of concern. 'I was puzzled, sir, very puzzled at the committal proceedings ... I don't think you can have known about it ...'

'Go on.'

'Well, sir, your wife, sir – sorry, girlfriend, Miss West, I mean, of the Crown Prosecution Service,' to prove she understood exactly Helen's dual importance. 'She brought Evelyn Blundell into the committal proceedings. They sat at the back and listened to the pathologist.'

'They what ... Helen?' A remarkably satisfying jump.

'Yes, sir. I'm afraid so. Not from the beginning. I was just checking the public gallery halfway through when I saw them. Your ...

Miss West saw me; she grabbed Evelyn and they left together. I thought I'd better tell you.'

'Thank you,' he said drily. 'No doubt there was some purpose in it. She works for Mr Redwood; I'm sure he approved.'

'He didn't know, sir. Not until I told him.'

You would, wouldn't you? Well done, Amanda, and what are you hiding with this taking-the-wind-out-of-my-sails kind of exercise? Shrugging it away, pretending to do so. 'You're sure there's no jewellery in Blundell's house?'

'Only what she left, sir.'

The revelations about Helen had the ring of truth, were in any event verifiable and therefore not the subject for lies, while the helpfulness of surly and difficult John Blundell had the tincture of dishonesty, but for the moment, Bailey was too dispirited to persist.

'And were the Featherstones co-operative?'

'No, sir, not very.'

Good, serves you right, but I'll remember the bit about the garden shed. If our William starts fires, he also stores paraffin. That will do, Amanda, you have played your upper hand with great effect; you deserve an Oscar.

Helen, why did you do it? How dare you interfere with such crass, such unbelievable insensitivity? He could not believe it, had to believe it: Amanda would never lie with such vulnerability. He had been aware for a little while now that she was in the habit of lying, but never where she could be caught. He wondered how much her impressive record owed to lying and to her delight-ful habit of always ducking the sort of awkward situation where careers were blighted. The question of Helen dogged him more hour by hour, often minute by minute; an explosion of incredulity, not yet anger; an indignation of disappointment, still capable of being placated by reasonable explanation, but hardening into firm belief of the worst without scope for forgiveness each time he rang either her office or home to find her defiantly absent. Who did she think she was? Frustrated detective, trying to fiddle with the jigsaw pieces to find a reaction? Mad scientist playing with poison on a younger life? He had gone home early to expiate the anger, bring forward the explanation, forced the same anger to new heights in the long hours of waiting. The anger was overlain with appalling anxiety as he listened to the rain, pacing the modern room he privately hated, smoking cigarettes he felt inclined to grind into the carpet, too sick to eat or drink, apart from two furious whiskies consumed without effect. By now anxiety had the winning streak, a tyrannical fear, premonition of Helen's loved body broken by bus or train, victim of something or someone; some tentacle of this case reaching her in punishment for her wilful involvement. He could recall as vividly as the shape of his own hand feeling the same anxiety the last time she had been hurt and he had seen her as battered and bruised as he now imagined her, obscenely injured.

Half past eight o'clock: no phone call. No word from this woman of his who was punctilious in such courtesies. And then she knocked at the door. He pulled it open, expecting some bearer of bad news, finding her instead smiling, carrying a bag. Been shopping. Like a father finding a lost child, his first reaction was the sheer fury of relief. He wanted to shake or hit or shout at her, to establish the reality and let her know she had cost him about ten years of his life. Of course she had neither wanted nor needed that. And even when he had yelled at her, shortly after the slap, he shouted, 'What were you doing bringing a child into court to listen to her mother's

death being rehashed? How could you do it?' He witnessed her disbelief that he could ever imagine she had done such a thing, heard
the reply that she had removed the girl, certainly, yes, but never
conducted her there. He knew it was true, it still did not shift the
anger. Anger remained with him like a leaden weight throughout
the rest of her words. The slap and the guilt rendered him impotent
to change his feelings; even when he saw how white and drawn she
was, and he pretended to listen, the anger, like indigestible food,
refused to shift.

'Listen to me, Geoffrey: I'm too tired to talk long. I'm sorry I
slapped you, sorrier that you should think so badly of me, but listen: I took Evelyn out of court; she had sneaked in without anyone seeing. We had a chat afterwards. I saw William Featherstone
recognize her; then I saw them together today. They're buddies,
probably something more. He adores her, but I got the distinct
impression that she was trying to push him under a train.' Bailey
did not interrupt this recitation to ask for details, and in the light
of the living room it did indeed seem incredible enough to defy
elaboration. 'Anyway, she ran off, and he pretended she'd never
been there, some prearranged story in which he was well drilled,
but then he let it out. He seemed to like me.' She laughed shakily.
'He also told me that both of them saw Mrs Blundell dead after
having seen her perform live. He was very distressed in the telling,
acted up a bit. He's not with it, Geoffrey, this William, and he's got
the hormones of a raging bull, brains seated in his underpants, and
a weird gentleness with it. Don't you think it's probable he could
have done something to Mrs B? He'd do anything to protect Evie, I
don't know from what, or keep her. Perhaps he's bedding her.'

It sounded to his ears like so much nonsense. 'She's only fourteen, Helen, for God's sake.'

'So what? They begin at twelve elsewhere; you know that as well as I. But not in Branston, where they're civilized by nice houses, is that it? Suppose he thought Mrs Blundell was on to him, they watched her, maybe she watched them. Suppose—'

'For Christ's sake, stop supposing, Helen. Will you let that bloody imagination of yours rest? Go to bed. You've been sitting in a clapped-out train listening to the ramblings of a crazy boy, and you've constructed a whole scenario out of air. Who knows what he's read in the papers or imagined for himself?' Then in a gentler tone, 'You're whacked, Helen. Go to bed; I'll bring you a drink.'

She looked at him, defeated. 'All right,' she said. 'I'll stop thinking too. Like any policeman.'

And then, in the bathroom, Bailey saw Helen washing, half crying, grey and tired, fingerprint bruises on her upper arm, similar to the marks he had seen on countless prisoners arrested in struggles: the autograph of heavy, sometimes careless, needlessly painful hands. Bailey was appalled. 'What's this, Helen? What the hell is this?'

'Nothing,' said Helen. 'Absolutely nothing. I told you William Featherstone was violent. You weren't listening.'

'Oh Christ,' he said taking her limp figure into his arms. 'Oh, Christ almighty, Helen, I'm sorry, darling, I'm so dreadfully sorry. Tell me—'

'That's quite all right, Superintendent.' She spoke brightly, her voice brittle with pride, eyes sparkling with quiescent tears. 'Perfectly all right. No problem at all. I'm going to sleep now. You can do what you like.'

CHRISTINE SUMMERFIELD GOT up to tend her garden, intending it as therapy organized for a day off, but found it already tended, the same therapy last empty weekend having rendered it cleaner than a new pin. She got in her car and drove doggedly to Antony Sumner's deserted cottage, to which she held the only key at his request and despite the wailings of his parents, relatives, and colleagues, who suggested selling it, burning it, or ignoring it as if he were already dead. Christine Summerfield had cleaned it; that was therapy, too. The place had never been so clean or she herself so bare of hope. She was sickened by her inadvertent discoveries, made while she was in search of the inevitable bills, which were not suspended during his imprisonment, and she was dismayed by her own resilience. She moved towards the cottage like an automaton, trying to think of him and resurrect her early belief that this was all a mistake and one day he would live there again, even live there with her; it was larger than her place. But that early optimism had faded despite her persistent nurturing of it, turned brown and desiccated like the leaves in the garden, helpless in the temperature of her own cold realism. She had little faith in a system of justice that spewed so many of her clients into her lap, but was fair enough to realize the same system, clumsy but relatively incorrupt, got it right at least half of the time and was as necessary as breath. She knew very well how casualties were created by life itself, not by authorities, and was also aware that Antony, her lover, had been treated as fairly as most. It was nothing as simple as the system that begat her own tremor of doubt; it was Antony.

While tidying his study in search of the gas bill – this indescribable mess of a man was so hooked on the printed page that he could never dispose of a single sheet of paper – she had found the beginnings of a novella, snapshots of his childhood, which made her weep, pictures of previous girlfriends, which made her peculiarly, possessively irritated, and a little bundle of fairly recent love letters from an unknown pupil, sadly signed in childish, educated script with the anonymous words, 'Yours Ever,' which made her furious. She knew they were recent because of references to local events, such as 'I saw you at the carnival last week, by the rose float; you looked very handsome'. She knew, too, he would never have responded to this moony devotion, but he should have established through the handwriting who had written them, returned the first letter with an admonition and surely not accepted more. Encouraging students to make a habit of writing was one thing; keeping the results was another. Whether he hoarded from carelessness mattered not. Whatever would he do for flattery, such a precious gift to him, poor man, the same weakness leading him to dead Mrs Blundell and all of this betrayal? Before the discovery of the letters, Christine had always respected Antony's integrity despite his mistakes, liked his enthusiasms despite his excesses, cherished his affections with all their past lack of discrimination, but on sight of those letters, the whole image of him began to slip, the respect fading by a dangerous degree, tinged by treacherous memories of his passion with its underlying violence. Were all men thus, madness lurking in their veins, following their organs to disaster because of a kind word, blindly obedient to subliminal commands? She suspected they were, was very tired of the breed, angry with him for what he was.

An element of disgust began before the committal proceedings. Evidence had unfolded while more doubts formed like a mushroom cloud. Christine sat beneath it humbled to camp follower and only supporter, fighting back reluctant belief in what she heard, while there gathered behind her eyes a huge resentment. Not for what he had done to Mrs Blundell – she could not in all honesty bring herself to care about that, although she wished she could – but for what he had done to her. For better or worse, from poorer to poorer, she knew, whatever the outcome, she could not forgive him. She had seen him in a new light while trying to shade it, viewed what she should never have seen, found him lacking, and wondered how she could ever again love him, and she was full of remorse for having come to doubt him. Even when she had never loved anyone half as much before, her mind had already moved to planning life without him, just as she was constantly advising her clients: Think of yourself, dear, you must, you know, no one else will. The last rat leaves the sinking ship; I don't know how love goes, but when it's gone, it's gone. Not without a self-hatred so acute it left her breathless.

So this was duty, obdurate, labour-intensive duty to prove to herself she still cared; she owed him that much, at least. Thou shalt not be guilty, dearest Antony, before trial, but after that, my pet, I shall have to leave you. I cannot sacrifice my life to you, only part of it. Tears hot on a flushed face, attacking this messy garden of his. Oh, why did he never do anything about it and why did he shatter my peace of mind? Look at this mess. He never looked after it, lived here three years and never raised spade or trowel. How could he? What a waste.

The previous owners had made an effort, left him with a format. It was a tiny garden: small patio from the kitchen, twenty feet of lawn bisected by path, shrubs standing like soldiers against each fence, a miniature shed, and a patented compost thing looking like a large and ungainly dustbin. She raked the overgrown lawn and the scrubby beds free of leaves. She had carried her rake here for the purpose. Why had he never bought one of his own? Sweeping up leaves awkwardly, putting them in the compost bin with disgust. That was where he had put the dead woman's clothes and handbag – sorry, someone else had put her clothes and handbag there. That was what Christine was supposed to believe and couldn't any longer. Strangely, that piece of evidence had failed to register with her at all until she had heard it read out loud, hadn't thought of it until it slapped her in the face. Now she did, and she was suddenly arrested by its incongruity with everything she knew of him. That he would strike the woman, yes. Take her money and jewellery, no. Put the remnants here, no: he simply wasn't materialistic enough.

The gate at the side of the cottage clicked. Full of sinister thoughts, she turned in alarm, faced Bailey, dear Superintendent Bailey, the bastard, standing in his workday suit, beginning to speak. She stood up like a lioness in a cage, snapped in a voice that was all teeth, 'What do you want?'

'Nothing specific. Passing, and saw your car.'

She was angry, turned back abruptly, and began attacking the leaves, which floated from control, presenting her behind conspicuously, determined to ignore him. He simply fell in, grasping piles of damp leaves with skill and efficiency, shoving them into the compost bin, pressing them down, going back for more, quietly ignoring the effect on his suit and hands. They worked in silence for fifteen minutes, clearing the leaves with speed, she found herself oddly mollified, disliking his presence less and less. She even felt the beginnings of a faint amusement, glad of the company. 'All right,' she said finally, flinging down the rake. 'You win. Now, what was it you really wanted?'

She sat on the single dirty patio chair. He sat on the wall next to it.

'I was wondering,' he said mildly, as if the conversation was the most natural in the world and this was the middle of it. 'Looking at this garden, I was wondering how Antony ever knew where the compost bin was. Or that he had one at all. Surprising. Not a keen gardener, I take it.'

'No,' she agreed curtly, suddenly reminded of the incongruity that had struck her before he arrived. 'He usually forgot he had a garden. Didn't really recognize its existence.'

'I see.'

He did see, she thought; he saw what others had failed to see. He was all nerves and nerve, a complicated man, looking for something. In one fleeting instance she could imagine what Helen had found in him.

'Did you like him?' she asked gruffly. 'Antony, I mean.'

'I didn't – don't know him well enough to say. I do try to distance myself from suspects, murder suspects particularly, because I hate, loathe, and detest violence. I find it difficult to take the rest seriously, but violence sickens me.'

'That means you don't like him.'

'It means I don't dislike him too much. I can't afford to.' His eyes strayed to the compost bin. 'But I don't see him as a thief. I wonder if I could look at his desk, even though we've looked at it before. I don't want to remove anything. Simply look.'

'For the investigation or for your conscience?'

He laughed. 'Helen's my conscience.'

'You've got a bloody cheek asking, but yes, you can. I doubt he would have allowed it, but I shall.'

Sun shone directly on her face, exposing the lines of worry and grief, making her look older and harsher than her years. The suggestion in his words of the case being incomplete did not bring a glimmer of hope as it might have done even days since; it created no bloom of excitement in her very pale cheeks.

'How's Helen?' Faintly polite and dim memory of manners, but a blank face.

His brow furrowed into lines. 'While quite understanding why you avoid her, she misses you greatly. She finds it very difficult to live with a policeman, I think.'

'Oh.'

It provided a strange relief, hearing about the difficulties of other couples; it was oddly comforting. Christine wished Helen no ill, could not contemplate that, but all the same she would not have rejoiced in her happiness. This phase of her life would pass, she hoped, but at the moment the transparent contentment of others made her feel faintly sick.

'May I look, then? Do you want to come with me?'

'No, I'll trust you. Can't quite understand what you're doing, though.'

'Listen,' he said, standing above her like a slender and gentle giant. 'I may not like Antony, but I don't want him convicted of something he may not have done. Helen's always thought I didn't look far enough, doesn't realize that I never stop looking in my own way. If I find anything helpful to his defence, I'll tell them. I always do.'

'Oh save your energy. He did it all right.'

'Do you really think so?'

'Yes, I do. Look, what's the point? Don't pussyfoot around here piling on the agony. Oh, shit. What I really mean is that whether he did it or not, whatever the verdict whenever it happens, it'll all come too late for me. I can't even apologize for sounding so selfish, but that's what I think. I can't even think of him. It's too late for us.'

'Perhaps not,' said Bailey, well used to the aftermath, the grateful media-blessed reunions of the acquitted and their families with whom they would never again live in peace. He was using tones of brisk optimism, a voice she recognized: nurse addressing the patient. 'Supposing he was acquitted. He'd get back his job, hasn't lost it yet; he'd come home. Life would go on as before.'

'No,' said Christine. 'Don't give me that shit. No, life wouldn't go on and couldn't. You know that very well. And you don't have to answer.' She spoke quietly, turning her face away from the sun as if ashamed of its resignation. 'Now bugger off and look at his desk. I've put the correspondence in piles. There are some letters from a schoolgirl that are particularly entertaining. They were of no interest to the others who looked. See yourself out.'

Bailey knew better than to repeat his platitudes, knew when and where he simply could not help, departed indoors for his unofficial exploration, his patient retracing of all the tracks he had delegated to Amanda Scott. Leaving Christine trying to erase from her eyes the relief of tears, looking at the garden denuded of all the early autumn leaves, feeling older than winter and already bereaved. She was right; she knew she was right. What was it she had said to him? 'Whatever the verdict.' The great big irrelevant verdict. Mrs Blundell had won after all.

HELEN HAD YANKED herself into daylight, redeemed into humanity by Bailey's kind but speechless provision of coffee, the rest of her stiff and immune from touching. Get in car, go to office, court this p.m., home early given a single chance to duck, more sleep if possible. Anger and pain were dissoluble in sleep, especially an insufficient, dream-filled sleep like hers. Her normal good nature reasserted itself and gave her enough cheerful self-control to reach her desk without hitting anyone *en route*. 'See Mr Redwood' – a note falling on to the blotter, which was covered with telephone numbers and shopping lists, slipping out of an in-tray the size of a house end. If yesterday had been the proper cue for an easy day today, someone somewhere had forgotten the lines.

Red Squirrel was suspiciously bright and know-all. 'Ah, Helen. Tried to get you yesterday, but you were off.'

'You're dead right I was, in all senses. But I did buy a coat,' she added irrelevantly. The coat continued to comfort. He looked puzzled.

'Little matter, Helen, of the Sumner proceedings. Why were you there? You were supposed to be in the office.'

'Ah, yes. Well, I wasn't; I was at the proceedings. I did the office work first, of course. Why was I there? Curiosity. It's also good for me to see an expert like you at work.' He would miss the irony and take the compliment; she knew he would. 'I asked Harmoner if he would object if I watched; he didn't, so I did.'

The pace of this left him slightly disconcerted. He cleared his narrow throat.

'Detective Sergeant Scott says she thinks she saw you with Evelyn Blundell at the back. She thought you arrived and left together.' Questions and accusations hung in the air. 'I rather had the impression she must have been mistaken about the arrival. Others saw the departure.'

'Evelyn came in after me. I hauled her out. I knew her by sight and thought she had no business there. That's all.' Helen was sick of this explanation and could have done serious bodily harm to Amanda Scott. She was relieved and grateful to see Redwood nod his acceptance of her explanation.

'I rather assumed something of the kind. You're rather too headstrong, Helen, but not lacking in wisdom.'

'You believe me, then?'

He looked surprised. 'Of course I do.' The fairness was reluctant, accompanied by another clearing of the throat. 'Whatever else I think of you, I've never known you to be other than professional. You might be rash sometimes, but you do have judgement. Of course I believe you.'

Which is more, Helen thought sadly, than dearest Bailey bothered to do. He didn't give me the benefit of the doubt, didn't make a single check before doubting my judgement, did he? But then, how could he? Whatever the verdict, patience and understanding had played no part in it. She listened politely to the guinea pig delivering a lecture.

'Miss West, you should not have been in court, should not have abused office time. Keep your nose out of other people's cases, do you hear?' This was not entirely sincere, since he was beginning to wish he had never interfered and had left her to it. The Sumner case weighed on him and he wanted help, but he could not concede out loud that she was the best person to give it, so he lectured her instead.

Helen, on the other hand, felt entirely disinclined to confess her extramural activities which had resulted in knowledge of the dual entanglements of Featherstone and Blundell. Nor did she wish to reveal her own frightening suspicions. Let Redwood speak directly or not at all. He had his case and his corpse and was going to run with it. Funny, seen like that: she could imagine him lugging a corpse across a courtroom floor. Her mind had slipped long before the end of the lecture and only shifted gear when the hectoring tone, mercifully mild, moved back into the conversational and she noticed the subtle way he had of soliciting opinions. She decided he had left it too late.

'Anyway, the committal went well,' he said. 'Very efficiently run. Sergeant Scott must be a great asset. I can see why Bailey was able to leave her to it.'

'Yes,' Helen said vaguely, not tuned in to praise for such a little telltale, still perturbed by the way Bailey appeared to have listened to her. 'Well, I'm glad everything's fine. Miss Scott's obviously the flavour of the month.'

Redwood disliked her quiescence, her equanimity in face of speeches from the throne, and the absence of anything suggesting co-operation or even acceptance of what had been his own version of an apology. He wanted to shake her, undermine that unnerving composure.

'Yes,' he said, rising to finish the interview. 'A highly successful case so far, but keep away from it. It's not yours.' He moved by instinct into a heavy teasing vein. 'Bailey owes a lot to Amanda Scott. Attractive girl. I should look to your laurels, there, Helen.' Playfully delivered words, like a punch in the arm, a kind of revenge.

'If you mean by my laurels my own superintendent,' Helen replied, returning the smile with saccharine, 'she can wear him around her head for all I care.'

'Oh. Right, then.'

And that was all she needed in order to ignore the rest of what he had said. For the remainder of the day she only recalled the last bit. She needed, she decided, a full frontal lobotomy, a new job, and a long holiday. And all she had was a new coat, while he, dear he, had brand-new Amanda Scott. Well, so be it. He was welcome to her. Jealousy was beneath Helen. Her instincts told her simply to give up.

EVELYN WAS PROFOUNDLY suspicious of her father's cheerfulness. Only that morning he had suffered an attack of meanness, going on about housekeeping and other mundane activities, chuntering through a lecture on the cost of living, but now the desk in the back of his office was littered with brochures, each featuring on its cover people smiling in bikinis and swimming trunks of indecent size, bikinis to the fore, each couple in Evelyn's eyes as identical as the grains of sand on which they sat. 'I was thinking,' said her father, 'of going on holiday.' Evelyn, fairly slow today, had gathered that much. He was looking at her with questioning anxiety. 'Some- where exotic. There's no trade here at the moment … well, not much. I want to leave all this unpleasantness behind. I need sun, sea, sand, all that. You've wanted to travel since you were ten, you always said you did. You'd like a holiday, wouldn't you, Evelyn?'

In another age, when she had still asked for things, before she gave up asking, when there was less to do, yes. 'When?' she asked with visible alarm.

'Oh, as soon as possible. Travel agent can get us a discount. In a day or two? Next week, maybe?'

'No,' she said loudly.

He looked at her dumbfounded. There he was in a sudden effluxion of energy, and yes, a touch of guilt, planning treats for a daughter and a suntan for himself to take away some of the years he would need to subtract before grappling with one Amanda Scott, and darling child said *non* with all the defiance of a General de Gaulle. 'Why?' he asked stupidly.

'School starts next week.'

'But you've spent all summer gummed up with books, haven't you? Never let up for a single evening, ever since Mummy … left. Missing a week's school won't matter, surely?'

'Yes, it will.'

'Oh, Evelyn, please.'

Oh shit and blast and bloody hell. Tears again, lurking in his eyes. More therapy indicated. The sooner he went back to ignoring her the better. Look at him with his beseeching eyes, like an ancient puppy with none of the appeal. 'Later, Dad, later. Take someone else. I'll be all right on my own.'

'No, you won't, of course you won't. I've had that Mr Bailey in here only this morning asking about you. All about homework, washing up, and did you have a bicycle, for heaven's sake. Everyone seems to think I bloody neglect you and I'm not having them thinking that. What would you do if I left you here?'

Meaning what would they think, all of them out there. Mind my own business, that's what I'd do, if you and everyone else would only mind yours. Words at the back of her throat ready to be shouted in sheer exasperation and gut-wrenching panic: Why don't you leave me alone? Can't you see I've got far too much to cope with already? It's a bit late to look after me now, Dad.

'Later, Dad, like I said,' stammered in a voice of wheedling humility. 'I couldn't cope. Not just yet. I'm not quite ready.' A better note to strike with him unable to see her little fists clenched behind the desk.

'Sure, darling child, but I don't see why.' The eyes filled with tears again. God, he had an inexhaustible supply that his customers never saw. He came around the desk again with his automatic gestures, automatic voice, patting her back.

"S'all right, Dad. 'S'all right, really it is. Let's just stay still awhile, shall we? After that man's been tried, Daddy, then we'll go, shall we?'

He thought of the hideous expenditure he was offering and might be avoiding, considered the business he might miss if he went away, thought of the evening ahead with delicious Amanda

Scott, found himself suddenly less tearful, and patted Evelyn's behind in turn. She leapt away like a scalded cat, calmed immediately, and sat down away from him, smiling her placatory smile.

'OK, darling child. Anything you say.'

EVELYN COULD HAVE wept during her afternoon of industry, ploughing through the list of shopping he had given her and she had not dared refuse. Father was watching her: it seemed everyone was watching her: she felt it when she walked down Branston High Street like a grown-up with a grocery bag, sick of it, very sick. She was even watched when she was out of bounds with William. She'd been seen on a tube platform, and he'd gone home alone, saying God knows what. If they found out about William, and what darling child did with William, that would be the end of holiday plans, school, and just about everything else that made life tolerable, like being ignored, for instance. William had to be protected and that was all there was about it. Going on holiday and leaving that vulnerable lump was quite unthinkable. He had to be protected from himself was what, and both of them had better stay protected from the outside world.

'Buy more groceries, will you, darling child? Especially washing-up liquid?' As if she was the skivvy her mother had wanted her to be. 'I don't know what you do with it,' he'd said. 'Do you drink it or something?'

'I like the dishes clean,' Evelyn had said primly. Yes, she would love the holiday, even with him – she could lose him somewhere; he would soon be bored with her – but it was impossible. She bought the washing-up liquid, cheapest brand, like he said, looked at it quizzically. Quite impossible to leave now. Not without William sorted out first.

Chapter Eleven

THE FLAMES WERE still murmuring towards the beginnings of stars when Bailey arrived at this fire. The fury of them had diminished, but the display and the noise were still significant. Most of the noise was the row of human endeavour, but as he walked towards the scene, there was a cracking of glass above the shop yard, then warning shouts as broken windowpanes clattered into the tiny yard below, musical and sinister, loud above the spitting of flame. The fire had long since engulfed its own beginnings. Bailey knew on first sight exactly what fuel had been used, watched the hungry heat that had stroked the windows into explosion. A low pyramid of boxes was tumbled by water. The firemen always used too much water, causing more damage than the fire. It was dramatic but pathetic, the whole sight, but it was under control. He noticed Amanda Scott's presence and her slightly festive clothes. Beneath her cloth coat, he could see the shiny material of an unusually flamboyant blouse catching the reflections of the dying flames, which also threw into focus the hard planes of her face. Her eyes shone like crystal: she was stiff with resentment at the interruption of her evening. Without a word she handed him the souvenirs she had found so efficiently, knowing he disliked her for it. For one bizarre moment, Bailey imagined her incandescent with malice.

'Coming out through the front, sir,' said another voice, irritatingly cheerful.

'Thank you.' He ducked down the smoke-filled alley beside the shop, followed the light to the road beyond.

'No problem here, sir, no one dead. They're in shock and all that, shock and smoke. One of them is cut. They live in the flat upstairs, sir. No, they're not the owners. They're an elderly couple who were watching TV, saw the flames at the back, and panicked. Couldn't get out, smashed the front door of the shop.'

Cut and crying, controlled tenants who lived above an upmarket gift shop in peaceful disharmony. Now they were consigned to a night in hospital and a lifetime fear of flames. The ambulance rolled away. One panting key holder was conferring with the fire brigade on the boarding up of his shattered plate-glass window, moaning about ruined stock already accumulated for Christmas, what a mess, what a bloody mess, a man disliking his life in the semidarkness and the acrid stench of the smoke. Bailey was momentarily oblivious of the fate of the survivors. His mind was busy with its own stock in trade; he was puzzled, alarmed, quietly angry. Deep in the pocket of his raincoat – Burberry, generously bought by Helen, stained by the smoke and by his having stooped to examine the dusty ground beyond the shop's back yard – his long fingers closed around the discordant collection of things given to him with such lack of ceremony by Amanda. Strange things to the uninitiated eye, so obviously placed, almost trampled in the rush as if the depositor of the incrimination, with a greater faith than Bailey in official vigilance, had wanted them found and relied on the eagle eye of a policeman to do so. Souvenirs. To Bailey's mind, in the sight of anyone with even primary knowledge of the boy, souvenirs with the hallmark of William Featherstone, almost bearing his autograph. A pile of bus tickets, a piece of chipped enamel half fashioned into a brooch, William's jewellery and William's favourite pastime scattered on the ground like his flag.

Early yet. An early dark, as if this arsonist had seized the first opportunity evening offered for the kind of display that would be spoiled by daylight. Even the timing served to illustrate how easy it would have been for him to arrive and depart prosaically by the bus that stopped outside the shop, timing his operation perhaps in accordance with the fictional timetables that only became fact in the early part of the evening, buses disappearing into total silence with the onset of night. Nine forty-five now. The work of minutes to stack boxes as he had done before; apply paraffin, as he had done before; discard the tickets and the shiny thing by the gate, as he had never done before. Flung apart from the other souvenirs was an empty washing-up liquid container, cheapest brand. Bailey thought fleetingly of the Featherstones' brimming sinks, the ever-expensive tastes, the mismanagement of provisions, buying the best and misusing it. It was too impractical a household for economy, not parsimonious enough. A richer, more successful household would feature such cheeseparing.

He thought of William with savagery. You have gone too far, boy, and you wanted to be discovered. This time you endangered lives; you could have killed that elderly couple with your flames. No, I have gone too far with my strange reluctance to arrest you sooner. This is my fault, you little bastard. Those deaths would have been on my conscience; now it is only these lives. Tramping back to the front of the shop, he regarded the damp but tasteful stock, saw in the key holder's hands the smooth edges of dull and tasteful jewellery, smooth handbags dusted down, and wondered with one slight tremor of shock why William had chosen such a place, so different from the tacky glitter he preferred. Looking at the damp tissue paper billowing in the road, the broken display stands crashed into by the old couple in their panic to escape, he had a sudden vision of the leaves strewn about in Antony Sumner's garden, the letters scattered on his desk with the same manic untidiness. There had been such control in the lighting of this fire and the others, such a sense of order; he could not equate this with an untidy mind. Again he thought of Antony Sumner's garden with the dead Mrs Blundell's clothing folded with such precision and placed in his otherwise disused compost bin. Her jewellery and her handbag, both purchased in exactly this kind of expensive emporium. Image crowded upon image. Untidy minds, unhinged minds, like William's. Bailey hunched in the street, trying to fathom how minds worked, confused by all the images in his own. Perhaps in William's swimming grey cells there existed this sense of order, imposed on his actions to save himself from the constant mess of his environment, but suddenly Bailey doubted it, doubted everything, sensed at work an alien mind devoid of William's clumsiness. He remembered the boy's lumbering, his strange popularity with the elderly on the buses, what Helen had described as his weird gentleness. Despite his violence, Bailey could not see him doing this, despite the evidence.

For once Amanda Scott would have to forgo the chance to make an arrest and be allowed to go home to her interrupted evening. For once, he would not phone Helen. He ordered a cursory search for William in the vicinity but not at home, please, I'll see to that. Then he went back to his office and the murder file – all the material, snippets, nonsense, rumours, documents marked 'unused' and labelled 'irrelevant' – and started again.

ALL RIGHT, SAID Helen to the kitchen ceiling. All right, all right, all right. He hasn't come home: he's doing to me what I did to him. Surely not: I've often wished the man would do something petty like this, allow me the excuse, once in a while, for a tantrum, but he doesn't, he won't; he's far too reasonable. So where the hell is he? Working, as usual? Spending his time productively? Or is he telling me something? Is he reconsidering his position in this bloody-minded household? Look at this squarely: none of it computes. His work rarely involves being away from a phone for hours on end; he had only to snap his fingers and someone would make the phone call for him; Amanda Scott would even snap his fingers for him if his knuckles were tired. Oh, be quiet. As with Bailey the night before, concern and anger intertwined in a mixture of growing unreason. She looked at the clean kitchen and envisaged the contents of the fridge: special foods, peace offerings, a good bottle of wine, rehearsed words now chilling with the rest. Bailey, we have such capacity for happiness. We must talk, or if you won't talk, at least tell me a story. I've made all these efforts with all this food … Was that what she was reduced to – Branston housewife in newish home seducing spouse with tidbits? Helen snorted, nine months' experience of domestic bliss, even with the long spells of contentment, curdling into a shout of resentment. I hate to cook, I hate to play second fiddle; I did not join this partnership to be a drudge, to sit around waiting for the man as if he kept me. She paused, struck by the imminence of yet more furious resentment, sat on the modern sofa. Wait a minute. There is a corollary to this: you are hooked on the man; he is a superior policeman; his partner must have self-sufficiency and endurance, and if you stay, this will be the story of your life. It cannot be otherwise, would not be otherwise were he doctor or parliamentarian; you would still be left waiting, and you would not like it, not like at all the fact that he has, in the scheme of things, greater value to the world than you. But I have even less importance here than I had in London. Branston diminishes me and no, I do not want artificial aids to fill the gap of uncertainty joining a club or taking evening classes. I cannot stay in a position where I am scolded like a child, I cannot live with a man who won't talk. And at the moment I need to talk; it's the only way I can find perspective on anything, so I'll go out and find some company, dammit, out. Where? Out. Somewhere.

Suspending judgement on her own reaction to the possible sight of William Featherstone, Helen flung on a coat, not the new coat, left Bailey a note mentioning her whereabouts and walked to The Crown. Let Bailey find the note and meet her there. Better a meeting on neutral ground: if he walked into that anonymous living room now, she might stain the walls with shouting. Not that The Crown's discordant atmosphere was likely to provide balm, but it was 'out', and the walk to reach it was preferable to static impatience, which was fast creating in her a kind of destructive electricity.

"Lo, Helen. How you been? Not seen yourself in ages. Too smart for you, are we?'

Bernadette Featherstone's greeting was offered from the depths of indifference, or so it sounded, surfacing against her better judgement; Helen found it cheering all the same. There was a party often in the bar, rowdy, post-races, post-wedding somewhere else, the revellers having found the only pub on a deserted road now had Bernadette to serve them with sullen efficiency.

'Where's Harold?' Helen asked, missing his presence leering over the counter.

Bernadette kept her eyes lowered, a posture that Helen did not know well enough to recognize as the symptom of a lie. 'Gone out with William. To the pictures.'

'Oh.' Helen found that surprising, given her knowledge of the Featherstones' habits, unprecedented even, but why not? It was pleasing news. She accepted it as truth, no real reason to doubt it.

Bernadette passed her a glass of wine without glance or comment. She was not about to confess that dear Harold was snoring like a drunkard, dead to the world upstairs, the combined effect of a bender and a row with William, whose whereabouts were currently, not unusually unknown. For once, Bernadette was conscious of her lack of control in her own family, bitter and ashamed of it. She was worried enough for her mind to be crossed with the idea of asking for help, but the thought died in passage.

If Helen had hoped for some biting conversation, perhaps a piece of invective, she was disappointed, but relieved all the same to retreat to a corner with a newspaper and book, only half of her waiting for Bailey; if she'd stayed at home, she would have waited with deathly, furious concentration.

'Himself coming down tonight, is he?' Bernadette shouted from the bar in the second tribute to manners.

'Maybe, maybe not. He'll please himself. I don't know.'

'Bloody men,' yelled Bernadette, startling the customers, granting Helen a transitory sensation of solidarity.

She read, drank a second glass of wine, watched through the door daylight fading with reluctance, the sky clawing at the remnants of summer, conscious in herself of the trickling away of patience and concentration. She had resisted the impulse to swig a couple of large gins, but in the bloodstream of her thinking, the dry red wine provoked slow ideas, speculation, and the return of the restlessness that had driven her out of her home and into the harsh plush of the pub's seat. With all this itching, she had deflected her mind from her own condition into thinking of William Featherstone. She remembered his reference to the summerhouse den, his retreat, a place that somehow offered him a curious safety and comfort. Helen felt a childish wish for the same sort of hiding place. She wondered if Bernadette knew of it, imagined she must; surely she did. There must be some place to which you consigned a child such as William with your blessing for his absence. Helen's desire to see this refuge became suddenly overpowering; this impulse was not entirely the effect of the liquid, more the last resort of a weirder kind of stress. But the drink always had this kind of effect on her, making her wilfully stupid when she should have been cautious, active when passivity was appropriate, talkative when silence was better advised. She wanted to see the den so much she did not have a choice; it was like that coat, there was no choice at all. There was this den, something to be discovered before darkness was complete, something to do. Professional solicitor plays amateur detective. How rude, how intrusive, how silly. She reflected she was merely curious after the most vulgar of fashions; she had no right to explore or trespass and would not have done so without the wine or the constant irritation of Bailey's absence. She got up and went to the bar.

'You trying to tank up or something?' said Bernadette briskly, avoiding her eye.

'Listen,' said Helen, 'you've got a summerhouse bar or some-thing like that, in the garden, haven't you? Can I look at it?'

Bernadette blanched, grinned, and frowned in quick succession, looking in one moment the image of her uncertain son, mirror-ing his vulnerability. She forgot the obvious remark – 'What's it to you?' – and all the aggression that usually followed any question she regarded as impertinent. Her shoulders sagged and her face crumpled instead. There was bravado in her voice, but not in the way she stood, like a rag doll.

'Yes, there is. A bloody great shed. Want to buy it? It's Wil-liam's, you know.' This she said in a great rush of confidence. 'At least I think it is.'

'I know. He told me.' Tactless, thought Helen as she said it, very tactless.

Bernadette's face showed a whiplash of hurt. 'Did he, now? Well, I won't ask when and how, bugger never talks to me. Look all you want. Why should I bloody care? He never tells me anything, that boy, my bloody son. And if he's out there, send him in.'

'You said he was at the pictures.'

'So I did, so he is, of course, with his dad. Sorry I spoke. At the flicks.' Moving away in dismissal. 'Go on if you're going. Look out for the tree on the path. Sod you.'

It was this invitation that committed her; that and her own tactlessness dispatched her on a mission. Explore and report back, discover this den, since you already know more than Bernadette. Report back with reassurance if you dare, damn you, some hurt to be justified. Crossing the dark path leading downhill from the kitchen, Helen was defensive rather than fearful, bold rather than afraid, ridiculously active in any pursuit rather than sitting still.

After clambering over the fallen tree, still visible in the semi-darkness, she saw the shed looming before her and almost laughed out loud. It was a ridiculous lopsided structure, a Featherstone masterpiece. Oh, what a fine abandoned dream, lovable on sight, redolent of her own childhood, a place she would have adopted, woven ghosts for, dreamed of, kept a secret from sisters and brothers, loved. Still aware of the unkindness of her mission, the rudeness in her curiosity, she determined not to linger despite her delight in this eccentricity. She would take one quick look around the back, a few more glances of furtive admiration. Then she'd go back inside, make peace with Bernadette, walk home, and face whatever music happened to be playing when she arrived. She was making for the window when the door of the shed creaked open like a prop in a horror film, and there, squinting into her own startled face, were the equally startled features of one William Featherstone.

'Who's that?'

She could not open her mouth.

'Oh. It's you.' He stood with his arms by his sides like a gorilla, face in a frown of confusion, unable to decide between anger, irritation, and relief in the knowledge that the eyes which met his own were neither unfamiliar nor unsympathetic. He flushed with disappointment, searching his mind for some sort of precedent or rule that would cover this situation. Evie had never mentioned or rehearsed him for this: he did not know what to do, but found in the end that anger was impossible. There was something here he liked; he could not remember what. He rubbed his hands across his eyes, felt exposed, while some strange code of manners afflicted him. Lumbering alongside the remnants of social graces forced into him as a child and all but forgotten now, there lingered his pride in the den itself, his own creation, something he had always yearned to show while knowing he could not. And Evie was not here to forbid it. At this time of night she would not come here, and if she did, she would be angry, he knew it. Yesterday she had abandoned him to this woman; today she might have done the same, no telling.

Helen smiled, the expression intended to cover a feeling of fear still half formed. William found himself smiling in return. 'You'd better come in,' he said, and tugged her arm in clumsy invitation.

She was suddenly diffident, genuinely shy herself. 'Should I?' she asked. 'Are you sure? You don't have to show me …'

'Course I'm sure. Come.' Some equally strange code of manners made it impossible for her to refuse.

He went back inside the shed. Helen followed, seeing herself in one brief glimpse in the window as the kind of character she had always hated in films, the one who walked off into the dark danger by herself with the whole audience shouting, 'Don't do that, you silly bitch. Can't you see it's the last thing you should do?' After negotiating the lethal steps and entering what appeared to be a kind of shallow grave, she found herself in a haven so bizarre she almost giggled with relief.

William lit the lamp before she descended the broken stepladder, something he could always do in the dark. Then he stood by like an anxious estate agent showing a house, waiting for her reaction, hoping for approval. With his arms extended, he could almost touch both walls, his head nearly touching the ceiling. The den in Helen's eyes was cluttered but reasonably clean, equipped with all the necessities of life, like a fallout shelter prepared for a siege: a few tins of food, two piled-up mattresses, a cupboard on which was pinned, quite incongruously, a bunch of tinsel pinched from the gaudy supply of The Crown, William's latest homemaking attempt, glittering foolishly in the dark. Helen had a fleeting picture of submarine life, men living in restricted airspace that smelled like this, of bodies and dust and perspiration, a threatened prison bedecked with pathetic tributes to ordinary humanity in an ordinary world.

William regarded her hopefully, his face a question mark, his mind working out why he liked her. Oh, yes, she had not told on him about being in London. Was that it? Something of the kind registered, and, oh, yes, she had a coat she had shown him, pretty. She was old, of course, teacher-old, one of them, but nice. He had longed for adult approval, longed to show this place to someone other than Evie, who visited with intermittent grace and who was frequently critical, rarely admiring. His longing was a version of domestic pride. 'I made all this,' said William, the excitement of the achievement clear in his voice, 'and no one else comes here, except—'

'Except Evelyn,' said Helen neutrally. 'Of course she does. William, it's wonderful, really it is. Where did you find all these things? Oh, look at that, you've even got cutlery. You could live here for ever and no one would know.'

The thrill of approbation seemed endless: he shook with it, mumbling in shy embarrassment, remembering again his strange and erratic code of manners. 'Sit, sit. You want tea? Only I got no milk. Plenty sugar but no milk.'

'Black tea, plenty sugar, will do fine.'

He was busy, flustered beyond efficiency, managing nevertheless to heat water on the other arm of the gas camping stove that held the light. He put tea bags in mugs surprisingly clean, and finally, after providing a running commentary on each of his own movements, brought forth tea of a kind. It tasted as it looked, lukewarm, flavoured in her mind with the smell of butane and the heat of the camping stove, the taste at odds with the last of the red wine. The place had ambience, she decided, suppressing hysteria by concentrating on the tastes in her mouth. The scents of the room were both domestic and animal. Her wandering imagination, which had lit first on the image of a submarine, dwelt next on the notion of a fox in its lair: William must not be made to feel at bay. With the image of a fox prancing through her mind, her hands curled around the mug and she remembered Mrs Blundell's fingers, thought of her predators, human and animal. She looked at the hulk of William sitting beside her on the makeshift bed, talking as if there were no tomorrow, benign, amiable, dangerous.

'I keep my tools in here,' he was saying, eager to display anything and everything there was.

'Do you, now? And did you make the cupboard?'

'Yes, of course.'

'Why do you need so many tools?'

'For making things, of course.' He threw her a look of condescension reserved by males for silly females.

'What things? Can I see them?'

A sigh of exaggerated, completely hypocritical impatience, 'Oh, all right, then, I s'pose you can ... You won't tell?'

'Why on earth would I tell?'

'Don't know, but you might. They'd laugh.'

'I promise I won't tell. And I shan't laugh, either.'

'OK.' It had been enough to stroke William's burning impatience to show off his handiwork. He opened the crooked homemade compartments of the cupboard, showing his collection of polystyrene figures, recognizably human but odd. 'I don't do these any more,' William remarked in passing. Then he revealed things carved in wood; then rings, bangles, and strings of strange glass beads spilled into Helen's hands. 'I like these things best,' he said simply in explanation for their existence. The shelf below this treasure chest held a hand drill, hammer, pliers, mallet, and the dull gleam of a blade.

Helen dragged her gaze to the glitter he held out for her inspection, and even while murmuring in genuine amazement, 'Oh, William, what's that?' or 'How on earth did you make this?' let her eyes go back to the knife on that shelf, an old horn handle and the pristine blade of a single-edge working knife, settled as comfortably as a carving knife in a kitchen. She admired William's possessions, silently remembering courtroom descriptions of wounds to the throat made by a single-edge knife that was never found. Oh, don't be silly, the world is full of knives. And throats cut within a half-mile of this shed?

William's sharper instincts caught her second glance at the weapon. He reached into the cupboard with the swiftness of a snake and pushed the thing to the back, looked at her in doubtful trust, withdrew it again. 'I saw you looking,' he remarked. 'You may as well see. Nice, isn't it?'

'Lovely,' said Helen. 'Only I don't like knives much. They frighten me.'

'They don't frighten me,' said William. 'I know what to do with them.'

'What do you do with them?'

'Oh, carve things most of the time. And kill people.' This was a boastful shout.

'I don't see why anyone would want to do that,' said Helen.

'I did,' said William, puffing out his chest.

'Oh, put the knife away, William. I like the jewels better. Show me some more.' He did as he was asked, anxious again to please, his memory as short as the moment.

Against her will she was impressed and frightened. 'Perhaps you could make things for a living, William. I mean, you could learn how to do all sorts of work ... oh, I don't know, carpentry, making pretty things like these. You'd be earning your own money. Wouldn't that be nice? Would you like that?'

'Oh, I would, I would.' He looked so vulnerable, like a bull terrier puppy, all pale snout and clumsy power, musclebound brain, confused reactions of confused strength.

'Perhaps you could talk to your dad about that.'

'Perhaps,' he said gruffly. 'But I don't talk to Dad much.'

'Why not?'

'Evie said not to. She says when I talk I always talk too much, and if I talk too much she won't come here any more, not even on Sundays. Besides, I don't like talking to Dad. I'm no good at it.'

'You need more practice. Then you'd make more sense. You get better at everything if you practise.'

He was not insulted. 'Practice? You mean like I got better at making things by doing it all the time? That's funny. Talking to Dad's not like that.' He laughed, a yelping, snorting sound, unnaturally loud, and she laughed with him.

'No,' she said, 'talking isn't quite like that. But the idea's the same.' Dear God, Bailey, where are you?

But the laughter had stopped, William fallen into a dreadful stillness as sudden and complete as a paralysis. He grabbed her arm, fingers digging into her wrist, face paler than a ghost.

'What is it, William? What is it?'

'Shhh.'

From above their heads there was a whisper of movement, then a silence unnervingly complete. Into the silence crept the sounds of the gathering night, the faint and distant noise of wind in the trees, the tiny whisper of an aeroplane overhead, nothing suggesting an intruder. William loosened his grip on Helen's arm, the puzzled look still stuck to his features, mouth open, eyes wide and clownish, softening into repose. "S'all right,' he said in a whisper. 'Mices, I think. Keep quiet, though.'

She sat silent and obedient, relaxing slowly, recognizing in him antennae that she did not have and a wariness she could not share. Then, as William opened his slack mouth to speak, there was a flurry of steps, a grunt of effort, the expulsion of breath in one great gasp.

Over their heads the trapdoor slammed into place, knocking aside the ladder and filling the cellar with choking dust and debris. Both of them gasped, retreating to the farthest corner of the room, she upsetting and extinguishing the lamp in the process, he turning off the hiss of the gas in one swoop, actions felt rather than seen in a darkness that seemed total. Then silence fell again for one pregnant and endless minute, full of the sound of breathing. In that long interval her eyes adjusted, sharpened by overpowering claustrophobia, until she could see the cracks between the wooden slats of the trapdoor and the shape of the trapdoor itself. She stuffed her fist into her mouth to prevent herself from screaming, choked on her fingers, and grabbed for William's arm, anything to touch. As she groped for him, he hugged her with one paw and wrapped the other around her neck. He placed his hand over her mouth, gently, but brooking no argument.

Silence followed the thunder upstairs. Then a sensuous scraping as if an animal or a human had lain across the trapdoor. There was a long, contrived sigh, an adjustment of clothes, then the sound of humming.

'Evie,' William screamed. 'Evie!'

A muffled sob, then heels drumming on the trapdoor, stopping as the voice began, petulant, seductive, and slow. 'You told, William Featherstone, you told. Crybaby, telltale. You told.' The voice was hardly recognizable as Evie's, a droning monotonous adult whine.

'I didn't, I didn't.' A responding shriek from William. 'I didn't, no I didn't.'

'Did, did, did.'

Helen struggled briefly against William's grip. His bitter-tasting palm remained clamped over her lips, forcing her to be silent.

'What did I tell? Who? When?' Another shout, irritation mingling with fear in his voice. 'What'm I supposed to have told?' This he repeated on a rising note of hysteria. Fumbling in the dark, Helen shuffled closer to the trapdoor, one arm feeling for William's shoulder, leading him in a single step, smelling the stale, earthbound smell of him, sensed the beginning of his tears.

The figure moved on the slats of the trapdoor, face pressed to the wood, voice more composed, louder, but still an insistent drone, monotonous, childish. 'You told, William, didn't you?'

'No, Evie, I didn't. Open the door, stupid.'

'Don't call me stupid.'

A silence of great length, William controlling his breathing, Helen standing absolutely still. Then, peculiarly, Evie sobbing, lying on the dirty door above and whimpering, whether in rage or in grief it was impossible to determine.

'I can't let you out, William. They'll be looking for you, all of them, I thought you'd be safe, but you aren't. I know you've told about us, and you'll tell the rest. So soft you are, William. You can stay here now, in the dark. Then you'll know better.'

'No, Evie, please.'

''S'all right William, I'll be back.'

There was scuffling, shuffling, thudding, a dragging of something heavy across the floor, sounds of more effort from Evelyn. William screamed again. 'Come back! Don't go, Evie. I'll tell them whatever you want. I'll tell them I did everything if you like, everything.'

'Did everything what, William?' Evelyn's voice was sharp and normal now, but fatigued and impatient.

He hesitated before answering in quieter tones, sinking to a mutter. 'Don't know. Everything.'

There was a tut-tutting of annoyance while Evie digested this and Helen stiffened. 'No,' said the upstairs voice, leaden with despair. 'That isn't what you were supposed to say at all, is it? You can stay here now until you remember what you should tell them if you're daft enough ever to say anything. That way people will leave me alone. So if you want to say anything, you can tell them you saw Mummy's boyfriend kill her, which is just what happened, isn't it? But you're useless. You've got to stay here now.'

The object she had pushed and pulled across the floor was shoved once more, falling on to one side against the slats. Liquid began to trickle through the wood in a steady stream, striking their upturned faces, hitting hair and clothes until William dragged Helen back out of reach, his hand still clamped on her mouth. Evelyn's quick footsteps died away; the door of the summerhouse banged into silence. William released his hand, slumped on the mattresses, began to sniff, while Helen felt the strongest urge yet to scream into the darkness, a reaction suppressed only by the more pressing need to cough and choke. He recovered, banged her back, unaffected by the smell that filled the place.

'Silly,' he muttered, an adult attempt at bravery, taking strength in the act of patting her, 'very silly, it'll be all right, you wait. Not to worry, missus, I can get out of here easy. When I can see,' he added, shuffling around on the floor, then standing and feeling in his pockets.

'What do you want, William? What are you looking for?'

'Matches,' he answered. 'Ah, found them.' Somewhere beyond his head, the liquid was still dripping, hitting the stone slab on the floor where the ladder had rested. Helen grabbed at his arm. "S'all right,' he said again. 'I can get out of here easy, once I've found the lamp.'

'William, do not light a match, *don't*, whatever you do.'

'Why?'

'Because,' she said, speaking slowly and carefully, enunciating each syllable, 'because Evelyn just poured this stuff all over us. You must not light a match, William; we are covered with paraffin.'

She could hear the rattle of the matchbox as he dropped it to the floor. 'Oh,' he said. 'I see.'

Chapter Twelve

BAILEY DISLIKED THE exterior of this pretentious house and took particular exception to the gravel outside the front door, placed there for the sole purpose of making a sound of satisfying richness. *Nouvelle richesse*, in Blundell's case, no worse than any other kind, simply more offensive. The snobbery of it appealed to Bailey's own subdued inversion of snobbery, which had prompted him to allow Amanda Scott to deal with this man and his neighbours instead of doing the job himself. Bailey knew he had no right to his prejudices. Some people chose houses that advertised their wealth, but they bled and suffered the same as those who had failed to make such conspicuous improvement in their lives. Still, the gravel irritated his soul. So had Blundell on their first meeting, when he had been diffident, sedulous, and crawling to please in a man-to-man kind of way, even when reporting the absence of a wife. 'Sorry to bother you, old man,' he had said. For God's sake.

Whatever resentment Bailey felt then would be reciprocated now. No man enjoyed visits from the police at eleven-thirty at night unless he was in pain or truly desperate for company. Only the form Blundell's resentment would take remained to be seen. PC Bowles, large and uniformed in the car outside the gate, could lend an air of officialdom if necessary, but Bailey hoped not. He knew the purpose of his visit to be tenuous, knew his pocket should contain a search warrant, and had already rehearsed the alternative approach, an example of the kind of benign trickery he had often used: 'If you won't let me in to look at your house, sir, I'm sure you won't mind waiting with this officer here while I go and wake up a magistrate to supply me with the piece of paper that will force you to comply. Up to you, sir.'

'And why do you want to search my house, Mr Bailey?'

'Well, I don't rightly know. There are questions lingering here.'

'Get out, Mr Bailey.'

He tried the garage first. Open and empty, nothing to steal apart from a bicycle – old, battered, hidden by a tarpaulin. Clearly labelled in Bailey's mind were two preoccupations: letters, and the gleam of gold. Letters taken from Antony Sumner's desk, the ones Amanda had failed to secure so sure was she of their irrelevance. Perhaps other, similar letters she had failed to discover here. And maybe the jewellery worn by the dead woman, the bracelet, earrings, and necklace that Blundell had described so uncannily well, as if he had seen them very recently. Bailey could not rid himself of the conviction that they were still in this house. Certainly the man was mean enough to keep them and claim his insurance, but Bailey doubted if that was all he'd been up to. He was clever enough, or maybe simply rich enough, to deflect dear Miss Scott. 'And every time she shouted "fire," the people answered, "Little liar".' Bailey recited the old rhyme to himself, stopping to survey the front door, trying to decide upon the most appropriate pleasantries for the occupants. Sometimes he managed the most sophisticated approach of all, making himself think and feel like an ordinary visitor, imagining himself with an invitation and sure of a welcome. People allowed extraordinary privileges to their guests, showed them the sanctum of their own lives, displayed everything from the beams to the contents of the bathroom cabinet without turning a hair. If Bailey could think of Blundell as his host, he might influence events. Then again, he might not. He could not imagine John Blundell offering him a drink, and the thought reminded him not only of the taste of whisky but of how difficult he would find it to refuse. A whisky would be nectar.

But within feet of the front door, he knew the house was empty, giving off from itself the scent of vacancy. He had spent enough of his life approaching doors and windows unbidden, in the dark, in daylight, in the eyes of storms, and instinct told him immediately when human life was absent. He had learned in the bitter experience of failure how to avoid the pitfalls, and how and where a man could hide indefinitely, learned to sense emptiness and its opposite. He had sat in a room for two hours on guard, uncomfortable, but unaware of the one silent Indian hidden behind a wardrobe two feet from his own back and still carrying a knife. Now he knew when to turn, when to look, when to ignore logic and obey his instincts. There was nothing live in this house; he was sure of it. But for all that, the place was lit up like a Christmas tree. Blundell, it seemed, was losing his grip: door unlocked, lights on, not a soul to be seen, like the *Marie Celeste*. When Blundell left, he had believed his castle to be still occupied.

Bailey shouted into the empty hall and was relieved by the answering silence. Acutely aware, if only for a second, of the dubious legality of his presence, he began to walk from room to room. Kitchen empty and tidy, heart of a heartless house, two glasses on the table. Living rooms and handsome stairs muffled by carpet and soft beneath the feet. Calling 'Anyone at home?' he trod heavily up the stairs, moved along the hall and into the largest room, being deliberately noisy, both as a warning to others and as a sop to his conscience.

He was indifferent to the fact that this exercise could blight his career, a consideration that had persuaded him to leave Bowles behind to avoid tarring him with the same brush of disgrace for so flagrant a breach of the rules. Bailey forgot the professional madness of his illicit search as soon as he stepped into what was obviously Blundell's room. Handsome mirrored wardrobes lined one whole wall. Wealth consumed by vanity, thought Bailey, opening the first door. Good God. A row of shredded garments hanging from padded hangers like streamers, resembling tired flags ripped by a malicious wind long after the celebration. Another door revealed more of the same, rags replaced neatly as if the creases of them still mattered, zips gaping like wounds, sleeves in shreds. He was stunned, closed the doors with something like reverence, furious with Amanda Scott, his mind jangling with possibilities, entertaining the thought of Blundell as murderer. Then he put the thoughts back into order, stored the vision of this graveyard of clothing for future reference, went back to the first purpose of his trespassing, left the room, and went to the next.

An unpromising door, bolted from the inside, light from the interior colouring the dark floor in a brilliant band. He had quickly identified the remainder of the upstairs rooms; this door was the only one left for the daughter of the house. Evelyn, darling child, whose writing on a shopping list seen in John Blundell's office bore such a striking resemblance to that on juvenile love letters to a teacher currently in prison. He did not know what was in his own mind other than writing, the gleam of gold, and a familiar feeling under his skin.

Bailey put his shoulder to the door, felt the breeze from the open window beyond as the softest splintering of wood shrugged off a cheap bolt, clumsily constructed as a barrier against a world that had never wanted entry in the first place. More a symbol, this bolt, effective only because it was completely respected. On the other side of the door, a room so Spartan it almost defied occupation: small bed, tacky wardrobe, cheap wooden desk bought for a child, spitefully at odds with the luxury of the rest of the house. A plastic skeleton hanging from a cupboard and a hoard of books, tidily placed. Thin curtains moved in the breeze, flagging the presence of Evelyn Blundell's own back door. A small transistor radio was playing quietly but insistently. He sat in the childish chair by the desk and began to open the drawers. Somewhere out there, walking the streets in the quasi-countryside of this artificial part of the world, looking at the better life, was darling child, a malevolent, determined, and beautiful presence, perhaps protecting a murderer. Somewhere in this anonymous room was the rest of her, arrogantly undisturbed.

EVELYN SAT AT the edge of Bluebell Wood, half frozen. She had embarked on her evening enterprises dressed for action, but her cotton T-shirt was inadequate against the cool night. The wood behind her was black. She had no fear of darkness but was chilled by her impatience and the cold. From this end of the wood, she could just see the outline of The Crown in the distance, partially obscured by trees, nothing else visible: her eyes fixed to a point between trees and horizon. Do it, William, just do it. Put your hand in your pocket, feel your silly plonker, leave it alone, and get out the matches. I couldn't, but you can. Go on, you just don't understand fires; you never did, not even after the first one I made you try. You were too thick; you couldn't even see it was fun. You only like doing that thing. You don't really like anything else except all that foul jewellery you make and, even worse, what you steal, and putting your plonker in me, and I'm so bloody tired of that, really I am. I'm sorry, though. All that fiddling about wasn't enough to keep you quiet; it makes me mad. I can't stand all that squidgy stuff. You'll talk to that woman you went with yesterday, went back on the bloody train with her, too frightened to go on the tube by yourself. It's no good, William, no good. You'll be like putty. All those questions, it's no good, William; you've got to go. Out like a light. Oh, I'm sorry, I shouldn't have said that, shouldn't think it, even without anyone hearing. She giggled at her own bad taste. I'm sorry, William.

Her shivering was becoming uncontrollable. She remembered the bicycle rides, huge physical efforts, the sensation of palpitating heat as she had watched the first of the flames outside the shop, then more pumping of pedals and heartbeat and emotion as she had entered the summerhouse, flexed first her hearing, and then her muscles to drag the paraffin across the floor, having closed that door. She had not intended to use the paraffin at first. A spur-of-the-moment stroke of brilliance, the same ultimate solution she had played with yesterday, not really intending to use it until she had seen his cringing and knew despite his denials that he was slipping. She'd heard the lie in the shrillness of his voice and had realized in the same moment that the general discrediting of William by having him labelled a loopy arsonist as well as a thief was not going to save either of them; all it meant was that no one would believe a fire raiser. He had to be put away where no one could talk to him at all. Now, in the absence of any flames hitting the sky, the sight for which she had grown hungry, she doubted her own wisdom, wondered if she had underestimated him. Surely not, she decided. She contemplated going back, but no, let him face his family stinking of paraffin if he got out – family and policemen, if they had found her clues. What difference would it make? They would never listen to him now.

The field below her inclined gently toward The Crown, the stubble of it shining like dull gold. Slinking down one side, barely visible, was the fox, a mere suspicion of movement, a flash on the eye like a ghost in motion. Its presence was a blow of surprise, a dark premonition of disaster, filling her mouth with vomit as she watched to see how close the thing would pass before detecting her presence. She loathed the sinuous progress of it, Mama's fox coming back, the one that had bitten off her hand, or so she had heard in some eavesdropped aside. No animal, no living thing, should have the teeth or temerity for that. Mother had been hers, the revenge all her own. Evelyn jumped to her feet, shouted wildly. 'Go away, go away,' waved her arms, watched the fox freeze, flatten, turn, and double back into the undergrowth at the foot of The Crown's jungle of a garden. She was shaking with relief; she kicked her feet and wagged her hands, jogged on the spot, circled the tree against which she had sat, settled down again to rest, flexed her fingers, looked at her watch. Midnight.

When she got home, she would write it all down, the way she wrote so many things, as Antony had taught her. It's all in your head, Evelyn: writing is only learning how to get it out, make sense of it. She remembered the alien familiarity of her room, the papers in it. They were safe, of course, the mildest of risks, because Papa could be bribed with the gold in the end, and no one had ever wanted entry to her sanctuary. No one ever had. Her only risk was what she had written; her only legacy from the teacher. Her eyes began to close.

She would wait one more hour. Then she would go and see.

Still no sign of fire.

WILLIAM WAS SINKING into sullen inactivity, shuffling and speechless.

'Cheer up. Nothing's ever as bad as it looks.' Helen's voice rang false in her own ears, repeating a cliché she hated.

He grunted with short laughter. 'Nothing looks like anything in the dark. We can't see anything in the dark.'

'OK. Sorry I spoke.'

'Not your fault.'

'Couldn't we try again, pet? You lift me up, I push the door?'

'No, I can't. I don't even want to. I'm tired.'

So was she. Their several attempts to shift the trapdoor with a certain clumsy co-ordination but without the benefit of the shattered ladder, had resulted in nothing. The first shove had shifted the paraffin container, dousing them further, while the second had damaged their ankles and knees. They were filthy and stinking. Helen's hope for eventual rescue via Bernadette, whose punishment for her interference would surely not be as extreme as abandonment, had sunk to a dull glow of optimism. Her greatest fear was the return of Evelyn, but her fear was William's greatest wish and she tried to distract him from it. Even in the course of their efforts, in the flow of her own chatter, the odd joke which had succeeded in making him laugh, William's stone mill of a mind had been grinding out conclusions. She had begged him to think; now she wished he could stop.

'She isn't coming back,' he said.

'Well, she's obviously cross about something.'

'I don't mean now. Ever.'

'Oh, I expect she will. People don't stay cross for long.'

'She tried to kill us. No, me.'

'Oh, no, William. This is just her idea of a joke.'

'She knows I don't understand about fires. She tried to teach me, but I couldn't learn.'

Helen paused, unwilling to stretch him further but desperately seeking clues as to how to deal with the dreadful possibility of Evelyn's return.

'Why is she so cross, William? Is it about you and her being special friends, you know what I mean, going to bed together? Is she afraid her father might find out, or what? There's more than that isn't there?'

'We weren't always special friends. She wouldn't let me ...' He wavered away into uncertainty. Helen imagined Bailey as interrogator. How quickly he would persuade this boy to tell, shuddered at the thought, listened. 'I suppose she didn't like it very much. She only let me after ... Oh, never mind.'

'After what?'

'After her mummy was dead. I cried. We buried her, Evie's mummy. She hated her mummy, but not as much as she hated the man she says killed her mummy.'

'Oh.' Helen cleared her throat. 'What about her mummy's coat and things? You know, the things women always seem to have, rings and bracelets and handbags. And clothes of course.' She could sense the puzzlement she could not see. William had lost his power to contrive, forgotten his small ability to keep secrets.

'She didn't have any clothes and things,' he said finally. 'She was all bare. Like a big chicken.' He gave a giggle of embarrassment.

'Goodness,' said Helen. 'And how did you dig the hole for her?'

'With our hands, mostly, and Evelyn's knife. The ground was very soft.'

'Is that her knife you showed me?'

'Yes. She told me to throw it away. I didn't, though. She never looks in the cupboard. I thought' – he struggled with the idea – 'I thought afterwards, long time afterwards, she might have wanted me to say I killed her mummy. I always said I would say that if she liked, I'd say that again and again if anyone ever said she'd done it – Evie, I mean.'

'You go to prison for things like that, William. For a long time.'

'So what? Doesn't matter for me,' said William stoutly. 'Why should it matter for me? But Evie's clever, going to be a doctor. Only Evie matters, not me. I love Evie better than anything. Only Evie ever cared about me.'

'She didn't—' Helen tried to make her questions as diffident as possible. 'She didn't see someone kill her mummy, did she?'

'I don't know,' said William hopelessly. 'I don't know, and I wouldn't care if she did. I don't know anything any more.' Sobs were rising again like a storm. 'I don't know. Her mummy was horrible. I only wanted to help. And now she wants to kill me.'

'Of course she doesn't. She'll come back.'

'She wants to kill me,' he repeated. 'And I don't know why.'

Helen put her arms around him, prayed for rescue, hugged him, and rocked him to and fro, a part of her wishing in fury a fate worse than death for Evelyn, the other part wondering how long it took for paraffin fumes to evaporate. The skin of her face felt flammable, her arms were weak, and the boy was growing ever more helpless. Wait for daylight. Another thought occurred to her with appalling clarity. 'William, will you give me the matches? I'd feel safer.' He handed them over. Her recognition, in this simple demand, of his despair and his longing to be dead made him cry more.

'There, there, no crying, love. Think about something else. There'll be nice things to do in the morning. Shh, now. Listen, I'll tell you a story.'

'I'm frightened,' said William. 'Hug me. No one's ever going to hug me again.' It was said with utter and final conviction. She hesitated. Hugging William, even in this filthy pit, was a dangerous activity for a boy who could not distinguish between affection and desire. She hugged him all the same. They might neither of them see morning.

'MY MOTHER NEVER hugged me,' Bailey read. 'Never did anything like that, ever. Dressed up and all that all the time, but never went in for hugging; it smudged her. Don't like her a lot and reckon she hates me. Jealous as sin. Hates me having friends. Always calls me darling child, like I haven't got a bloody name.' Bailey was examining one of a hundred fragments he had found in the desk in Evelyn's room, a mess of paper crammed into drawers, half-written letters and portions of school essays.

This page was mildly corrected in Antony Sumner's hand: 'Evelyn, no need to swear in essays. It diminishes your considerable talent for description. Please remember to write in full sentences, not a series of fragments. Try this paragraph, "A Description of My Family" again.'

She had tried again on the bottom of the same sheet: 'My mother is always staring into the distance and prefers I do not have a real name or identity. She has never loved me and always tries to prevent me having anything I want. The more I treasure something, the harder she will try to take it away.'

'Much better, but give examples,' Sumner annotated in a bored hand. 'An essay should illustrate the points it makes.'

'Well, she took away my camera, my new desk, my best clothes. She would never let me have friends or anything,' Evelyn had continued on an uncorrected sheet, apparently written for her own benefit, the standard of the English beginning to slip. 'Amazing she lets me have these English lessons. Because I asked Dad first, because it's pretty cheap and because she doesn't think it would be any fun. Didn't know, did she, how I love you. Thought she'd just be keeping me indoors while she's so bloody fat and I'm so thin. Ha ha.'

Beneath these fragments, of which Evelyn had kept dozens of pages corrected in Sumner's handwriting, Bailey found a pile of poignantly incomplete letters on primrose paper: 'My darling Antony, I love you so much it hurts. I want to kiss you all over, I'll do whatever you like. No one else listens to me except you and no one else notices me. Even if I had any friends, I couldn't bring them home, especially not Will. So I'm free to love you to pieces, and I do, I do. Hope you got my Valentine. Now that we have lessons with just us, I shall have you all to myself. She doesn't know. How can I write how much I love you?'

Scattered among the sheets of compulsive writing were random diary jottings, as if Sumner's tuition had brought about an obsessive habit with the pen and a constant urge to record, albeit incompletely. On scraps torn from exercise books lay the evidence of a saga of bitter disappointment. 'August 5: Mummy losing weight like an Ethiopian. Ha ha. Buying new things. I wonder if she wants him. Oh, God, she can't, she's old. Why? Because he's mine, that's why. I watch them going out for drinks. Dad pretends he doesn't notice.'

Next, a torn sheet, crumpled, straightened out again, kept against her better judgement: 'Watched them in the woods. Disgusting, yuck. He sucks her big tits, puts his thing in her, grunting like pigs. Why, why, why? I would have. I'm going to find William. Must stop crying. Can't stop crying. How can you do this to me? I hate her, hate her. Only thing I ever really wanted.'

'October 4: Dad buying things for her, only she never lets him buy anything for me. Gold stuff, lots of it. Suppose she thinks she looks bloody wonderful. Dad trying to buy her back. Silly wanker. Antony talks to me, nice to me, but pathetic, head somewhere else. That gold stuff is mine by right. What about me, Daddy? What about me, then? I am beginning …'

'November 10: Where will they go in the cold? Not Bluebell Wood. In his car? Yuck. A whole winter in a car? That won't do. Ha ha. I wonder about telling Dad but what difference would it make? I got William to rap on the car window and scare them.'

'March 15: She's gone funny. He's gone off her; I knew he would. Now he'll come back to me. I want to, I want to, but he's making excuses not to come any more for my lessons. Why not? What have I done? How can he leave me? Surely he knows I don't mind about bitch face as long as he comes back.'

Then a flat statement on May 10: 'Followed him again. He was with someone else, kissing. Watched them a long time. He doesn't come here any more and doesn't even say hello to me.'

A gap of weeks and then more animation: 'Mummy phones him all the time, but he won't come back. She's done it, hasn't she? Driven him away. She doesn't know I can listen to her on the phone, doesn't even care if I do. Jangling gold and making phone calls. I can't say how much I hate her stinking face. She took him, she took him. Serves her right. Hate him, hate him, hate him.'

'June 5: She gets him to meet her! I'm going, too. With my k ...'

Bailey paused in his reading, opened the next drawer. More paper, roughly torn sheets with crossings-out, sketched maps, a tube map of London, and a picture of a local craft shop, one of William's favourites, Bailey seemed to remember. There were lists, terse reminders on paper: 'Get washing liquid, v. useful. Hide bike, ask Dad for new one, don't tell.' Interspersed with the lists were strange descriptions, like brief catharses, literary attempts to distil an experience, full of slang in a deliberate and rebellious departure from the favoured style of the essays. A passage dated the day of Sumner's committal: 'You'd like this, Mr Antony fucking Sumner. Ain't this kind of neat? You were in the wood again with the old sow who wants to shag you like a bitch in heat – she never let me have a dog, so I don't know how I know. Says she'll run off with you, doesn't give a fuck for her daughter, husband, etc. Tell me news. Ha ha. Ants in her pants, ripping off clothes. You hit her with the stick and leave her there with her bum in the air and your stick on the ground. Gives me the idea. So I tiptoe up with my knife and then I tiptoe away again. Get *my* gold later, also clothes. I want to ... Go on, then, rot. Daddy's the same today. In I come in the evening, go downstairs. "All this time studying, darling child?" he says. "Of course," I say.'

Bailey put down the page and found his hands were trembling. Sifted through the rest finding none of equal length or savagery, some of a similar degree of crudeness: 'At least I now know How to Fuck. William taught me. See what you missed, A.S.? Ha ha.' A few expressions of regret about something: 'Shouldn't ask Will to help, have to do something about Will.' Nothing else but reminders, dates, and scribbles, staccato scrawls like spittle on a page, a mind seized by itself, each day a new plan. On the desk itself, a notice to the occupant: 'Holidays, Dad. See to W. Buy: (1) …' The remainder of the white sheet a panic-stricken blank until the tiny scribble at the bottom: 'People watching me now.'

Oh, you are wrong, my dear. People have been entirely consistent in their failure to watch you. You might have known, thought Bailey, they would not change. We should all have watched you sooner, and where the hell are you now? He visualized her approach to the sobbing form of her mother, knife in hand, seeing in one wide-angled glance the evidence left to incriminate another, using the same neatness to litter the ground by one of the fires designed to discredit the hapless idiot who had assisted, perhaps, in the burial. What had one interfering policeman found here? No true confessions, but enough to release one Antony Sumner, that teacher of impossible stupidity, who had nevertheless taught her a powerful use of the written word. Not evidence enough to convict the darling child. And here she would sit in her room, keeping secret her books and her contempt, aware that someone must feed her.

He froze at sounds from outside: car door, footsteps on gravel. With systematic speed, he began to search the remaining drawers in the desk, refusing to acknowledge the distraction. He registered an explosion of argument inside the front door of the house. Raised voices: Amanda Scott, John Blundell, and the patient, apologetic drone of Constable Bowles. At that same moment Bailey's hand closed around the semi-chill of metal. In his fist was the gleam of a gold necklace, heavy, elegant, dull-coloured. He might have known. Of course William Featherstone would never have craved this. And William Featherstone was never watched either.

'IF YOU'RE so bloody worried, you go. Why should I be woken up? Let the little bastard get on with it.'

'He's not little. That's the problem. And he's not a bastard.'

'Yes he is. You've only to look at him. He's not my flesh and blood, is he, Bernadette?'

'Oh, so that's your excuse for never watching him, is it? Can't stand the thought he might be your responsibility after all this time? Well you can't get away with that, however hard you try and God knows you've tried often enough. Fucking's the only thing we ever got right, and he's the result. Now go and find him, fuck you.'

He recoiled from the explicit crudeness. Bernadette swore, cursed, and abused frequently, but rarely so personally. Harold was half awake, shaken from fully dressed sleep, dragged into his kitchen and his life disbelievingly, bereft of anything but slight shock and the merest semblance of cunning.

'In the summerhouse, is he? And that copper's woman went out there three hours ago? You've taken your time, haven't you, sweetheart? No worry like real worry. She'll have gone home hours ago, interfering bitch. What'd she be doing with a great dolt like William?'

'God alone knows, but she never came back. We'll both go, if you're too frightened.' For once he was not defensive, but did not move.

'Course I'm bloody frightened. Bloody summerhouse. Lights and ghosts, full of them. I've seen 'em. So've you. It's you who's frightened.'

She was pulling on a coat, stubbing out her cigarette, simultaneous movements of fury.

'It's two in the morning. Leave it out, Bernie, for Christ's sake.'

'Two in the morning, he says, as if it can wait. We've a violent son at large and a missing copper's wife. Does it never occur to you, Harold, that two in the morning means that by now someone, somewhere, might come looking for her if she hasn't gone home? Like now, for instance?' Bernadette's eyes were levelled over his head towards the kitchen doors leading to the bar. Slowly Harold turned, imagining the presence of a silent blue-uniformed cavalry. Through ill-focused eyes, he could see nothing but emptiness, a sound suggesting the approach of car engines. With one automatic movement, he stuffed lighter and cigarettes into his top pocket, grabbed her by the arm, pushed and pulled her through the back kitchen door. Down the slope with stumbling, cursing steps, around the tree with ease, ceasing to hold Bernadette, who plodded behind.

The night was completely still, apart from the slightest breeze, a self-satisfied stillness auguring heat and lassitude under a late harvest moon, the garden awash with half-light, to which the eye could adjust easily. The summerhouse loomed ahead. Harold paused, listening for sound, hearing a muffled banging as he approached the door: *boom, boom*, weak inflictions of wood on wood almost below his feet, the sound of ineffectual effort, pausing as he paused, unconscious of him while he was acutely aware, all trace of whisky gone now except for the bile in his throat. Inside the door, voices, thank God, some normality. And at the opposite window, a fleeting, pale image of a face he had seen before, glimpsed quickly and gone, ignored for the moment.

Inside, the shed was half lit by the moon. Harold could see the trapdoor weighted with one full paraffin can, another one lay on its side. He remembered these surplus containers, heavy as hell, but he could not remember their purpose, strode towards them, began to heave them aside, conscious of spilling the last of the liquid from one, disgusted by the smell. Stopped to the sound of a muffled question from under his feet.

'Evie? That you, Evie?'

'No, it bloody isn't, son.'

'Oh, God, it's you.'

Harold was repelled by the leaden disappointment in William's voice, audible through wood and heavy with rejection, even in extremis. It carried the sudden, strangely unacceptable truth that the loathing he felt for his son was entirely reciprocal, and it angered him. The voice continued with dull, indifferent calm.

'Can you open the trapdoor, Dad? You pull from the left.'

Harold felt splinters enter his skin as he scrabbled for a gap on the left of an ill-fitting door, scarcely remembered now. He pulled, surprised by the ease of it until he saw the pale glow of Bernadette's hands pulling beside his own. Breathless with effort, he peered downward into the pitch, saw two upturned faces.

'Hello,' said one. 'We're very pleased to see you.'

Harold swore, passed his hands across his eyes, squinting. The cigarette lighter fell from his top pocket, plopped on the earth below. He had the vague, irrelevant sense of William stooping to retrieve it. In the distance, his ears caught the sound of a siren, an intrusion in the night, sounding the imminence of invasion. It increased his anger beyond his own believing.

'You're a filthy little bastard, William, that's what you are. Bringing women here, are you? Saves them looking at you. They'd need the dark, you pathetic little shit. You can stay in this stinking pit for ever, as far as I'm concerned, you little sod.'

'Oh, be quiet, Mr Featherstone, will you,' said the other one, only now discernible as Helen West, speaking in a tone of almost pleasant urgency, not free, he noticed, of a slight overtone of disgust. 'Just shut up and help us out, will you?' She touched William's arm in the vain hope of giving him the comfort of conspiracy. 'Someone locked us in here by mistake. And the ladder's broken.'

'Take her, Dad.' Instructions from William, now utterly calm. He seized Helen by the waist and lifted her on to his shoulders. 'Reach, missus, go on.' Miraculously swift, one balletic lift and an agonizing yank of shoulders taking her through the aperture virtually into Harold's arms. She pushed him away, knelt by the opening.

'Now you, William. Come on, the air's fresh up here.' Fresh with newly spilled paraffin seeped from the empty flagon, fresh with sour whisky breath, controlled rage, and the whimperings of Bernadette. Apart from the relief of escape there was little to recommend such freedom for William. It was unloving, threatening, full of retribution.

'Go away,' said William. 'Leave me alone.'

'I'll tan your bloody hide,' roared Harold, his fists clenched.

'Belt up,' said Helen. 'Go and fetch a ladder, will you? And keep your mouth shut. He doesn't deserve that. Your bloody son deserves a whole lot better than that.'

Her furious face was upturned, eyes glittering in skin streaked with dirt, making Harold recoil in shock. He moved to the open shed door, Bernadette retreating with him, obedient.

''S'all right,' William said to Helen. 'Honestly, 's'all right. I can get out now. Just let me stay still a bit. Till he's calmed down.' She nodded agreement.

And then, from beyond the summerhouse came flashes of light and crashings of sound, footsteps thundering from the direction of the pub, crashing through bushes in directionless haste, men searching with raised voices, Helen at the opening:

'Wait here, William. You'll be out soon. And you won't be in trouble, I promise,' leaving the trapdoor in response to one familiar voice, running outside to find it. She had heard Bailey. She was sure she had heard Bailey, saw nothing but torchlight approaching the shed, the sound of male humanity, indistinguishable as anything but a ragged procession, the first breaking into a run, wavering torch beam catching first her own face, then something farther distant.

'There she is, there she is.' Bailey incredibly running into her, touching her shoulder *en route*, not in comfort, simply to deflect her from his path, running beyond her. A scuffle out of sight in the darkness, the meshing of several urgent bodies in an orgy of contact, the tableau of Helen and the Featherstones standing still, oblivious to what was happening outside their view at the boundary with the field. Then, snarling and screaming, one girl child embraced by many hands, spitting like a cat, swayed back towards them in a fierce huddle that squirmed to a halt, still moving. The space outside the summerhouse door was suddenly crowded. Bailey transferred one arm of the cotton-clad figure into the grasp of another large form. Evelyn Blundell slumped between them, and the officers now grasping those thin arms tightened their hold to keep her upright. Three more men hovered breathlessly behind. Bailey's face was a mask of incredulity, the voice short of breath but accusingly calm as the beam of his torch caught first Bernadette's pallor, then Harold's sweating skin, Helen's face last as if noting them for memory. He spoke with a final weariness. 'What the hell are you doing here, Helen? Go home.'

Evelyn looked up, face contorted, towards Helen's familiar face, the Featherstone parents, the dreadful presence of her captors. Helen's own reactions to Bailey's words, those verbal slaps to her own existence, might have been more audible than her own recoil of rejection had the girl not interrupted, flinging back her head, arching herself forward, the lithe body jackknifing itself straight in a moment of enormous strength. An officer twisted one arm up her back with sudden brutality. She did not scream in reaction, simply screamed like a howling animal, long, loud, and pained, words clear in the vicious harmony of her yelling.

'William … you bastard! You told, you told, I hate you …' A scream going on and on and on, until Bailey slapped her hard. Her head jerked back with the sheer violence of the blow and the scream stopped. Their ears rang with the sound and the message of it, spitting hatred, the echo of it floating and settling on perspiring bodies and stunned minds, until slowly, very slowly, the group began to shuffle and re-form. Into Helen's numbed consciousness there floated the image of William downstairs in his den, listening to this crescendo, thinking slowly on what he had heard. First abuse from a father, then Evelyn yelling condemnation like a valedictory curse. William, searching for the matches that were safe in Helen's pocket, thinking, thinking: Evie came back, she came back, and she hates me. Wanted to kill me did Evie, and I thought she loved me. No other bugger does. The thought in Helen's head became an arrow of alarm, a sense of his loneliness, sharper because of her own in the face of Bailey's vituperative stare.

Alarm became a premonition of fear, turning her back to the door of the shed. She ran the few steps forward, shouting, 'William, William, it's all right.' Bernadette running with her, both guilty for momentary forgetfulness of his presence, victim of them all. As she reached the door, there was an internal explosion like the long-delayed lighting of the gas in an oven. She felt Bailey yank her back with enormous force, sending her sprawling to the

About the Author

FRANCES FYFIELD has spent much of her professional life practicing as a criminal lawyer, work which has informed her highly acclaimed novels. She has been the recipient of both the Gold and Silver Crime Writers' Association Daggers. She is also a regular broadcaster on Radio 4, most recently as the presenter of the series 'Tales from the Stave.' She lives in London and in Deal, overlooking the sea, which is her passion.

www.francesfyfield.co.uk

Visit www.AuthorTracker.com for exclusive information on your favorite HarperCollins authors.